"If you liked *Divergent* and *The Hunger Games*, you're going to love *Ways of The Doomed*. Moira McPartlin's prose is rich but unpretentious, her storytelling, thumping. An exciting new voice in YA fiction." HELEN FITZGERALD

"Chilling, intelligent, and thought-provoking, this richly imagined vision of the future gripped me from the outset. Beautifully written with fully realised characters, vivid settings, and a clever and playful use of language, *Ways of the Doomed* makes for a thrilling read. I loved it! My only complaint? I can't wait for book 2." CHRISTINA BANACH, AUTHOR OF *MINTY*

PRAISE FOR MOIRA MCPARTLIN'S DEBUT, *THE INCOMERS*:

SHORTLISTED – Saltire Society First Book Award 2012

"A graceful, searching tale of a stranger in a strange land. Its emotional resonance and narrative sweep fascinate to the end." ALAN BISSETT

"Graceful, delicate stuff that masterfully builds as it goes, painting a picture of a time, place and people that is never less than engrossing." DAILY RECORD

"Raises issues of estrangement vividly and compassionately." NORTHWORDS NOW

ALSO BY MOIRA MCPARTLIN

THE INCOMERS

WAYS OF THE
DOOMED

BOOK 1 OF THE SUN SONG TRILOGY

MOIRA McPARTLIN

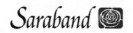
Saraband

Published by Saraband,
Suite 202, 98 Woodlands Road
Glasgow, G3 6HB
www.saraband.net

ISBN: 9781908643889
ebook: 9781908643902

Publication of this book has been supported by Creative Scotland.

ALBA | CHRUTHACHAIL

Printed and bound by
CPI Group (UK) Ltd, Croydon, CR0 4YY
on sustainably sourced paper.

1 2 3 4 5 6 7 8 9 10

FOR COLIN

Part One

Base Dalriada

Lesser Esperaneo

2089

Chapter One

The last time I saw my mother was three days after my sixteenth birthday.

The wrestling bout was on but already I was pestered by the morning winterlight blighting the Games Wall and reflecting dust onto the rim of my headgear. I don't know how many times that native had been told to suction this room to full proof; the lazy bint never did.

My parents' prime birthday gift to me was the Cadenson Wrestling Station, the most excellent deluxe model with a hyper-pain module. Epic. For five months already I had to endure Jake Hislop bragging about his CW stat. His parents, being Upper-Corp, had access to mega leisure bars. Jake only had to snap his bony fingers and his wish was granted. He never had to wait for his birthday. It was beamervilles enough having only Mid-Corp parents without the added reds of waiting an era for their weeny leisure bar quota to mount up and eventually get the gift of the century. Now the CW was mine and I'd been locked into a Jake grudge match ever since I peeled the wrapper off.

That day as Ma stood in the doorway dressed in her crisp grey uniform, Jake's impression held me fast in a stranglehold. It was like he was right here, in the room with me. I could smell the oats he had for breakfast – rank. The machine began to count. Soon it would cancel me out and shunt the victorious Jake back to the reality of his unit to gloat. I kicked the wall and twisted from his grasp. The room tossed as I heaved his impression off me, I head-dived over the low table, bounced backwards, and landed on top

3

of him. He side-shifted, rolled his skinny impression under the table, hove from the other side and, snatching my hair, viced my neck with his arm.

'I'm leaving now, Somhairle.' I heard Ma's voice but saw only her feet, shod as always in polished military boots. As I flailed my arms to grab a corner of Jake, I skittered and raked at his face; the warmth of imagined blood tickled to my wrists. His return blow to my belly was exact and buckled me, forehead to knee. I bent double like a native working in the fields, winded and almost beaten.

The machine called break and began to count again.

'Somhairle, switch that off for a minute please. Send Jake back. We need to say goodbye.'

'No, not now, I almost have him.' I took a knee and knuckle, long enough to catch some O_2. The room swirled with invading dust. 'Ma, the dust. Close the damn door.'

I looked up and caught the eye of the native, ever faithful. She stood tall in the shadow behind Ma.

Ma was going on another mission. So what? She'd been going on missions all my life. What was the big deal this time? She'll be back in a couple of days. Then Jake offered a hand, I took it, he yanked and threw me over his shoulder like a sack of laundry. When I landed I twisted my ankles round his lower legs, flipped over and brought him down. Before he reacted I had him pinned.

'Unu, Du, Tri, Kvar, Kvin, Ses, Sep, Ok, Naŭ, Dek,' the machine counted.

'VICTORY!' I roared as Jake's image evaporated.

'Nice one Sorlie,' the machine purred. I fired up my communicator and watched Jake slouch in his unit, an empty sack waiting to be carted to the recyk midden.

'Jake the snake, crawl on your belly, loser,' I voice-overed. 'That's called a supreme advantage wipeout.' I cut the connection before he had a chance to spit back.

4

What a crazed game. Oh man, I could join the ladder league and reach the top in click time. I glanced round for Ma's approving smile but she'd gone. Only the native remained, and no smile cracked that face.

I looked around me. The room was trashed. The table lay upended, a pile of regulation magazines were scattered and the Games Wall was marked with a boot-heel score the length of my arm. Pa would rage about that if he saw it. All the utilities should have been moved out before the bout but, you know how it is, time's short. The battleground debris belonged more to a battalion than a couple of teenage boys. I ordered the native to pack the Cadenson Station and clear the room, but she didn't move. Her breasts pushed for freedom under her drab green overalls. I could feel my face pink at the memory of my nocturnal fantasies of her and wakening to the familiar crusting wet patch on the sheet. She was just a native for jupe sake, just a Celt. I shouldn't even be considering her and she was old, at least twenty-five. But there was something about her that made my skin prickle. It was more than her breasts. She was nothing like the other natives on the Base who were bland; she freaked my friends with her presence, but that never stopped them ogling her.

And now Ma had left me yet again in the native's care, as she had done since I was small. Only this time, because Ma refused to wait, we didn't have a chance to say goodbye properly.

'What are you waiting for? Clear up this mess. That wall needs cleaned, native. Attend to it.'

She tiptoed into the room as if her feet were made of china and would shatter if weight bore down too hard. It was a disconcerting trait that always left me searching for her in the house just to make sure she wasn't spying. Everyone knows natives spy on their Privileged owners.

'Your Ma has left for the Front.' Her soft voice held a steely note. She reeked of the workfields but it didn't hide her overriding stench of pickling vinegar.

5

'She'll be back in a couple of days.'

'You think so?' She had the cheek to turn her back on me as she tiptoed from the room.

'You haven't cleared up,' I shouted after her. 'If it's not done by the time Pa comes home you're in deep trouble, missy.'

• • •

The native did put the room to rights after a while, when it suited her, and before Pa was due to return. She had vanished to the fields by the time I surfaced from my pit next morning. A bowl of breakfast oats sat on the kitchen table and a prepared lunch of beans and wheat paste still steamed under the cooling hood.

After lunch I heard Pa's Jeep turn into the block. I wanted to run to him and smell that peculiar foosty smell that clung to his clothes whenever he worked on the Base, but I stuck to my room and listened to the Jeep reverse into the garage, waiting for the connecting door to slam. Let him come to me.

After an hour, when he still hadn't appeared, I ventured into the bare corridors of our unit and found him in the store room, dragging camping gear into the middle of the floor as if he were preparing a bonfire.

'What's going on?'

He recoiled and flexed his gun hand. The already sunken sockets of his eyes were rubbed red. He wiped his nose with the back of his hand then stretched it out for me to take. It was cold and brittle, just like the man I saw before me, withering before his time. My stomach lurched and blackened. I could almost smell the snuffed-out candle of our previous life.

'What's happened? It's the Hero in Death thing, isn't it?'

Chapter Two

You get used to being a military kid. In fact, my first memory was of Ma and Pa deserting me, of being scared of that now familiar grey uniform – especially Ma's. I remember the first time they disappeared as an epoch spent under the tyranny of a dour-faced native nurse who treated my toddler tears as a minor inconvenience. When I clamped my jaws shut, refusing to eat her disgusting gruel, she skelped my bare knee; this brought about a scream which she used to wedge my jaw open with thumb and index of one hand while shovelling the food in with the other. I choked on oats mixed with my tears and snot. The witch stood and smirked as spew and urine puddled at my feet. By the time Ma and Pa returned, the chubby, cheerful boy they left had morphed into a skinny, feeble sniveller who had learned to eat up then hide. Whenever they left, after that first time, I would scream and kick and beg them to stay. Ma would sometimes cry, but the State was more powerful than my tantrums. It wasn't until the witch suddenly left in the night and my parents openly welcomed this strange new native who tiptoed into our household that the nightmare eased.

I remember once when I was about ten years old, Ma was talking to the native in the kitchen. Miss Tippie-toes stood with head bowed, cutting vegetables; a sullen pout plumped her mouth as if she had something in her teeth she couldn't shift. She caressed the paring knife with her thumb and hitched her hip as if she carried a weight there. Ma's voice stuttered with urgency.

'If word comes back from the Service of our release, take Somhairle to his grandfather.' She handed a thick biobag packet to the native. 'Give the old bastard this; he'll know what to do.'

7

'Natives aren't allowed presents,' I piped up. 'Where's my present?'

'I'll bring you one back, Somhairle. I promise, if you promise always to remember me when I'm gone.' Ma kissed my head then hugged me to her. 'You must remember me,' she whispered, 'because memories are the one thing the State cannot take from you.' That was the first time she spoke this mantra, and she never failed to repeat it each time she left thereafter. 'Memories are the one thing the State cannot take from you.'

Unlike Pa, whose smell changed depending on whether he worked at the Base or not, Ma always smelled sweet, like the fields of the Pleasure Lands we always visited in the second quarter. I would discover years later the sweet aroma was lavender. Pa too kissed me goodbye that time. His earthiness overpowered the essence of Ma, and it was this earthiness I took with me when I lay in bed that night wondering what present Ma would bring back. Maybe Pa would bring me something too. Looking back on this now, it must have been the desire for presents that stopped me asking the obvious. Who was this grandfather, this old bastard? I wasn't to find this out until much later.

When Ma came home that time, her eyes were panda'd with black smudges, her sweetness had fled; she stank of diseased animals, carrion left out in the elements to be picked clean by scavengers. When I asked her where my present was she squeezed me so close my skin nipped. 'I'm so sorry Sorlie,' was all she said. That was when I knew something was wrong; she never normally called me by my anglicised name.

Pa arrived home from his mission a few weeks after Ma and although he didn't look as tired as she, I knew better than to ask for a present. His silence simmered as he moved his kit from the room my parents shared into the sleeping quarter next to mine. The native melted into her tasks and manoeuvred me away from parental contact for the rest of that day.

My parents never spoke to each other after that time but I often caught them communicating with their sorrowful eyes.

'They are forbidden to speak to each other,' the native confided to me.

'Why?'

'Your mother has received instructions to be a Hero in Death.' She held her hand up to halt my question. 'Don't ask me what it means. Just accept that our lives will change. Don't mention this to your parents,' she added, 'just be kind to them while you can.'

Sometimes in the night I heard Pa thump his bed like a punch bag and gasp as if in pain. The sadness never left his eyes even when I performed well in school or we spent time together fishing in the Designated Water Parks.

• • •

The day after my sixteenth birthday Pa drove me to the coast for the first time.

He had to stand on tiptoes to set my hat straight, not that I would have let him. Body hair was appearing in every crack and orifice and my voice took regular trips into far-off octaves in search of that perfect pitch. When he first announced the trip, I resisted; it was my birthday after all and the Cadenson Wrestling Station grudge match beckoned, but Pa wanted to leave the next day.

We were sitting at the kitchen table eating the celebration meal prepared by the native who, as usual, tiptoed around the edges of our life with barely a breath out of place, lifting bowls and filling beakers as she went.

'It's time,' was all Pa said, but his face said much more.

Why did they have to spoil my birthday with this? I looked to Ma for support, but she only nodded. Lately she had grown silent and as haggard as the old crones who cleaned the Base latrines, but that evening she changed from her uniform into one of her prettified utility suits. The native helped her brush and style her hair into the fashion she preferred when I was a tot, and they painted her face from a dried and crusted palette Ma produced from the same memory box she used to store my 'firsts'. Before she retired to her solitary room for sleep she packed Pa's bag with care, even though it was the native's duty. For once the dark circles that plagued her eyes faded into the blush of her cheeks as she smoothed and folded each item of Pa's clothing, finishing by tucking a small sprig of lavender under the collar of his sleepwear.

That night through the thin walls of our unit I heard Pa fight hard with his pillow.

• • •

It was the end of the third quarter, between soft and hard harvests, when most vegetation withers and browns and the natives scrape and gather what they can for the Privileged stores. We drove past gigantic rusting pylons and through vast cracked grey concrete forests of derelict wind-turbines – evidence of failures from the century's hardest winters, when the developers ran to the sun, leaving behind their crumbling installations and a country struggling to see in the dark.

'Look at them, useless creatures, impotent and ugly,' Pa said with relish as if he enjoyed the way the words 'impotent and ugly' lassoed his tongue.

The vehicle we travelled in was his military Jeep. On our journey of several hours we passed only one other vehicle, also military.

'When I was a boy,' he said, 'the roads were jammed with cars and trucks. Even ordinary natives had vehicles.'

'No way. Natives can't drive.'

'In those days they could. People from these communities mixed and married. Some natives even married Privileged.'

'No way!'

'Mixed marriages were only banned after the Nationalist uprising, when the Purists came to power. And then ten years later the Land Reclaimists mounted the coup and banned all native and non-military transport in a futile attempt to save some of Esperaneo's environment and to conserve the dwindling fuel supply. Natives used to be just like us, only difference was they had predominant Celtic genes.'

Why was he spouting this crazy talk? My mouth dried with the taste of the unknown and forbidden. Suddenly I wanted the Jeep to be pulled up at a checkpoint and for the Military to take me back to the Base. Then he smiled.

'You think we're in trouble? Well maybe we will be, but not yet. See.' He thumped the roof of the Jeep, he played drums on the dashboard, he stroked the door as if it were a cat. His laugh was the deep hearty eruption I remembered from before the time he moved into the room next to mine.

'See, Sorlie? No surveillance. It doesn't work up here. The mountains block the signal.'

'What about the satellites?'

'They can't listen to everyone, so they ignore these isolated parts.'

He must be lying.

'What about our chips?'

'Oh, they know we're here. I'll be disciplined for leaving the Safe Zone, but so what?'

Pa was a quiet man who normally spoke only if he had something important to say. That day in the Jeep his stories made my head fizz; he infected me with his history. He spoke of his upbringing on the small arable farm his family had owned and lost to the Land Reclaimists, of how his position in the Military ensured that his parents would be looked after in their failing years. I never knew my grandparents, but when I asked him to elaborate he jumped topic, swatting his history dead like a swipe at a mozzie. Then he slipped into dwam-time, silent, staring at the road ahead.

Memories are the one thing the State cannot take from you.

The Jeep rumbled over a broken and potholed road not much bigger than the path to our front door. Climbing higher up the mountain side we ascended into a soupy clag that clung to the brown bracken and obscured the view. The wipers squealed into action on torn rubbers, making little headway on the rain-splattered screen.

Pa wasn't fazed. 'Remind me to report that fault,' he said as he halted the offending blades.

At the summit, the cloud lay behind and below us. Pa pulled over and stopped in a car park strewn with cairns. To the west lay an expanse of water that I took to be an enormous lake. In parts I could just make out a farther shore, at others the water reached the horizon. In the near distance, the smoky mountains of an island danced in silhouette against a streaked crimson and pink sky. The dimmed headlights left us in the gloaming, and we climbed from the cab, spellbound in the grip of the sunset. Great gulps of cold sweet air quenched my urban-stained lungs; I'd never tasted anything so clean, so sweet. The air chill tweaked my nostrils, making me sneeze. The wind brought tears to my eyes.

'What do you see, Sorlie?' Pa asked as he threaded his arm through mine.

'I see mountains and water and an island. I see a great blood-run sky and cairns piled like pagan charms around the car park.'

Pa remained quiet as if waiting for another answer.

'What do you see?' I asked, not wanting to fail.

'I see freedom.' He pointed to the northern horizon, where no islands could be seen. 'It seems distant but it's there. It's where we'll be heading one day soon.'

'Where? I don't get it.'

He continued to peer into the distance. I shivered at the thought of heading there now, leaving behind Ma, and home, and everything.

I coughed. 'I'm quite happy at the Base, thanks very much.'

He hugged me then. 'Oh Sorlie, you don't know what freedom is. That's reason enough to fight for it.' He released me from his arms. 'Come on, we're not going home yet. Let's go and find our own little piece of freedom for a while.'

A shadow of doubt wiped Pa's face when we spied a trio of vehicle lights travelling in convoy towards us on the great main road that stretched below and back to the urbans. We sat together on a cairn and waited for them to arrive to take us back, but they never did so we moved on.

After a bowel-squelching descent down a precipitous track, Pa pulled the Jeep off the road and bumped over rough, rutted terrain until a mound of reed-stubbled sand barred our way. Something different in the air nipped my nose and mouth this time as I climbed from the cab. I licked my lips and tasted salt. A constant crash like the booming of traditional artillery sounded from beyond the dune. The scarf Ma wrapped round me before I left protected my eyes and nose against the sand gusts peppering the air.

Pa grabbed my arm and hauled me to the Jeep's tailboard.

'Come on, let's set up camp and build a fire,' he said.

'A fire? Is that allowed?'

'Don't be such a worrywart. The State has more pressing things to deal with than a camp fire.'

He pulled camping gear from the Jeep and louped up the dune while I tried to follow. Sand dragged my feet into its mercurial folds, spilling over my boot tops, burrowing deep to scratch between my toes. It was nothing like the sand back at the Base, used for mending roads. I was fair puggled when I reached the crest, only to be blown back by the wind and the sight that greeted me. White froth thrashed the shoreline, wave upon wave slurped and gobbled a bank of pebbles then spat them out as they turned back on themselves. I held my arms wide and felt my blouson balloon with air. I half expected to rise from the earth like a kite.

While I Da Vinci'd, Pa collected a scattering of wood from the shore.

'Come on, are you going to help or not?' He dragged a piece of tree-trunk the size of a bench towards me.

'Wood – on a beach?'

'Aye. It's submarine peat. This will be an escapee from the nets of the moor-logging trawlers. The natives who live in these parts comb the beaches and collect it for fuel. If we chip bits off this beastie,' he slapped the trunk, 'there's enough for a kindling.'

Once the fire was crackling, I knelt on the sand and Pa draped a blanket over my shoulders. Soon the battered, blackened pan he'd dug out of the Jeep was bubbling with water. I felt a warmth I had never experienced before, even though the air was cold around me and the wind off the sea bristled my cheeks.

'Tell me more about freedom, then,' I said.

A shower of sparks erupted from the fire as Pa poked it before he settled back on his heels.

'It wasn't that long ago when we were free. At least, people thought they were free. They were too wrapped up in their own greed and pleasure to see what was happening. All they were interested in was celebrity trivia and petty parochial affairs.'

He raked at the fire again, sending a spray of sparks too close to my blanket for comfort.

'And all around populations were growing, unemployment was high, natural resources were running out and people began to starve. There were threats from the East, threats from the West. All the countries in what was then Europe faced the same challenges. That was when the State of Esperaneo was formed. You would have thought it would have brought people together but the situation deteriorated. That's when the Nationalists and Conservationists began to take power and divisions widened. Neighbour turned on neighbour, families fought amongst themselves.

There was no security over energy and the lights went out for a while. And when the lights go out chaos follows. It was worse in the urbans.' He stopped suddenly and waved his arm as if to wipe out his memory of that time. 'I was just a small boy during those dark days but I remember the cold most of all. I was scared of the dark and somehow my mother always managed to keep a light burning for me.'

The daylight was fading, washing out towards the western horizon, and with the drawing over of night, five small lights appeared out at sea. 'Look,' he said pointing to the lights. 'Why do you think they need trawlers to deep trawl for wood? It's ridiculous.' I jumped when he spat his words into the fire and they sizzled. He pointed back to the trawlers. 'Look beyond the boats. The small islands out there were cleared of their inhabitants so they could be turned into penitentiaries. You can see their lights twinkling in the distance. The pride of Esperaneo's Criminal Justice System.'

His arm circled me and the blanket pulled round us both as we huddled in the sand, our bodies warm against the sea chill. He remained silent for a few minutes and the steady rhythm of his heartbeat replaced the lull of his voice. A crust of tears linked a chain down the cheek I had pressed to his chest. Black and white birds teetered at the tide line on spindle legs, stabbing the wet sand with scimitar beaks.

'Why are you telling me this?' I said.

'Because you need to know,' he said. 'Not all taught history is true.'

I felt stifled by his closeness; I was no longer a child. I moved from him and we both lay back on the sand; he understood. The sky had cleared of its clouds, which left an ominous chill in the air. As we lay with backs moulded into the sand I looked up at the satellites tracking between the stars. The sky was silted with satellites. Something was chewing at Pa; he'd been silent for too long.

'What are they all for?' I asked. It was time to get Pa to crack open the topic he'd been hoarding, but he needed a nudge. 'Maybe you're wrong about them not listening.'

At first I thought he'd fallen asleep. His breathing was quiet and even. When he eventually spoke the edge to his voice scraped like the blunt blade he took across his neck in the morning, ready to nick and draw blood.

There was no preamble as he slipped straight into a well-rehearsed litany – 'i's dotted, 't's crossed and wax sealed with a capital 'D' for Doom.

'David Pringle is the warden of Black Rock Penitentiary,' he began. 'The furthest penitentiary from our shores, at the edge of the Western Sea. Black Rock was one of the first of its kind to be

15

established because of its location many miles from land and with a dangerous coastline. It was perfect as a deterrent.' He dug his elbows into the sand and shucked himself to sitting. 'It was once a hidden bunker base.'

'Have you been there?' I sat up to join him, and cooried into my jacket.

'I was there once and never want to return. It's upgraded now though. To something even worse.'

'Worse?'

'David Pringle is your grandfather, Sorlie.'

They used to call it *dropping the penny*, then *connect shit*; now I don't care what it's called, every scrap of information Pa told me over the years slotted into my logic store and calculated a huge heap of trouble headed my way.

'My grandfather lives on a prison island in the middle of the ocean?'

'Yes, as I said, he's the warden there.'

Memories of the day Ma gave our native the present flooded back.

'So why tell the native to take me there?'

'What?'

I tried to remember Ma's exact words but they were gone. 'I heard Ma tell the native to take me to my grandfather.'

'She might have to, one day.'

'Why?'

'Because we might not have any choice.' He picked up handfuls of sand and let them trickle through his fingers. 'Look Sorlie, there are some things you need to know. About your grandfather; about your mother.'

As if on cue the normally elusive moon pulled up from the dunes behind us and lit a lamp just bright enough for me to see my father's ravaged face.

'Your mother was brought up on a farm by her grandfather,' Pa said. 'Your great-grandfather, Sorley. Your namesake. Same name, different spelling. Her father, David, left her there while he bigged it up in Beckham City.'

'What about her mother?' The wind picked up and slapped the curtain of cloud back across the moon's face.

'I'll come to that, but let's get under cover first.'

As Pa and I battled the tidal gusts to erect our sleeping pod, dark clouds converged in the south, obliterating the satellites and stars. A storm was coming, in more ways than one.

'Don't you think we should head home?' I asked as we crawled under cover.

Pa shook his head. 'It's better we stay here tonight. Your mother needs rest.' He took out his thermo wand and began to boil water. I wondered if he would fess about the Hero in Death stuff and why he and Ma weren't permitted to speak to one another, but dwam-time claimed him.

We huddled in the open doorway of the pod and watched the moor-logging trawler lights in the distance as they dredged the deep.

'They seem hardly to be moving,' I said to break the spell. 'Even in this squall.'

'That's because they use low grade fuel. It's hardly worth the effort.'

Pa pointed across a short stretch of water to the nearest island. One by one the small lights pinched out for evening shutdown, leaving only one harsh white beacon searching in its clock face. At one point on its revolution it kissed the beam from the neighbouring island's searchlight like lovers cast adrift, destined to be apart and yet given the brief intimacy of that one touch.

'Energy must be conserved but not at the cost of security, eh?' Pa leaned forward, the wind flattening his hair as he poked his head out the pod door.

'What is it?' I asked.

'There, the intermittent flash. Do you see it? That's it, that's Black Rock.'

There were two beams, one constant like the lover's kiss and another, smaller light that clicked on and off in its own particular way as if it had a loose wire that needed fixing.

As I sipped my bowl of grain soup, Pa rigged a dim halo from the strap on the roof. He settled back in the pod and we sat facing each other like yin-yang, watching the halo swing then buckle as a gust hit the pod side. I would have been happy if the great magma eruption had happened just then and we were captured like this for eternity in an avalanche of ash.

'This tent's too small for us,' he said. 'Look at you, almost a man.'

'Come on Pa, spill. You were telling me about you-know-who.' I thumbed to the pod opening. 'And what about my grandmother?'

He cleared his throat. 'Vanora, your grandmother. After your mother was born, Davie took Vanora with him to Beckham City. He had fine ideals at that time and believed that he could better himself. Until he met Vanora he'd been a contented landowner. She was a town girl. He met her at a pagan festival dance. Halloween, I think it was called. His parents were unhappy about the match, but it made no difference. Davie was set on her.'

'What was she like?'

'She had exotic good looks and intelligence. Apart from that, your mother remembers little of her. It is now forbidden by law to speak of her.'

'Why? What happened to her?'

Pa's eyes shifted to the ground. He was millisecs from telling me something, I knew he was, but he shook his head and said, 'It's not important at the moment. It's Davie you need to hear about. He and Vanora married and lived on the farm and your mother was born there within the year.

'Your great-grandfather, Sorley, blamed Vanora for Davie's discontent. He was wrong. There was always a blackness in Davie's soul.'

'Why are you telling me this? Why isn't Ma telling me?'

'Your mother has a restriction placed on her, you know that.

She can't leave the Base unless on military business. The surveillance there prevents her telling you anything. Lately she's begun to worry about your future and wants you to know these things.'

'How do you know what she thinks?' I asked. So what if my words hurt. 'You're not permitted to speak to each other.'

Pa didn't even blink. 'The State is not always as wise as it thinks it is. We don't need words.'

A light rain pattered on the pod fabric, the walls flapped in the wind. Pa zipped the night out before he continued.

'With your mother safe in the hands of her grandparents, Davie and Vanora lived the high life in Beckham City. They'd been there for almost a decade when the Purists took power. Things changed overnight. People started to disappear, even before the ethnos were deported back to their ancestral lands. Often Transports were ambushed; there was widespread killing and kidnappings by the opposition party, rebels; they were all at it. Even the Noiri.'

'The Noiri? I thought they were neutral – just out for profit?'

'They are, but there's plenty profit to be had in revolution. Something happened to David at this time. Your mother remembers him coming back to the farm without Vanora – he said she was visiting her parents. Then she turned up a couple of days later, bruised about the face and head. She slept in your mother's room but left with him soon after. The next time he returned he again came alone. When his parents asked where Vanora was he just said, "No more."

Pa picked at the stitching of his sleeping bag and rubbed a loose thread into a bobble between his fingers. 'Soon after, he was appointed warden of Black Rock. It was supposed to be a reward. In exchange for the honour, he agreed to send or sell – choose any word you want – your mother into military service. She was thirteen. The farm stayed with her grandparents until they both died soon after she was conscripted. Then David turned it over to the State as part of the deal. He must have known his parents wouldn't survive such a betrayal.' Pa unzipped the pod door and threw the bobble out, grabbing a mouthful of air, like a resuscitation, before he closed it again. He poured water from a flask and placed a purifying tablet into it. It had hardly dissolved before he slaked his thirst and handed the bottle to me. Our eyes met and he looked away too quickly.

'Wait a minute. Why are you telling me this now? You're not planning the same thing? Not combat? I've already been deemed psychologically unsuited for combat.'

He grabbed me and held me in a tight bear hug. I could feel his heart battering through his jacket; I could feel the heat of his breath and smell his scent of polish and steel.

'We would never do that to you,' he hissed. He released me to arm's length and this time held my gaze. 'I'm telling you all this now because I fear a catastrophic change is on the way.'

My nose had started to run and I knew what was coming.

'Does this mean there could be another war alert? What about our defences? You and Ma, is that not your job, to stop this happening?'

'Yeah,' his laugh was bitter. 'Your mother especially, but she has resisted her status as far as she can. She's done it for you – for us. But she can't hold off much longer.'

The side of the pod sagged when Pa rested back. He wiped sweat from his brow with a handkerchief that I was sure smelled of Ma. 'Look Sorlie, I've said too much. Just be aware that I may not always be around. My work is difficult, and one day, well – you know the score.'

Death, he meant death, something military kids were taught to deal with.

'Your history is more important to your future than you realise. Believe me,' he said.

'What do you mean?'

'I'm not the one to tell you and I pray to the stars you need never find out.'

Chapter Three

The native smelled of vinegar, always. Even on the days when she dressed in her best green overalls and walked from the Base to the market in the nearest urban.

• • •

Her name was Ishbel. I knew this because I overheard Ma call her name once when I was small and playing my favourite game of spying under the table.

'Ishbel, can you try and find some fresh dairy products for Somhairle? It's difficult I know, but you can do it.' There was a little laugh in her voice of a shared joke, as if the native was her friend. Then later that same afternoon Ma found me in my spying den and went radge at the native for no good reason.

• • •

When Pa and I returned home from our trip to the coast we found the native stationed at the inner garage door. The taillights of the Jeep shone on her face, making her pale skin glow ruddy red. She was taller than both Ma and Pa, and carried her height well, as if she had a cord running from the top of her head that was constantly being drawn to the sky. I knew she was strong because she could open the sticky waste recyk unit door with ease and even Pa struggled with that. The sleeves of the green uniform always rolled above the elbow and showed off her bulking arms, and her shoulders stretched the seams. When I was very small, about six or seven, she would take me for walks in the nearby hills. There was a small lake nestling in a valley where the natives swam for pleasure, being forbidden to use the Base pool. On these walks Ishbel cajoled me into my swim suit, then coaxed me to the freezing water's edge. At the first step my little feet would turn blue and I would scream for effect and it worked. She would park me beside one of the other green-clad natives and I spent the rest of the time watching her thrash her athletic body around the lake. At these times I thought she should be the one in the Military and not my mother, who was slight, almost childlike.

Although her uniform was drab it suited her copper hair and her eyes, which always reminded me of pieces of amber. Each time I looked in their shiny brightness I saw something 'far away' trapped there. Sounds lame, I know, but it's true.

In all the time she lived with us she spoke few words to my parents. When I was small she told me old tales of men and women who lived long ago on those islands now inhabited by prisoners. She sang me stories in her ancient language and promised to teach me the words of her long-dead ancestor's songs, but that day never came. Her greatest trick was to imitate the birds that lived in the Designated Park areas. Her other good game was to draw pictures of extinct birds and animals that inhabited these shores up until only a decade ago, then get me to choose the picture that matched the weird sounds she made. Sometimes the sounds were so bizarre I giggled till I almost wet my pants.

When she laughed, which was rarely, normally at something daft I did, her whole face moved. She'd throw back her head so far her throat stretched like a swan and I could see right past her white shell-like teeth to the pink of her gullet.

I asked her once if she was happy. She just smiled and brushed the hair from my eyes before returning to her many tasks.

• • •

The stories and music stopped the day after I joined Academy and I ordered her to tidy my room. I found I no longer had time to sit in the kitchen with her while she sang and spun her stupid tales.

• • •

That day after our camping trip I wanted to get straight to my Cadenson Wrestling Station, but the native barred the way, her

22

hands thrust deep in her pockets. Something was wrong.

'Get out the way.' I nudged her, but she didn't move.

'Enough, Sorlie,' Pa shouted. 'What is it, girl?'

'She's been summoned.' She looked at me and started to let me through but Pa signalled her to stay.

'She's received orders,' she said, almost in a whisper. 'Another mission despite her appeal.'

Pa covered his eyes with his hand, but she was not finished.

'They told her it was her last chance to be a Hero in Death. If she did not succeed this time there would be serious consequences for you all.' The native stood wide of the door and corralled us into the kitchen.

'Come, I have prepared some proper food for you.' Her tone and pitch changed so dramatically I thought she had taken a benny. Didn't she know the domestic surveillance picked up on that sort of thing?

'You must be starved after your trip,' she continued in a breezy manner, most unbecoming to a native.

Pa looked as if food was the farthest thing from his thoughts. 'Where is she?' he asked.

'In her quarters, preparing,' she said in a low voice. Then, loudly again, 'I have cooked your favourite, Sorlie. Maize chips.' She had gone mad – I've always loathed maize chips.

She pushed a plate to Pa. I saw him pull a ragged slip of white linen from under it and bunch it in his fist before pushing the food away.

'I can't eat this muck anymore,' he said and went to his room.

'What's going on?' I asked.

'What about you? You not eating either?' she quipped. 'If not, you can help me with something.'

'Help?' What could a Privilege help a native with?

'Yes, help.' Her voice sliced my question to ribbons, which she tied into silence by taking my hand in her sweaty palm and hauling me from the seat as if I were a toddler again. I tried to shake it off but she held me fast as if saving me from drowning. The surveillance dot above the kitchen door seemed to blink several times but nothing else happened. The message started to sink in.

The pantry was in a cellar beneath the house and as soon as she opened the door the smell reminded me this was where she did her pickling. Even though she grew heaps of fruit and vegetables in our garden, she still went to the market every other day to barter for more. What wasn't needed for our own use was pickled. The shelves were lined with rows and rows of full jars

'Why do we need all these?' I asked now as I started to fill the empty shelf space with jars of new preserves.

'One day you'll see.'

As long as I could remember we hardly ever ate any of the pickles she made, yet each time we added jars to the shelves there was always room for more.

'Where do they go?' I asked her once.

'Maybe our ancestors carry them to the other world,' was her dumb reply. Did she not realise that I was Privileged? She was native. There was no way our ancestors shared the same road.

'Do you think Pa will help me set up my Cadenson Wrestling Station?'

Without warning she slammed a jar on the shelf so hard it shattered, spilling slivers of glass and stinking vinegar-soused vegetables to the floor. She had some cleaning up to do.

Chapter Four

'They said she was not a Hero in Death but that's a lie.'

Pa sat on the store room floor, building a fortress of gear around him. His crazy red eyes avoiding my stare. He wiped them with the heel of his hand. 'I can't allow her name to be tarnished like a criminal. Your mother was a brave warrior. You have more of her in you than you have of me. Be brave.'

It was kind of freaky that he referred to Ma in the past tense. 'What's happened? She's coming back, she always does.' I watched as Pa began to pack his bag. 'You're not leaving? Where are you going? Can I come with you?'

I grabbed his arm. He shrugged it off with as much gentleness as his urgency allowed. 'Don't leave me, please.'

'I have to. You don't understand, your mother's name needs to be avenged.'

'Make me understand. Ma wouldn't want you to leave me,' I pleaded.

His eyes daggered me with sudden fury. It was hopeless.

'So when will you be back?'

'I don't know, Sorlie.' Like a moth against a flame his anger burned out as quickly as it flared. 'Be good, follow your conscience, and do what Ishbel tells you. She is more to you than you think. Much more. Here.' He handed me a small device.

'What is it?'

'It's a plug-in for your communicator. It has a powerful transmitter for picking up and sending old-fashioned radio signals. It also has a cracking imager. You'll find it fun once you work out how to use it. I doubt you'll be able to find the manual on FuB though.' He snorted. 'FuB by name Fat useless Bastard by nature.' Even in his distressed state he couldn't resist his habitual derision of the State's Official Information Hub.

Pa turned the plug-in over in his palm and with his thumbnail picked open a small lip.

'There's an extra battery in here. It's very special and very delicate so don't force it. Here, give me your wrist.' He connected the plug-in to my communicator. It clicked in place mitre to mitre as if it belonged there and had only gone astray in the manufacture.

He rose to go.

'Please,' I pleaded again, 'don't leave me.'

But his gaze and his mind had already left the building as he kissed my forehead. He did not take the Jeep; he walked out the way of the native, through the front door, rucksack slung over his shoulder, and headed towards the main gate of the Base.

• • •

Silence menaced the house. As if forewarned, even my tutors did not call me to my workstation for lessons. I felt I had been quarantined for a disease I didn't have and couldn't name. The stupid Cadenson Wrestling Station goaded me with guilt about Ma until I smashed it into smaller pieces than the shattered pickle jar in the pantry. There might have been tears but there was no time to regret my action because the native cleared all evidence of the wreckage by the time I surfaced from my teenage gloom. My quarters became my world, my quilt my warmth, my bed a cave into which I crawled and cried. No doubt the native heard these bouts of grief as she tiptoed to and from her cell but she never let on. She brought meals for me to move around the plate. Nothing else happened. The silence ticked by as I listened for Pa's return.

He didn't return.

• • •

Two days after his departure the silence and quarantine ended. I was shaken awake.

'Sorlie, we must go, quickly.'

'Ma?'

'No, Sorlie.' It was the native wearing a military coat. My thundering heart sank back to the pit it had grown accustomed to.

'You're wearing Ma's coat.' Why was the bitch teasing me?

She looked down at herself.

'This is not your mother's coat,' she said. 'Now come on.'

'No.' I grabbed my quilt. She slapped my hand and hauled me off the bed.

'Stop being such a child. We must go. Now!' She threw clothes at me. 'Get dressed, quickly.'

'Where are we going? When are we coming back?'

'Never.'

'But Pa? He'll not know where to find us if we go.'

'Your father will know where to find us. Meanwhile, your mother asked me to look after you, so that's what I'm doing. We must leave this house now.' Her tone was authoritative, and even though she was a native I found myself impelled to comply.

'Why? Why must we leave?'

'Too many questions,' she snapped as she threw my warm coat over my shoulders. Then she relented a little. 'There's trouble in the Urban and Purist rebels are making their way to the Base. Now come, before it's too late.'

That seemed rubbish talk. The Base valley where our domestic dwelling was situated had been attacked before and each previous attack had been preceded by sirens and heavy truck movements and commotion. Tonight it was quiet. The search light spanned my wall as it did every other night, every fifty-three seconds. It had been a constant babysitter that helped lull me to sleep when my parents missioned and left me alone with the native and her mutterings in the dark. I would count the seconds, count the revolutions, and listen for a shot that never came.

The temptation to dig my heels into the hard concrete floor was strong but the native was stronger as she hauled me from my quarter, down the stairwell and through the kitchen to the internal garage door. Her strength was awesome. If I struggled I risked having my shoulder dislocated.

In the garage Pa's Jeep sat beside an empty space with an oil patch on the floor – the space left by Ma's army vehicle that day we didn't say goodbye, the day she didn't return. She never even came home draped in the flag of Esperaneo as was her right. But then no one had actually said she was dead.

The native pushed me in the Jeep and climbed into the driver side. She started the engine and opened the garage door with the remote. As soon as it was open enough for the Jeep to clear she pushed her foot down and released the brake. The Jeep leaped forward and stalled. She fumbled to start it again.

'Do you want me to drive?' I said.

'Shut up,' she snapped.

'You can't talk to me like that. I could have you executed.'

She slapped me, hard, right across the face. 'You have no idea how long I've waited to do that,' she said.

Shit, I started to cry, I couldn't stop myself. How could this be happening to me? Insubordination was a crime. So was kidnapping. It happened sometimes to Privileged kids – kidnapping by native pirates. But Ishbel wasn't a pirate, she was Ishbel.

She released the brake again and this time shot out of the garage.

The gates to the camp were always locked and guarded. When the native pulled over a light shone on the vehicle and a laser began to work its search from the back through to the front. She dropped her window.

'Unlock the gate,' she said. 'The boy's father is sick. I have an instruction to move him to his family in the South.' She held up a pass to one of the gate's scanners.

A voice said: 'We have not been informed of that instruction.'

'That's your problem,' said Ishbel. 'If you don't want to be on report, get your jobsworth arse into gear, scan the code and unlock the damn gate. The boy will have died of old age by the time we get there.'

She put her hand in her pocket; her neck was tense like a penned wolf waiting to enter the fighting ring. I realised she was holding her breath and probably clutched a gun in her hidden hand. I had no clue what she was talking about, but I too held my breath waiting for a bullet to puncture the native's head.

The light blacked out and the gate cranked open.

The native released a long whistle through the gap in her front teeth and I heard myself laugh like a hyena.

'Don't get hysterical on me,' she said.

'How did you forge those instructions?'

She kept her eyes on the road. 'Anything can be forged for the right price.'

Once through the gates she pushed hard on the accelerator.

'I'm not going to my grandfather's place, am I? He sounds horrible.'

She didn't answer.

'D'you know when Pa will be back?'

Silence.

'Is he at Black Rock? How will we get there? Will we get on a boat? Will we have breakfast on the boat? I'm starving.'

She remained silent.

'Is my father really ill?'

Nothing.

'Why won't you tell me?' I could hear my voice rising into the whiny tone I had kicked out of me sharpish on my first Academy day.

'I'll tell you soon. Now let me drive or we'll end up in a damn ditch.'

• • •

We headed northwest. The road bit a line along the base of high mountains with scalloped ridges, climbed, then surfaced on a wind-scoured plateau. The native wrestled with the wheel as the Jeep buffeted and bucked against erratic gusts. The sky in the west was black as bit-u. In the east I saw a single tree teetering on a boulder; its spindly boughs, pointing in all airts like some mad totem guarding the glen, were silhouetted against the coming light.

The native's face was set, her jaw viced to the point where the vein in her neck trembled. If I had a knife I could have reached over and popped it. I hated her for hitting me. Her eyes fixed on the road ahead, both hands gripping the wheel. The dash-light reflected off a large device she wore in place of her native command band.

So many forbidden things this native now touched. This native who was kidnapping me had always been biddable, considerate even, never insolent or cheeky. Now she'd packed up her reason and gone *freneza*.

'I'm *starving*.' I winced at my kickshit voice. I coughed and roughed it up a bit. 'I need food.' She should remember who's boss.

'In the bag.' She signalled towards the holdall on the floor, the only thing she had taken from the house. I unzipped it and reached in. There were clothes and a thick biobag package – the present Ma had given the native when I was small. At last my hand fell to a tuck box and water bottle. I rattled the box. The contents sounded like bog standard Fiver grain bars, which was what they proved to be. I chose the least boring oat Fiver and chewed it.

'What's in the present?'

Her face viced up even more if possible, torqued to the point of rupture. I was scared she was going to hit me again, so I shut up. The bar stuck like toffee to the surface of my mouth and tongue.

After I'd read all the ingredients on the grain bar label, I dared to look at her. 'I won't tell about you hitting me if you tell me what's going on.' She pretended not to hear.

I reached forward to launch some tunes. She slapped my hand away from the dial.

'Stop hitting me. You'll be in big trouble.'

The neck crank released a couple of notches as she glared at me and said, 'I'm sorry, but please don't put on the music. It's many years since I've driven and I need to concentrate.'

'Natives aren't permitted to drive,' I said, even though I knew this was a redundant statement.

Her eyes narrowed to the road as if she was an oldie who no longer qualified for Corrective-S and her eyesight wasn't up for the task.

'Please don't speak to me,' she said. 'We can talk when we get there. Be patient.'

'Get where?'

But she only gave me her teeth-whistle sigh again.

Chapter Five

'They call it the Dead Man's Ferry,' she said. We were parked, over-looking the docks, high above the port of *Ulapul*. Below, the chipped and battered hull of a ferry butted the harbour wall, its open mouth snarling at a commotion happening on the quay, its rank breath almost visible in the way the crowd shied from its hunger.

The native handed me one of the two mugs of brew she had just bartered from a rusty white Noiri van parked a few metres away. The brew was hot and black and sweet with an after taste of burnt leaves that soured my palate and made my cheeks draw in. Despite this I felt good. She watched me as I drank.

'It's black tea. Banned in Esperaneo thirty years ago after a health scare but the natives still find it cheap on the Noiri,' she said with certain pride. From her pocket she pulled a waxed packet and threw it in my lap.

'Eat. I don't know how long it will be before I can feed you again.'

The packet was warm and contained a substance I'd never seen before. It looked like a bread roll but it was white and inside was something pink and square and bumpy like a grain cake, but when I bit into it oil dribbled down my chin. The bread was cool but the filling roasting, blistering the roof of my mouth. It tasted spicy and made me feel happy for a moment, then guilty, like the time last year I tried hash; I knew it was wrong, forbidden.

'Is this meat?'

She nodded as she took a bite of her roll. Her tongue flicked out, catching a drip of a brown sauce that escaped the bread. 'It's called Lorne sausage.'

The words sounded foreign. Presumably its acquisition was something else the natives took pride in.

A rider on a gyrocycle skidded into the car park, idled by the van and shouted something incoherent towards the vendor before screeching away. The vendor chucked his wares into the hold, slammed the doors and kangarooed off in the same direction.

'Hurry with the food,' the native said.

When I finished she stuffed the wrappings into the mugs and took them to the side of the car park to stash behind a rock.

'What's Dead Man's Ferry then?' I asked when she returned.

'It takes the convicts to the prison ships.'

'But why Dead Man's Ferry? They're convicts, they'll get out sometime won't they?'

'Huh. Some do but not all.'

She swung round in her seat and faced me, her expression hard like a mask pulled so tightly over her face if she twitched a muscle if would crack and shatter into fragments at her feet. I could feel my palms begin to sweat. It was weird. I wanted to know what was going on but I didn't want to hear what she had to say.

'Your father is not coming back. And neither is your mother.'

My heart bounced over my lungs and hid, pounding beneath my ribs.

'You are an orphan Sorlie.'

She watched me as if I were a specimen in a jar, as if she could see my chest constrict, as if she wanted to see me in pain.

'I don't believe you. You said back there that Pa would know where to find us.'

'I lied. I had to say something to get you off the Base. Then was not the time to tell you.' She stretched her neck and peered in the rear view mirror as if willing an interruption, then took a big breath.

'Your father went off to avenge your mother's name. Up until her last mission she could never carry out her status of Hero in Death. She had been expected to die when she went on her missions. She was to walk into situations with the targets, then blow herself and them up.'

I held my hands over my ears but the native grabbed one and jammed it under my ribcage and kept the pressure on it.

'She could never carry the whole plan through. They said it was because she was a coward but it was because she loved you and your father too much. And even though she always managed to carry out her task and kill her designated targets without blowing herself up, the Military was not satisfied. Her survival was disloyal to the State. She was not a true hero. They warned her after the last mission that if she did not kill herself with her target the Military would take you away and train you as a first line suicide fighter. Your mother would never allow that.'

I gasped, and a hollow sound escaped me. I pressed my free hand to my mouth to keep down the food. My saliva was drowning me. The pain I felt from the native's fingers clawing into my fist was nothing as I imagined my mother strapping bombs to herself and walking up to her target. What was she thinking of when she detonated? Was she thinking of me, or Pa, or was she thinking of the pain it may cause? I thought of her blown into fragments of flesh and bone and hair and blood. Her soft hands that smoothed oil into my dry skin at night, ripped from her arms. That small white hand, her right hand that wore the opal ring I gave her for her birthday, charred and lying on a floor somewhere, discarded and swept up with the trash.

All these years I had no idea what Hero in Death meant other than that my parents were forbidden to talk to each other. Why had I never tried harder to find out?

Images of Ma's smiling face flashed through my mind and then of her in recent years – her sadness, her decline.

'I didn't even say goodbye.'

I hadn't realised I had spoken these words aloud until the native released her grip on me and said, 'You must forgive yourself for that, Sorlie. There is nothing you can do about it now.' Her words were words of kindness but the accusation resonated in the tone. 'After her mission, for reasons known only to the Military, they designated her Un-Hero in Death, and for this your father lost his mind. He assassinated her commander and was in turn executed. They say he wasn't even court-martialled.'

I stumbled from the cab and spewed the animal food onto the car park. Snot ran down my face; vomit clung to my nostrils and burned my throat. I wanted to curl over and lie in my own stinking mess.

She did not come, so I climbed back into the cab and took the wet wipe she offered. There was nothing else I could do.

'I am so sorry Sorlie, but this is why we have to leave. He tried to be a good man but in the eyes of the State you are the son of a traitor. Both your parents have been disgraced despite their years of loyalty. Your life at the Base has ended; you can never return.'

'Why? Why'd he do it? He must have known what would happen. He knew I'd be left alone.'

'His love for your mother was too great. He couldn't bear to live without her. And he knew your life was about to change no matter what happened to them. They wanted your freedom, a life free of military commitment.'

Freedom. That was Pa's word, his place, the place he told me we would all be headed one day. So how would living with my grandfather bring me freedom? He lived in a hellhole penitentiary.

Lights from an approaching military truck wiping over the native's face reset her expression to hard.

'Dry your eyes. Don't say anything,' she said. 'Try to look normal.'

Normal – after what she'd just revealed?

The truck stopped on the spot the white van had vacated. They shone a hunting light over our Jeep. One of the men got out, walked to where the native had stacked the mugs, and urinated on the gorse. The other climbed from the driver's side, spat on the ground and swaggered towards us. But before he got to the door the native jumped from the cab and flashed her ID.

The man stopped short as soon as he saw the military coat and saluted. He glanced in my direction and said, 'Sorry ma'am, didn't realise.' The snigger in his voice raised the native's brow but she kept schtum.

'That will be all soldier,' she barked.

He marched back to the truck and they drove off, throwing us an insulting blast of the horn in their wake.

'It's ok. They're searching for the illegal food, not us. The vendors will come back later to collect their mugs and rubbish.'

It took me a while to find my voice. 'What's going on? Where is he? Where's my father?'

'I'm sorry Sorlie. I told you. He's dead.'

My teeth started rattling like crazy, making my head thump big style. The native placed a blanket around my shoulders and hugged me. She was warm and even the smell of vinegar couldn't prevent me putting my head against her breast and allowing my tears to flow. Tears for Pa and the tears I hadn't yet shed for my mother.

'It's a shit situation, I know. This is the real world Sorlie. The world outside of military childhood is shit. There's nothing we can do about your parents, but we can try to make the shit smell a little better for those who are left behind.'

* * *

I don't know for how long we stayed like that but when she eventually pushed me back to my side of the cab I found my left hand had gone to sleep and my ribs ached from lying over the partition. When the blood began to flow again, the pain of pins and needles attacking my hand brought tears back to my eyes. I gulped them down and scolded myself. From now on I intended my mind to be a desert – dry, devoid of tears; that way nothing could hurt me again.

The native took my hand and rubbed it. 'Your pa knew something was going to happen. Before he left he reminded me of the packet your mother gave me many years ago, not that I needed reminding. He left his Jeep in the garage for my use.' She smiled then. 'He even backed it in. Thank jupe he did, I could never have reversed it out in a hurry.' She pulled the present from the holdall and handed it to me. 'Take it. Your mother asked me to deliver you to your grandfather and give him the package for safe keeping until you celebrate your coming of age, but that was before your parents were declared traitors. Also she did not know your grandfather as I do.'

'How do you know my grandfather? And how can you even dare to disobey my mother's instructions?'

Ishbel shook her head and pressed my hands over the present. 'You do not understand. This is your original DNA passport. Keep it hidden from him. He must never know you have this. Don't be tempted to look at it in case it's discovered.' She squeezed my hand hard and brought back the pain. 'Your life could be in danger if it is.'

'Why?'

'Because this holds the secret of your heritage.'

'So?'

'You need to be protected from the State. And your grandfather is still in their pay.'

'I don't understand. Why do I need protecting and how can you know my grandfather better than my mother did?'

'I just do and now you must go to him, much as I hate to take you. And as to your other question, well, we all need protecting from the State one way or another.' She tapped the present. 'Look Sorlie, there are some things you are too young to understand and right now I do not have the time to explain. Just keep it hidden.'

'But he's my grandfather. If I am in danger from him why do I need to go there?'

She whistled through her teeth. 'You are not listening. Your parents were declared traitors, and you, their son, are now an outlaw. And even though your grandfather works for the State, we are certain he will keep you hidden until the time comes for you to leave him.

'But what if my grandfather sells me to the Military in the same way he did with my mother?'

'He will not do it this time.'

'How do you know?' I could hear my voice rising, the pain of my parents' death replaced with an intense fear of what was to come. I had never met my grandfather; all I knew of him was what Pa had told me on our camping trip.

'You just have to trust me. He will not harm you.'

'Who are you? And who are we – you said we?'

'That is of no concern to you now. Let me just say, at the moment I am only one of a handful of persons in Esperaneo who care for your well-being.'

'Who are this handful? My grandfather?'

She looked to the sea. 'No not your grandfather. I doubt if he cares for anyone, but he has a debt to pay. I can't tell you any more so don't ask again. I've already said more than instructed. Come, we must go, or we will be late for our Transport.' She handed me the packet. 'Stow it on your person.'

I tucked it in my inner wear and hoped it wasn't too obvious. She threw the holdall onto my lap before starting the Jeep. I looked at the native, who had cared for me since I was small, who had told me stories and sang me songs, but who had never hugged me until today. She was a Celt, the underclass I was not supposed to associate with, and yet she had just told me that she cared for me with a warmth I had never witnessed in her before. Those amber eyes with the far-away locked in them told me she cared.

As if to confirm this she put her hand up to my face and said, 'I'm sorry I slapped you. I will try not to do it again.'

Who was she? She pulled rank on military personnel and was now speaking to me as a Privileged would do. Suddenly I wanted to go home with this new-look native to care for me; to be talking or wrestling with my friends or watching the Games Wall with my feet on the table and a tub of popcorn on my lap; to be back in the safety of my sleeping room, waiting for my parents to return from their missions. But I knew that safe life was long gone with my parent's deaths – their traitors' deaths. The native was right, life's shit.

Chapter Six

The road north dropped towards the town before resuming its winding way through the desolate High Lands.

'I thought we weren't going to the ferry?'

'We're not,' she said.

The road elbowed and almost doubled back on itself as if the engineers had intended to carry on into the town but changed their minds when they saw the wretchedness there. As we approached the bend, the native slowed to a crawl and hunched over the steering wheel to survey the shambolic harbour. A container truck spilled human cargo onto the concrete dockside where waiting guards kicked them into line and began shifting through them. They were natives, mostly men, some women, chained together by wrists and ankles. Some were in a bad way and needed help from fellow prisoners; the inert were unhooked from the line and dragged to one side, then carted off in another truck. It reminded me of archive fishing-trawler footage when the catch was hauled and the tiddlers thrown back for another chance, the only difference being the throw backs here had run out of chances.

The open maw of the ferry swallowed the remainder whole. We watched as they disappeared into the black, blinked out one by one like viruses being eradicated from a flash memory device. One caught my attention: a boy of about my age, with a shock of rust-coloured hair, walking straight-backed among the haunted and wasted figures around him. He twisted his body from the regiment until his hate-filled eyes sparked across the floodlit quayside to me. He did not belong there even though he was unmistakably native.

'Did you see that?' I said, even though I knew she had.

The native swallowed dryly and remained silent as she accelerated from the scene. It was bizarre, like some cameo play she'd laid on for my benefit.

'Why the chains?' I said to break the silence. 'Why don't they use the Tag and Stun?'

She snorted a bitter laugh. 'They wouldn't waste their tags here. These souls are addicts – alcohol and drugs. They're bound for the prison ships five miles out in the bay. They don't even make it to the islands. They're worthless to the State. Life expectancy out there is less than a year. Disease, starvation and deprivation kills them. It would be kinder to put them down. It's no better than the clearances.'

The native clearances of the late Sixties' Purist regime, when the natives from all corners of Esperaneo were purged from their land; this was taught history. Pa said Academy shied from teaching the wretched real history of Esperaneo, but some history they are proud of.

Once, a boy asked the tutor why the Land Reclaimists continued with the clearances even though it was originally a policy brought in by the Purists who'd been their enemies. The tutor's face turned purple before he ran from the class. Next day the boy was missing. He was never seen again. My parents knew the family so I asked why he no longer came to class. Pa's eyes flicked a warning and he pursed his lips as if to sound a raspberry. No need to ask what that meant. We could all communicate with our eyes – sometimes it was all we had. Only gouging could stop that, but that rarely happened.

Another boy once punted round an image of a book called *Everyone's Watching*. Perhaps he wanted us to read it and use it for code, but we never found out because he too disappeared from school. Pa said it was because he was specially chosen to be sent with the new military recruits to the borders. The only way this was special was because the boy was just nine years old.

Academy was a long way from the misery I had just witnessed on the dockside.

'Why did you bring me here if we're not using the ferry?' That rusty-haired boy with the fight in his eyes looked neither addict nor worthless.

'You need to learn something of the misery of others before you enter the Prison System.'

'You make it sound as though I'm to become a prisoner too.'

Her silence was unnerving.

Huge drops of rain pelted the windscreen as we left the dock behind. The native flicked the wipers on full, and as they screeched across the screen I held my hands up to my ears again to try to blot the painful sound out. Was it only a few days ago when Pa and I went on the camping trip and he'd complained about the noise?

With a muttering grumble the native clicked the wipers to slow.

The headlights on the Jeep intensified as we passed through a tunnel of trees and they remained on high because, away from the dock lights, the sky was growing darker. It seemed that daylight would never appear in my life again, and I didn't want it to. We pulled off the main road and bumped along a small single track until we came to a gate. The native stepped out to open it, then drove into the field beyond and cut the engine.

'We wait here.'

'Is my father really dead?'

'Yes. I'm afraid he is.'

The pity in her voice made me want to punch her and instruct her to stop lying to me and to bring my father back, but I knew she wasn't lying and it wasn't her fault. Instead I wiped my hand across my nose and mouth and asked the other question on my mind.

'How long will it be until we reach … our destination?' The name of the place stuck in my gullet.

'Soon a Transport will arrive and I'll take you to your grandfather. When I hand you over to him I won't speak to you. My mission will be complete and you may never see me again.'

She made me sound like a parcel of oats. I thought she was finished but as she looked up at the sky she said, 'I'm glad I was your native, Sorlie. You were a special child and I know that you'll grow into a very special adult. It's not been easy for you, but I suppose you've known no other life.'

'Why can't I go with you? I don't want to go to my grandfather's. I've never even met him.' My throat burned.

'Please don't cry.'

'Then don't take me there.' I could hear my screeching but didn't care. 'Why can't I stay with you? I want to stay with you.'

'Don't shout Sorlie; it will do you no good. I have other work and there is nowhere else for you just now.'

'What if the Military come to hunt me down? You said I was an outlaw. What about my chip?'

'Your chip is short range so you'll just disappear off their system. They might suspect you are in your grandfather's care, but if they do come looking for you, he won't hand you over, I'm certain.'

'You can't leave me with a stranger who lives in a penitentiary. I just know it'll be horrible.'

'It may not be for very long,' she said, still looking at the sky.

Thick silence fell over us like a plague, infecting my mind with dark thoughts. A couple of days ago I was a sixteen year old boy whose only cares were what grades the science project earned and who I would next wallop at wrestling. Today I was an orphan being placed into the care of an evil grandfather. It was like something out of the Games Wall multi-layer, not something real.

'You know him, don't you? My grandfather?'

'Yes, I've met him. Only once. But I know him better than he realises.'

'Well, what's he like?'

She picked at her broken nails.

'Spill,' I said trying to chase fear from my voice.

'Dark.' She sounded angry. Then she coughed and spoke as if she had rehearsed. 'Dark,' she began again. 'Not his hair, which is silver, but his face; everything about him is dark, from the wiry brows above his vicious blue eyes to the boots he uses to kick his way around. And cold and sharp, like a steel blade. But sometimes that blade reflects his past and his future and then he becomes just another pitiful old man.' In the space of one sentence her anger turned to sadness in this description of a man she had only met once. This was personal.

A sound approaching from above turned her attention back to the window. 'Let's go,' she said as she grabbed the holdall.

The sky ahead streaked with fork lights highlighting specks of rain dancing towards the sodden field. It looked almost pretty.

'Your name is Ishbel, isn't it?'

The tendons in her neck snapped with the speed of her head-twist to me.

'Forget that.'

'It's what Ma called you.' I wanted to topple her while she was off balance.

'Your parents were often lax.'

'Will I ever see you again?'

'I don't know, Sorlie. I hope we'll meet again one day.'

The Transport that landed in the field carried an insignia on the nose, a badge like an old heraldic shield, almost childlike: it showed a Celtic knot woven through with small white flowers. It was a most peculiar sight on such a battered old Transport, which was definitely non-military.

'I don't understand. Non-military flight is banned.'

'Some people can get past the rules.'

Yes, she had already proved that.

'What sort of Transport is this?'

'More questions I can't answer,' she said as she took my arm. 'Come on.'

• • •

It seems we had cheated the dawn as the Transport headed into a deeper darkness where light was endangered and warmth was extinct. The Transport was a small six-seater twin engine affair and deserved a lowercase status; everything around me rattled, including my teeth and bones. The rip in the red plastic seat I perched on bumfled with escaping wadding, and the torn edge scratched through my clothes. The seatbelt round my waist was frayed and held together with a dodgy buckle.

If I wasn't being kidnapped I might have enjoyed the thrill of the turbulent ride. As a military family, we used Transports to take us on our rare visits to the Leisure Lands, but those Transports were well maintained, unlike this rickety piece of junk. The native sat in the seat next to me, sending a message on her wrist communicator, even though this was forbidden to her. I knew I was staring but couldn't stop; I'd never seen a native on a Transport before. Although her brow was pleated in concentration, she was calm, as if this was part of daily life.

'Who are you?' I asked.

'I am your native. That's all you need to know.'

Chapter Seven

It was like being inside a game. If I held out my hands I could touch the pilot's seat, read the hi-vis green dial. If I had a hand-held with me I swear I could have flown the thing; I had played it often enough. Eavesdropping on the pilot's conversation with the co-pilot was difficult; they spoke to each other and communicated with some controller in a dialect of English that eluded me. It wasn't even like the new Garble language the State had tried to introduce last year.

We travelled low over the water and I spotted the light formation of those weird crawling moor-logging boats Pa pointed out to me from the beach that night. Through the rain-drenched blackness a few more lights emerged. Some seemed to trace us in their beams, searching, twitching to shoot us down. Each time a light bounced upwards the pilot manoeuvred the Transport to avoid it, slamming the throttle forward and throwing us back in our seats. I couldn't have done better on the Games Wall.

When the hard lights died, the clouds grudgingly parted to an indigo sky; the moon on the horizon bowed to the dawn. At last the day had arrived; maybe things wouldn't be so bad in daylight.

Ishbel hunched forward, jaw clamped, her eyes fixed ahead. Where would she go? Where did natives go when their useful life is over? A reservation, perhaps, far away from harm? It's one of those pointless mysteries that do not concern the Privileged.

In all the time she served us she'd never been absent, not even for a day. I remember during Academy selection periods, the only time we were required to physically turn up for class, she was there when I left home in the morning and there when I came home at night, food prepared ready for me to eat alone. When the meal was cleared she would help me with homework, then we would play chess. She was an excellent chess opponent; she always let me win but stretched the game long enough to challenge.

Last year when the Ento 3 virus erupted in Academy, she sat by my bed all night even though my parents were home. They needed to sleep, she said; their work was important to our Noble State. The spit in her voice when she said *our Noble State* struck me as strange and for the first time I thought about her life, though not for long. She never complained, she hardly ever laughed, she never cried; what more was there to think about?

Only once did I find her missing. I'd been sent home from Academy early; it was the beginning of the major power failures, before they re-commissioned the back-up nuclear stations. The house was empty and the rooms held a sort of chill as if an ancient ancestor had travelled through and stroked the hairs on my neck as they passed. I felt scared, worried that an unknown force had disabled the security surveillance and lay in wait for me. Pirates or rebels – there was always talk, kidnappings, disappearances. Pa constantly called me a worrywart, but still, sometimes worry-warts itch and bleed and after all, sixth sense was becoming the next big thing.

I climbed the stairs to the native's cell at the top of the house, unknown territory for me. It was the size of my bathroom with a bathroom the size of a closet. The bed was wedged into the corner leaving just enough space for a table and chair; all were plain white utility wood. No pictures hung on the walls, no mementos or trinkets lay around. Every surface was bare, all except a blue and white speckled pebble the size of a duck's egg. It had a dent in the middle as if it had been worn away. Why would anyone keep that? It wasn't even pretty. I left the room then; she wasn't there and there was nothing else to interest me.

· · ·

'Did you bring your pebble?'

'What?'

'The pebble, the one from your room, did you bring it?'

She said nothing.

'Remember that time I came home early and you weren't there. I looked for you in your cell and all I found was that stupid pebble.'

When she had returned that day she showed no surprise to find me there, but she did scuttle up to the cell before preparing my meal. On her return she looked flushed; her face rearranged in features of many expressions. I could see it moving again now in the same manner as if there was an intruder inside her body pushing and struggling to break free.

She put her hand in her pocket and pulled out the stone. It was smaller than I remembered but the markings on the surface were the same.

When she ran her thumb over the stone and into the depression, it fit perfectly.

'I rub it for luck. It normally lives in my pocket, but I left in a rush that day and forgot to pick it up. It's from my motherland, my home island.' She turned to the window. 'Look, you can see the lights up ahead. We're almost there.'

The Transport began to slow in its approach, buffeted sideways by the wind. It was almost full light.

White-crested waves crashed against a jagged shoreline above which towering black and white peppered cliffs hung in balconies decorated with vegetation and guano. Birds whirled and wheeled oblivious to the wind.

One would have thought the sea and cliffs would be deterrent enough for such a prison, but grey walls even higher than the Base perimeter fence formed an impressive crown on the clifftop.

A large **H** was red-painted on a central section inside the crown. In my Recent History class we learned the most common form of air Transport for short distance had been a helicopter. This **H** was a helipad. Helicopters had been banned as dangerous

47

and replaced by fixed-wing Transports fifty-odd years ago. The realisation struck me: Black Rock Penitentiary was over fifty years old. It was ancient.

. . .

The sharp, ozone-tinged air scratched my lungs as I stepped onto the **H** pad. The native followed and motioned me to stay put. An old man dressed in dull clothing stood watching our disembarkation; he tried in vain to smooth his long hair, which blew all airts in the wind. I guessed it was my grandfather, not because he reminded me of my mother, although there was a likeness, but because he matched the dark description Ishbel had given of him.

I hadn't believed her. I hadn't known what to expect: a little old man perhaps, an oldie who should have been reclassified long ago? Certainly not the reality of what strode towards us like some jackbooted history gag. On approach his height became obvious; he was many centimetres taller than me. His hair was the colour of palladium and now, under control, it swept back tight from his high forehead; a neat bristle beard sculpted his chin but not his cheeks, as was the recent fashion with other men of his generation. His dull clothing was a long grey coat of heavy waterproof material, the type worn by adventurers in the earlier part of the century. It brushed his worn calf-high boots as he marched towards us with the straight back of a military man. He had never been in the Military but his appearance defied that fact.

'Slow down,' I ground into my teeth, but he was there too soon. His stature was striking, but even more was the startling intensity of his pale blue eyes. In the synthetic lights of the Transport I could see they were almost wolf-white, shining above a flattened broken nose that gave him the look of an aging warrior. His face was not handsome, one to avoid, but magnetic. There was no smile for the grandson he'd never met, no friendly welcome. His eyes ranged over me, as if I were a piece of machinery to be bought and put to work. What did he look for? A semblance of his dead daughter or something he did not wish to find? That ancestors' breath touched my neck again and my feet flexed to flee. After an aeon of scrutiny he nodded to himself and turned his attention towards the native, who handed him a packet and said, 'This is from your daughter.'

My heart thudded in my ears as I mistook the package handed over for the one she instructed me to keep secret, which was stupid because I could feel its regular outline tucked tight under my belt.

The old man slit the packet open with a crooked thumbnail and stepped under the beam of the Transport's landing lights. As soon as he clicked the card into his communicator port and started reading, flashes of emotion passed over his features, ending in a thunderous scowl.

'You will find the Care Plan in order. Do you have any questions?' Ishbel braved. She faced him steadily, though he could probably have her put to death just for her tone of voice.

That primordial head jerked up from its reading to glower at her.

'I understand everything. Now get off my island, Celtic whore.'

She held his gaze for a beat, then turned and placed a hand on my shoulder. 'Be strong, and guard your possessions,' she whispered in my ear. Her amber eyes no longer held far-away in them but reflected my plight in their intensity and there was something else.

Hope.

I saw hope in her eyes as she took my hand and pressed her pebble into its palm.

'Take it, look after it for me. It will remind you of your past and the preparation your parents gave you.'

I placed it in my pocket and tried to decipher the message that was working in her earnest eyes. As she turned and walked toward the Transport, I felt an urge to run after her.

'Wait!'

I jumped, at first thinking I spoke my thoughts, but it was Grandfather who hailed Ishbel.

'Where's his passport?' he asked. 'The original?'

She did not look round. 'Your good daughter destroyed it.'

'You expect me to believe that?'

'Believe what you wish. It is destroyed,' she lied.

'Just as well,' he muttered.

He stood with me as the Transport door closed behind Ishbel but did not linger to watch it leave. The hand he put out to grip my shoulder came with surprising speed. I shrank from his touch.

'Over there and quick about it, the heat's escaping,' he barked, pointing to an open door.

The smell of institution, a particular mix of bodies, rubber-boot heels and pungent cleansing fluid, was my welcome to Black Rock. As the heavy metal door bolted and sealed behind us, the putrid air rose from below and the ceiling seemed to press down to crush me. I felt dizzy.

'What's the matter with you, boy?' His hand pushed me forward. I saw we were at the top of a metal spiral staircase. A light shone through the hatching from about thirty metres below.

'Take it if you're scared,' he said, slapping the handrail. It was more a challenge than a command.

My footsteps echoed in dull clangs as I descended. I began to count those clangs to take my mind off my shortened breath. With each step I became more stifled and had to stop once to loosen my tunic collar. He jabbed me in the back and said, 'Get a move on, I've work to do.'

It was one hundred and ninety-six steps to the bottom. There, he stepped past me and opened another door with a punch of a fingernail upon the button. Before he pushed me through I snuck a last look back up the spiral. I may not have arrived here on the Dead Man's Ferry but my soul had surely departed on the Transport in the keeping of the native, Ishbel.

Part Two

Chapter Eight

A long dark corridor lit only by floor spots stretched into an uncertain gloom. It was like one of the horrendous exercises the Military set to assess different stages of youth development where you're locked in an unlit room filled with keys in obscure places. Not only do you have to assemble the correct combination of keys to find the way out to the blinking dull-light, but as soon as the clock starts the room begins to shrink, hiding some of the escape doors. I was rubbish at it then and nothing had changed; that strangled feeling of entrapment persisted. At my hesitation the old man knitted his brillo-brows, so I tried 'a smile for a smile'. I was his grandson for jupe sake – there was supposed to be a bond.

I smelled the fear. Not from the old man: this was his domain and his confidence shone brighter than the buttons on his coat. It could have been my stench, but more likely it was seeping from the abyss ahead.

'We must pass some prisoners' cells to reach my private quarters. This will be the only time. After today you will never be permitted access to the penitentiary.'

What about when I leave? But the question stayed cradled in a pocket of worry at the back of my mouth.

'Walk by my side,' he said. 'Don't make a sound. Don't even breathe.'

I nodded. It seemed my voice had packed up and left with Ishbel.

Emerging from the shadows at the other end of the corridor a military-style guard stood rigid. His uniform was flat black and he carried an old-fashioned automatic rifle. A riot baton hung on his belt. His eyes never wavered from some fixed point above our heads, even when he clicked his heels in salute. My grandfather ignored him and poked me in the back with a sharp finger.

'Move!'

Blood thundered round my body and I put my hand to my chest to catch the pulse and quieten it. Could the prisoners hear it or did they have their own sounds? I imagined huddled beings, behind doors, ears pressed to cold metal listening for our footsteps. The temptation to flop on my belly and crawl the length of the corridor was so strong I hunched to keep low, afraid of disturbing the pregnant air. The sound of my heels clattered like hail on a snare drum. The locked doors crowded me; the corridor stretched, narrowed and with each step the guard seemed to move farther away. A voice from somewhere sizzled and singed the hair on my nape; Grandfather's step missed a beat, I lost my footing and tripped. He grabbed my arm, stopped my fall and jerked me forward like a naughty child.

Sweat soaked my oxters and groin and by the time we reached the guard I wanted to pee, but to ask seemed unwise. I probably couldn't do it anyway.

A metal shutter door slid open behind the guard. I stepped over the lip and was propelled right then left by my grandfather's arm. He waved his ring at a heavy pad and another door slid open to reveal a wide hall from the olden days. The air smelled different. The institution stench was replaced with the overpowering pungency of vanilla. There was the foosty smell of my grandfather with an undercurrent of something else, that powdery something I had only ever detected in the rare times I'd encountered oldies.

Cracked and veined paintings, the ancient kind still found in government buildings, hung on brocade-covered walls; tables carried lamps, china vases and bowls filled with dusty dried flowers; a museum. We approached ornamental wooden doors where carvings of huge oak hands the size of plates beckoned me. My grandfather produced an old-fashioned key and turned it, grinding the lock, moribund technology that should have been scrapped years ago.

The doors hushed open over a thick fabric floor covering.

My feet softened in the plush pile, my footsteps silenced. The room was brightly lit, busy and cluttered. One of those old lighting effects with glass crystals dangled from the ceiling. Scarred and scratched items of furniture were scattered lengthways and breadthwise across the room, leaving very little floor space. In the corner looking out of place on a small bureau, an obsolete workstation blinked. An equally incongruous white box hummed in one corner, water gurgling in its bowels as it sucked the moisture from the room, its frayed wire inserted into an electric socket.

The room smelled like the mouldy native rag sales Ishbel used to drag me to on Saturday mornings. The wall covering was strange: rectangles of varying shapes and colours. The walls were bricked with books – real books, not texts. I'd seen books before on field trips to native settlements but never so many in one place; I wanted to touch them but was terrified to move.

The expression on my grandfather's face was unfathomable. Was it pride?

'May I?' I asked, pointing to the shelf by the door.

He nodded. I picked off the first book that came to hand: Marcus Periwinkle's *The Loneliest Planet*.

We had been taught the text at Academy. It was deemed a classic but here was an actual copy. I rubbed my hand over the cover and opened it. It smelled of the dying leaves that fall and rot after the rainy season.

'It's a book,' he said. Yes, it was pride. He couldn't hide it in his voice. 'Read them if you like.' He waved his hand around the room like a magician conjuring up an imaginary world, except this world was too creepy to be believed.

'I detest text readers. Some of these books are banned.' He touched a spine of one with his fingertips. 'But I permit you to read them while you're here,' he said like an old sage. 'As part of your education, you understand.'

Was this guy real?

'Thank you,' I said with the required reverence as my hand

caressed the book. I cracked open the spine and pressed my nose into the crease between the pages.

Bad move. He whipped the book from my hand.

'You are to treat these with respect or I'll deny you access,' he said as he smoothed the wrinkle from the spine. The room was warm but I felt that chill again and I still needed to pee. This clutter must harbour colonies of germs; I could feel them crawling out of the books and fabric and into my immune system. I tried to imagine myself reading in this room and couldn't. I wanted out.

'I need to pee. Can I please use your facilities?'

He replaced the book in its shelf space and with precision aligned it with the others. Then his pale eyes hunted over me again. He looked as if he could murder me without breaking sweat.

'I'll show you to your quarters. Come, boy.'

Another wooden door opened into a white-panelled, sterile corridor. The smells of vanilla and leaves were replaced with that of synthetic pine. The corridor was long with perhaps six or eight doors leading off and a metal shutter at the far end. Half way along he lifted his foot and toed a partially open door.

This room dazzled in its whiteness. It was larger than the reading room, or seemed so because it was sparsely furnished. There was little more than a utilitarian bed, a desk and two chairs, all white. There was no Games Wall, just a prehistoric workstation that was totally obsolete – a beast station.

'Is this it?' I couldn't bite my tongue.

I dumped my bag on the bed and fought to stop my piss-hop. Where was the toilet?

'This was my assistant's room.'

'Oh yeah.' He probably died of white blindness.

At least there was a window, the first window I'd seen since I walked down those awful stairs below the crown of the perimeter walls. Until this moment I'd assumed the whole penitentiary was underground. It gave me a view to the sky and sea and circling birds. This window would be my salvation even though there was not one scrap of land to be seen through a fine mist.

I turned and caught his stare. He stepped back, then seemed to collect himself.

'What is it?' I asked.

'Your eyes. They're blue.' He seemed surprised at this fact, even after his earlier scrutiny.

'Yes. My mother's eyes were blue.' I waited to see his reaction, to see if he knew she was dead, to notice the use of the past tense. The horrible past tense. But there was no flicker in his expression.

'Your mother should never have been born,' he said, and left the room.

That hurt. He should have just kicked me in the balls. At least then I would know the pain would subside in a short while.

How could he be like this? Ma was so gentle. Had been so gentle. No way could he be my grandfather. Never. He must be an impostor.

These thoughts recurred over and over as I examined the room to find any hint of modern technology and determine the surveillance points. At the window, the sight of the sea sealed my predicament. It was as if I were on a raft, adrift; an orphan with no native to care for me; I didn't even have Academy to pass the time. I was imprisoned in a penitentiary, yet had committed no crime.

I peed in the white washroom and stared at my reflection in the mirror for an epoch to see if there was any resemblance to him. There might have been a camera behind it but I cared not one grain. Let them take my stare. What I saw was the same blue-eyed boy who woke a few days ago, excited on his sixteenth birthday. My parents had smiled and hugged me and taken pleasure in the happiness their present had given. Was that only a few days ago?

After a while prefab food was delivered by an insignificant native. He kept his head low and mumbled for me to leave the tray in the corridor when done. I considered firing up the beast station but it needed a key that was nowhere around. I connected my reader and watched some Snap TV. The signal was weak and the clips were repeats I had seen a trillion times before so I lay on top of the bed and watched the changing light, waiting for darkness to drop in. There was no moon, it was raining again and as I listened to the splashes on the window I tried to empty my mind. When tears threatened, I used Pa's trick and pummelled the pillow until my upper abductors ached. The ordeal of the past few hours had left my mind numb so it was no surprise I slept. When I woke it was fully night and for the first time I noticed the sound of the sea. And from then on the sound of the sea pounded my ears every minute of every day. The hammering of the surge on the rocks below my window was so hard I feared, and sometimes wished, that the island would erode at its base and the crown of the penitentiary would crumble and it and all its inhabitants would tumble into the raging surf and perish. Who would care if we did?

There were other night sounds in the lull when the tide receded. Screams. Not from the living quarters but from outside. Animal screams, perhaps a young rabbit hooked and lifted into the sky by an owl, but moments later a similar scream shuddered and I tried hard to believe it was not that of a man.

That first night I lay on my bed and watched the timer on the wall click its way towards morning. There was nothing to drink and no kit to test the water. If I tried to ignore my pounding dehydration headache maybe I would sleep.

A light from outside flashed into the room and across the floor. I counted the seconds, as I did for the fifty-three seconds of the Home Base perimeter light, but this light flashed again after nine seconds and then again after eleven. That can't be right. It must be a lighthouse but a lighthouse beam is constant. I counted the varying spaces until daylight began to creep across the floor and then I slept. I knew I slept because a slight shake of my shoulder woke me.

'Come on now, wake up pal.'

One eye opened to daytime. The dull light struggled through the window, casting a delicate halo around the dark apparition in navy overalls that stood before me.

Chapter Nine

'Ye've got tae wake up now and eat something, wee man.'

He was small with sandy-coloured hair and skin the colour of oatmeal. There was a definite native look about him, with freckles on his face and hands. His cheek bones and eyes were so hollowed it looked as though the skin on his face had been borrowed or stolen, pulled tight over his skull and vacuum packed. Grey eyes stared at me and crinkled when his smile revealed a mouth of discoloured, crooked teeth. That smile reached right into my soul and gave me a hug.

'Come on now, wee man, let's be havin' ye up and dressed and fed.' Northern native slang, not too strong but there all the same. As part of their Cultural Diversity programme, Academy gave demonstrations of different native slang, carving up Esperaneo into the native districts and showing how the language and slang dramatically changed according to those geographical districts. Up till now I'd never met anyone who spoke any form. The natives at the Base had their slang trained out of them. Apparently slang was heard at illegal sporting events when the pits were full of natives hollering and bawling for blood, but such events were a mystery to me. Ishbel, although a native, had a soft lilting accent not readily recognisable as native.

So this was my new native. He was no Ishbel for sure.

'Don't you be thinkin' ye'll git breakfast in bed every day wee man, jist the day, see'n as how it's yer first.'

'My name's Somhairle,' I said, hoping he would get the message and stop calling me wee man. I was, after all, taller than he, and it seemed too familiar a term for a native to use with a Privileged.

'Aye ah know yer name son, but it's a bit formal no? So ah'll jist cry ye Sorlie.' He held out a puny hand for me to shake but when I didn't take it he dropped it to his side and began smoothing down his tunic. 'Mine's Kaydon, but you can ca' me Scud, that's what aw ma mates cry me.'

'Scud? What sort of name is that?'

He shrugged.

'Why do they call you Scud?'

He shrugged again. 'No idea,' he said as he placed the tray on my lap. 'Now you be gettin' that intae ye. Ah'll be back in a mo wi some work fur ye tae dae.' He wandered to the window, cast a look then turned to me. 'Just cause yer here doesnae mean yer gettin' aff school work.' He thumbed toward the door. 'Auld Davie there thinks there's nithin' as important as a guid education.'

Still he didn't leave. He looked back to the window and sighed, in much the same way Ishbel sighed. I wondered where she was waking up this morning. The first morning in years she didn't have to prepare my breakfast. It was my turn to sigh and this galvanised my new native into action.

The funny little man hustled round the room tidying as he went. As he folded my outer clothes he gravitated many times to the window. Each time he caught my eye he grinned. His overalls were a sort of uniform, not like the guards or those of a civilian but an all-in-one with a series of symbols etched on it.

He eventually left me to my food which was warm with no added dairy. I detected a hint of added calcium, probably in powder form. My drink was water but it too had mineral textures and flavours added to it. So what, I was parched. My energy levels whooshed and I felt a kind of excitement at what was in store for me on my first day. As I leaned forward to place the tray on the floor I felt the pressure of the packet containing my DNA passport on my waist. Ishbel risked her life to give me this without my grandfather's knowledge. Why? Surely he knew what my DNA passport held: my ancestry line. And what was the difference between this original passport and the benign substitute? Before I rose I secreted it deep in the bag, mindful of hidden cameras – my earlier inspection had identified a small dot beside the washroom door as the most likely candidate. Even though it was an old installation there were no corners to hide and examine the passport. I'd bide my time. Grandfather's reaction to Ishbel was weird; although he didn't seem suspicious of her, he certainly didn't like her. He called her a whore – very quaint. It's a wonder he didn't search my bag when I arrived though.

There were two utility suits packed in the bag so I put one on without showering. Judging by Scud's body odour, I assumed the water restriction rules applied here too. One good thing, Scud had brought the key to the workstation. While I waited for him to return, I connected my reader and communicator and turned the beast on. After an aeon a screen popped up with the words:

"Welcome Somhairle to Black Rock. We hope you enjoy your stay."

'Ah jist thought it wid make ye feel at hame,' the scuttling Scud said on his return.

'You did this?'

'Aye – we aw huv terminals in our cells. We can send messages. Everything's monitored though.' He tapped the side of his nose with his finger, made a squinty mouth and hooked his thumb towards the small dot beside the washroom door. So I was right, there was a camera there.

'Everything is monitored but that little welcome message seems tae have been kosher.'

'You have a cell? Does that mean you're a prisoner? You aren't my new native?'

Scud walked to the window, placed his hands on the wall and took a swatchie at the sky. 'Aye a prisoner, that's me. And yer native,' he said without turning.

My grandfather assigned me a prisoner for a native. Great. 'What crime did you commit?'

'Nothing too serious,' he said, examining the command band on his wrist. 'Other than that ah cannae say.'

'Where's my grandfather?' I said to break Scud's sentinel at the window.

'Busy man, busy man. You mus'nae disturb him.' His voiced scurried like his body.

'He said I could read his books.'

Scud wheeled on his heels and peered at me with narrow native eyes. I was reminded of the cats kept in Academy science labs who stared down their captors with no fear even though they were doomed.

'Did he now?' Scud whispered. 'Did he now? Well then wee man, ye'll need tae nip along tae the library the morra after lunch. Davie boy always goes for a nap in his sleep quarters then and he'll no be wantin' you under his feet ony other time.' Scud took one final glance at the window before joining me at the beast station. 'But don't tell him ah told ye that – about the nap. He's not as young as he thinks he is and disnae like tae admit it. Aye, he'll come a cropper one day if he disnae look efter hissel'.'

The smile on Scud's face didn't disguise a certain menace present in his eyes, throwing doubt on the lack of seriousness to his crime. He seemed to snap out of that role and returned to the soft smile that greeted me on waking.

'Why can't I go to the library today?'

'Coz.'

'But why?'

'I need tae clear it with him, is all. But being yer new tutor that shouldnae be a problem for me.'

Snot erupted in my nose with that one. 'You? My tutor?'

'Who else?'

'What about Academy?'

His shifty look didn't pass me. And then it dawned: if I was an outlaw how could I continue with my education at Academy? Scud knew this.

Superb – no parents, no identity, no education, no snafin' future. Scud nodded as if reading my mind. His eyes changed again but this time to intelligence I'd never seen, or noticed, in a native – other than Ishbel. I wanted him to leave me but I had one more question for him.

'What were those screams I heard in the night?'

He grabbed his command band.

'Animals probably. It's a jungle out there.' He punched me on the arm. 'Better aff in here, eh?' He left abruptly and didn't return until lunch. Then he loaded beast-station with an old desk top learning system and left again. Each time I tried to speak to him he tapped his nose and brushed my questions aside. Some line had been crossed when I asked about the screams.

As he collected my lunch tray he smiled, almost apologetically. 'The morra will be different, eh? We'll git ye in tae the library, then ye'll find oot aw sorts o' things.'

'Will I see my grandfather tonight?'

He didn't even look round from the doorway as he said, 'Probably not.'

Chapter Ten

Of course the packet was still there – did I really need to check the holdall one more time? I did anyway. The sparse furnishings did not accommodate good hiding places so the only way to stow the holdall was to stuff it in the bedside locker.

The power shutdown happened sooner than expected. There was nothing to do but lie listening to the wash and pull of the sea. The sounds changed depending on the tide and wind and sea levels. That's when I noticed the lighthouse beacon again. Counting the erratic flashes was sure to put me to sleep, except tonight it was constant, every thirteen seconds. The pinlight of my communicator was pretty feeble but enough to aid my stumble to the window. It was impossible to work out where the lighthouse was and how it could shine in this room. There must be some deflection devices on the outside wall.

The overcast sky hid the stars and satellites, but far out in the blackness of the sea the lights of five bold moor-logging trawlers twinkled, as stationary as the stars seemed to be. Then something winked in the distance, just about where the horizon should be. A low star? No. It flashed, it moved, groping a way towards the island. A Transport. My heart walloped. She was coming back. The temptation to grab the holdall and stand by the door like a child waiting to be taken to the Pleasure Dome tugged me, but the gravitational pull of the window was stronger.

The approaching light never wavered from its line. Soon it would rise to the landing spot. It didn't. It kept on a trajectory, straight for my window. The noise of the engine growled, overwhelming the sound of the waves. It was going to crash. I closed my eyes and ducked, clattering my funny bone against the wall – nothing happened. The growling heightened to a whine. I rose to my feet, clutching my stoonding elbow, not wanting to open my eyes. When I did, I saw the Transport hover outside my window, like some weird firebug, two globes of light unblinking, as if trying to wire me a telepathic message. It was Ishbel. The Transport tipped its nose downwards in a bow then brought back to level. Slow to react, the lights from the perimeter crown decided to spark to life. Gunfire rained on the Transport before it somersaulted backwards and upwards into the night.

'No, don't go,' I said to the dark room and my surveillance. But she had gone. She'd left me again. I thudded my forehead on the cool of the window and thrust my hands in my pockets to stop me punching the glass. I fingered the pebble Ishbel had given me and rubbed the indentation of her own homesickness. Once our society believed in an afterlife; how I wished that were true. The breath of my ancestors deserted me now. Were Ma and Pa out there somewhere in the ether, looking over my shoulder? I made a wish on the pebble that Ishbel would come back for me and take me to her island, wherever that was. Maybe it was close to Pa's mythical land of freedom.

Even if she wasn't coming back for me just yet, she hadn't forsaken me; she knew exactly where I was in the Penitentiary. This time I left the pebble in my pocket and thumped the window with my fist until it hurt too much. The trogs behind the surveillance dot should have stopped me but they were silent, no doubt enjoying my pain. The pinprick light faded and little orphan Sorlie stumbled, lost in the dark.

• • •

Scud proved to be a daemon in native clothing. The curriculum he set was merciless although it was obvious that history was his thing. Even though Academy systems were out of bounds, somehow Davie had procured the learning modules. Scud scuttled around explaining how the desktop learning worked. He and it were about ten years past sell by and yet Academy modules operated on it. During the first level he peered over my shoulder. His odour had a ripeness of weekly washing and dubious dentistry breath, but at least he didn't smell of vinegar.

'Are you going to stay sitting here?' I asked, trying to sound pissed off.

Lessons should be done alone, everyone knows that. It was only when tactical assignments cropped up that the additional help of the native Ishbel had proved useful. Somehow she knew all the answers even though natives were not required to learn. I never questioned it at the time, but now I wonder what else she knew.

'Aye, ah'm fine here.' Scud showed off the command band on his wrist. 'Davie boy said ah wis tae make sure you studied and ah wis tae help ye if ye got stuck.' He tapped the band. 'If ah'm needed elsewhere he'll soon let me know.'

'And you'll be able to help me?' I couldn't stop the sneer in my voice. To meet one educated native was unusual but two was unbelievable.

'Aye, ah'm no as daft as ah sound ye know.'

The history module was 'Changes to the Government in the Last Fifty Years.' As each lesson appeared Scud would tut and mutter under his breath.

'Rubbish, utter tripe.'

'What?' But he would tap his nose and raise his eyes to the ceiling then right then left.

Next was maths – ouch. The standard deviation example was brutal. Two years I'd struggled with SD and none of my tutors satisfied my pleas for help. You could have wrapped me up and posted me to the moon when Scud explained the principles in SD for Dafties format. OK, so what if Scud's method was like cheating? It worked.

'Sorted,' I beamed.

He nearly smiled. But pride is a Privileged emotion so he stood

66

up, stretched his back and wandered to the window for a quick fix of ocean watching.

'Right ah'll go fetch yer lunch and then ah'll take ye tae yer precious books and ah'll git some peace and quiet.'

'Where will you go?'

'Back tae ma cell,' he said. 'This duty's a soft touch fur me. Every scholar in ma block wis efter ma blood when Davie chose me. But ah only huv the morning wi ye, wee man, that's aw. Then it's back tae ma cell tae recite the alphabet backwards.' He tapped his nose and clasped his command band.

'What do you mean?'

'Never mind son.' His voice was soft, low, almost a growl.

'Why did he choose you?'

Scud shrugged. 'Must huv looked through ma records and saw ah used tae be a university lecturer before the Purists came tae power.'

'How could you?'

'How could ah what?'

But I never got a chance to find out. A high pitch buzzing screeched from Scud's command band. He started to vibrate, his eyes rolled back into those deep-set sockets and his whole body rattled like someone shot by a stun gun. It lasted only seconds then he dropped to his knees and curled his head into his chest. I rushed forward to help him.

'Don't touch me,' he snarled through gritted teeth.

Bone by bone he uncurled his spine, rose from his knees to his feet. Beads of sweat drenched his red puckered face. He hovered his shaking hands in front of his chest. How long we stood like that, facing each other, waiting for his hands to stop their Saint Vitus dance and the pallor to return to his face – minutes? It felt like hours.

'There,' he said with a rasp. He coughed and licked his lips. 'There, that's what ah get fur opening ma big puss too wide.'

In slow measured steps he left.

An alert from the beast-station flashed an incoming message. It was from Davie boy, as I now thought of him: 'DO NOT CONVERSE WITH THE NATIVES. THEY ARE THERE TO SERVE YOU. NOTHING ELSE.'

Chapter Eleven

The lunch Scud served masqueraded as a grain mixed with an unidentifiable green vegetable substitute. It looked like the sludge dredged from the Base water pumps after each flood. It reeked of it too. There was no remnant of Scud's earlier shock; in fact he was chirpy, making a high-pitched sound through his teeth. It was the sound birds make from the trees in the morning and the evening just before dusk.

Ishbel whistled through the gap in her teeth when she was anxious but she never made a tune. Despite the warning not to converse I asked, 'What's with the noise?' What was I supposed to do, ignore him?

His wrist band hummed ominously.

'Sorry. Cannae help it. Ah don't even know ah'm whistling most o' the time. Hard habit tae break even efter twenty years.'

'Twenty years, you said twenty years – is that how long you've been here?' Panic shifted in his eyes, his head wobbled like some Eastern icon injected with akceli. Too far too soon, I'd need to learn to ride my cool.

'Can you teach me? To whistle I mean.'

'Ah don't think so, son. No allowed in here.' He collapsed into the chair and put his forehead in one hand and pointed to the food with the other. 'Wire in Sorlie, then ah'll get ye along tae the library.' He wiped his hand over his eyes and looked up at me. His skin was paler than before. It wasn't just the zapping: his stubbled head seemed blonder, and his grey eyes were now the colour of dried mud.

'Are you ill?'

'Just hurry wi the food.'

• • •

The library reeked of its dusty ancient histories, hidden and banned by successive governments. The flutter in my stomach was for the forbidden and also the fear of what I might find. I felt like an astronaut of old (in the time before space travel was limited to mineral extraction) landing on a far-flung planet, discovering a crusted tomb in which the secrets of whole civilisations were buried for their own good. As promised, Davie was absent; it seemed like years since I saw him. Scud pranced round the room, peering and clucking and sucking in, dancing some weird piss-hop.

'If you need to go pee, then go.' That stopped his trot.

'Pretty impressive, eh?' Scud said. 'You're one lucky lad being given this privilege. Ah wish it were me.' He rummaged with his finger millimetres from the books. What punishment applied to a native touching paper? I dreaded to think but Scud knew.

'Where do I start?'

'If ah were you ah would spend the day looking at only one shelf. Take yer time, ye've got until seventeen hundred hours.'

He circled the room of titles again then pointed to the shelves near the main door. 'Start here.'

• • •

The books in this section were fiction; some books I had never heard of, so guessed they were no longer permitted reads. Some were the same texts given to high ranking officers. Ma and Pa had some but not many.

Old names such as Tolstoy, Babel, Steinbeck; native fiction – Gunn and Gibbon; more modern classics by Klein, Ling and Pascal. These were the names of legends whispered of in the corner of the playing fields. As students we had tried to get hold of the texts but never quite managed it. There were rumours and boasts but that's all they were.

The fiction we were given in English was insipid, safe and easy to learn. Our tutor, Mr Elliot, often hinted there was more.

He would utter the names of the forbidden then bite his tongue and with a frightened stare waited for something unspeakable to happen in much the same way Scud looked at his command band. Nothing ever did happen during class, the surveillance trogs must have been occupied elsewhere. Academy trogs were inefficient in real time; playback was always their option. It was the sort of social control religion exploited in the olden days – you never knew if someone was watching so you walked within the margins and only dared dip a toe outside if the stakes warranted the risk. One time Mr Elliot signed into class the day after one of his utterances with a broken arm and a black eye; he apologised and said he'd slipped. At first his utterances seemed genuine mistakes, and then one day Mr Elliot disappeared. His risk must have been worth the beating, but maybe not what followed. And now Scud played the same game.

After Mr Elliot's disappearance the whispers on the playing field turned from banned books to rebellion, but what could a bunch of kids do? It was all talk.

Once, one of the boys produced from his sweaty shin pad a tattered copy of a real book about a spy named James Bond. He retold the story of the classic cars and beautiful women. This vicarious read made us laugh and we couldn't see the harm. Fleming was the writer's name.

Most of the shelves were arranged in alphabetical order, but there was no Fleming in F. Shakespeare was a name that struck a memory chord so I gave him a whiz – *The Merchant of Venice*. Venice was one of the first cities to disappear under water but I hadn't a clue what a merchant was. The language was freaky, a bit like English but not. At least the introduction was in old plain English. It told me the tale was of a Jewish moneylender Shylock. So merchant must mean moneylender. These were like the creeps and their bruisers that hung around the Base gates waiting for the natives to return from market, something to do with credit and bad vibes. So this Shylock dude must be the bad guy. The word

Jewish was alien, so I punched it into my hand reader. Nada. Even the worldwide translator blanked. There was a tattered old dictionary tucked into the bottom corner near the door but the word was not entered. Perhaps it was a misspelling; it happened in old text. Maybe fiction could wait.

The book I spent most of the afternoon reading was the history of the island. I found it by chance when I returned the dictionary to its corner. When I entered this room on my first day it was hard to imagine settling down to read here, but in an animal skin chair, the kind now forbidden by the LRP, I did just that. The chair was cool and soft and smelled of candle wax which neutralised the sweet foostiness of the room. The creamy pages of the book were smeared with what looked like cooking oil, the middle section contained monochrome photos of grubby men and women. Men in caps puffed smoking sticks, the women were bundled in scarves and wraps like washed-out Russian Dolls. They all looked as miserable as natives these days do; no wonder because they had lived off a diet of seabirds and fish – putrid puke or what? The seabird provided them with every need including oil for cooking and lighting – primitive. Then the book took on this preaching tone which pure grates my nerves to sawdust. It said, "Their demise proved to be a prophecy for the rest of the world, but as usual no one was paying attention. They took from the earth but did not give back, their lifestyle was unsustainable, and unlike the peoples of Esperaneo, their practices were not checked." You could tell it was written by a gum-bumping Land Reclaimist.

• • •

'What are you doing here, lad?'

The harsh voice jolted me from dreamtime and back to the room. The half-read book's pages were bent over, crumpled in my grasp, stuck like some smutty porno-card I couldn't shake off. I quickly tried to smooth the page but Davie grabbed it from me, almost pulling me out of the chair with it. My mouth was dry and my head ached. How could I have slept?

His face was centimetres from me, granite eyes throwing me back, impaling me to the chair.

'Well? Answer me? What are you doing here?'

'Em,' a small squeak uttered from my dry mouth. My swallow wedged in my craw, bypassing a sliver of saliva on the way. I choked. 'Em, you said I could read your books.' I stood, edging to the door.

'And did the native not instruct you to quit by sixteen hundred hours?'

'Seventeen, Scud said seventeen hundred.' It was neon and klaxons the minute the words left my mouth.

'Scud?' The word rumbled round the room, but he shifted and dropped his stare. There was confusion behind that roar. He banged his hand hard on the desk. 'I said sixteen, and since when does a Privileged know a native's name?'

'It… It isn't his real name.'

He arched an eyebrow in disbelief.

'It is just what I call him – to myself.' My palms were sweating and I became aware that I was scratching my wrist but at least I didn't have the book to worry. If I destroyed a book he would no doubt wring my neck.

He pushed me aside and sat in the chair, smoothing down the pages against his thigh. 'What have you chosen to read, anyway?' He pulled what I thought were fabled pince-nez from his breast pocket and squinted through them at the book. 'Pah, nostalgic drivel.'

'Could you suggest one, sir?' I asked.

'Don't use that pawky tone with me, boy! It won't work. Find your own way.'

I circled on the spot like a wolf before it settled in its den but there were too many choices. I was lost.

'What are you learning in class, boy?'

'The Purist Uprising during the collapse of the global market system in 2018.'

He pulled a small wooden box from his pocket, took a pinch of powder and sniffed it up his nose.

'Bit of a mouthful that.'

'Grandfather?'

'Don't call me Grandfather,' he said, blinking.

'What shall I call you then?'

He stared toward the corner of the room, his eyes clouded over.

'Call me Davie.' The glasses made him appear older. What was I afraid of? He was an oldie and not that much taller than me. The fact he needed glasses proved he no longer qualified for Corrective-S.

Imitating Ishbel, I clenched my toes and stretched to my full height before I said, 'I'm doing a project on flora and fauna and need to go outside.' This was a whopping lie, he only needed to check my knowledge log before I had a chance to alter it.

Those eyes crackled.

'No.' He pointed to a shelf of books. 'All the knowledge you need is here. Now get out. I have work to do.'

'Shall we have our meal together tonight?' I would work on him then.

He glared again but not before the hesitation dropped him a point.

'No.'

'Please Grandfather, I mean Davie. You can't keep me in solitary confinement.'

'What part of the word 'NO' do you not understand? Now leave.'

'Can I take the book?'

As he passed the book to me I noticed the liver spots on his plate sized hands were dotted with concealer that had not fully rubbed in. That was interesting.

'Don't forget to bring it back.'

Chapter Twelve

When Scud arrived later with my supper, his pallor was ghostly, almost translucent.

'What's crackin' wee man?'

'What's crackin'?' I pointed to his face. 'You, by the look of it. What happened to your face? You look like a shedding snake.'

He tapped his nose.

'But your freckles, they've gone completely.' His complexion resembled the aero flour and water paste we made at the Montessori by dipping straws into the mix and bubbling it up before mask making.

'How did that happen?'

He shrugged his shoulders. 'Don' know, nae great heartache, they wurnae ma freckles tae miss.' He cackled like a hag and started busying himself, as all natives do, with my tidying up.

'What do you mean, not yours – how could they not be yours?'

'Shush.' He bent low beside me and rapped his command band, then stood straight with hands on hips shaking his head.

'Ah have tae say you are the untidiest wee pup ah've ever come up against. Did Ish… ah mean yer mother never prevent ye getting intae such a bad habit? Ah would have thought they'd huv sorted ye oot, you being a military kid an aw.'

'Wait, you almost said Ishbel.'

He kicked the table, knocking the tray to the floor. 'Now look what ye made me dae.'

'How do you know I'm a military kid?' I whispered. There was a quiver in my voice, the skin on my body creeped as if I too moulted. What else did he know?

Scud continued clearing up the spilled tray.

'Military you say, did ah say that?' He scratched his head. His acting was chronic. 'Well, ah don' know. Ah must huv picked it up frae somewhere. Yer claethes spelt it out ah suppose.' He coughed and said, 'Anyway that's aw tae change.' He nodded to a parcel he'd dropped at the door on the way in. 'New overalls for ye. Ah suggested tae Davie boy ye might need them. Dae ye no think ye'll need mair than two sets o' claethes? No? The sea water we wash them in damages that cheap fibre somethin' rotten, even expensive cloth like yours'll take a pounding.'

Something was wrong. It was more than his skin. Each time he looked at the dark through the window his bottom lip quivered, like a baby missing its Ma.

'Are you sure you're OK?'

Scud wiped his nose on his sleeve, took a deep breath and said, 'Fine.'

He stared at some spot over my shoulder.

'Did ye ever dae art at Academy? Ah used tae be right guid at art.'

'Yes, sometimes, but it was difficult with the paper ban. We often painted and drew on recyk textile.'

Scud rubbed his hand over his aeroed cheek and chin. 'Maybe you could ask Davie boy fur art things, ah'm sure he'll have loads o' Noiri contacts wi supplies.'

'I think I would prefer to work on Davie boy's permission for my nature work – to get outside.'

At first I thought he hadn't heard, he continued rubbing his cheek and chin. He picked a scab off the side of his nose, examined it and put it in his pocket. 'Aye right enough wee man,' he said. 'Let's get on then.'

He insisted I show him again the work completed the day before. He shook his head and did that whistling thing with his teeth. He hovered over the history book that lay by my bed but did not touch. 'How much does Davie know about nature ah wonder?'

'He was brought up on a farm.'

'Uh, huh. Ah wonder if this farm wis close tae the sea?'

'I don't know.'

'What dae ye know about the birds young Sorlie?'

'Not much.'

'Not much or nothin'?'

'Nothing I suppose.'

He settled into the chair beside me, wafting rancid breath my way. 'Well there are birds here that aw you mainlanders huv niver set eyes on.' He shuffled his bum and moved closer to me. His unfortunate habit of invading my space irritated me. Each time I drew away he moved closer – very native like. He closed his eyes and struck a dramatic pose, holding his face in the direction of the window for full effect.

'When you lie in bed at night huv ye niver heard it?'

I recalled the night sounds I heard.

'Gulls you mean. I only hear the sea and gulls and sometimes screams.'

His eyes popped wide open and he made a 'shush' mouth.

'Not gulls.' He leaned forward and whispered. 'The special bird.'

'What special bird?' I whispered back.

'The corncrake.' He jumped up and did that prancing thing that set my nerves jangling just to watch. 'The corncrake, wee man.' This time he didn't whisper. 'The scrape and rasp like a rusty hinge trying tae break free.' He laughed wide and I noticed gaps in his mouth where his molars should have been. 'Ye must huv heard o' it. It's legendary. Here, look it up on FuB.'

Beastie wheezed and sighed as its ancient components considered the question, went out to lunch, took a nap and eventually ground out the answer. 'It says here that it has been extinct since 2017.'

'Aye, maybe in other places but if ye listen carefully ye can hear it here.'

'You wouldn't hear it above the other noises.'

But Scud was back on window duty. 'Now wouldn't that be a grand find for yer grandfather. An extinct bird. On his island. He'd be famous and the LRP wid hail him as a hero fur preserving this special environment that hus allowed them tae survive. The find might even pit a stop tae the Purist challenge.'

'Hardly. And how do you know about the Purist challenge?' This was political news rumbling around the Base.

He ignored me. 'Aye, ah think that you could locate that corncrake out there.' He tapped his nose. 'If ye were allowed out tae explore the island that is.' He propped his elbows on the wall, nose pressed to the glass and grinned like a daftie. 'What better nature project could there be than that?'

• • •

There was no mention of the corncrake in the island book, but with this new-found knowledge there must be something I could cook up into a stew to feed Davie.

Ever since I arrived on this island my physical stats had shown reduced readings. The non-colour white choked; the vastness of white walls and furniture suffocated. It was like being caught up in a crisp white sheet and wrapped tighter and tighter in its folds until it could be squeezed into a filament small enough to be fed into FuB and hurtled into the ether, a rough endless space with no idea where it would land. I had to get out of here.

Beastie had a few more facts to hand about the island's water purity, climate and vegetation – the usual gen – which I downloaded with some graphics to my hand reader and studied. Preparation was nine-tenths of the solution or some such scam.

There was one other thing that was dragging me down: that packet Ishbel had given me and why its discovery was so dangerous. If I got out there might be a chance to read it, a chance to escape or at least make contact with Ishbel. My worrying whittled away the rest of the evening until power shutdown. I looked at the all-seeing dot on the wall.

'Night, night,' I said. It didn't blink.

• • •

'Come on lazy, get out yer pit. Ye've a busy day ahead o' ye.' Scud's voice croaked as if he carried a glob of phlegm in his throat that wouldn't budge. Its pitch was higher too, almost female. It took a while to extract myself from the slugbag I slept in under the top cover. Scud moved to help me, but when I saw him I shrank back into my bag like a lug worm in sand.

'Sakes! What happened to you?'

His skin had shaded from pasty to barnacled. It was as if his freckles had been bleached and then baked.

'Don't worry, it isnae catchin'.' His mouthed pinched in hurt feelings and he retreated to rearrange my work area, leaving me yet again to struggle with the bag.

'What is it then? What happened to your skin?' I asked.

He looked at the back of his hand and shook his head then moved my reader to its original position on the desk.

'Well what is it? Stop fussing and tell me.'

'Ah don' know.' He didn't quite snap, that was prohibited, but there was an edge to his voice. 'It must be something tae dae wi the new vitamins they're giving us. Ah've been feeling a bit weird lately. Some o' the other guys at roster this mornin' looked a bit ropey too, especially the ging-ers.'

'What's a ging-er?'

'Ginger hair.' He grabbed his command band and took a shifty to the dot. 'It's as if we a' huv a virus or something but we can't, coz the guard couldn't care less about shoving us around. If it wiz a virus they wid be coorieing in their quarters and we'd be locked up tae rot.' The whites of his eyes pleaded as he looked from me to the surveillance dot. He grasped his command band so tightly the barnacles on his knuckles nearly popped.

'But your skin was different yesterday too.'

'Let's just leave it, OK,' he said, trying not to move his lips. 'Ma skin condition is nae concern o' a Privileged.'

'As you wish, but how do you know I'll have a busy day?'

'Don' know, just guessed – you being a bright boy, you getting access tae the library, you being stuck in here.'

'I need to do a nature project – look.' I reached to refresh Beastie, but it had powered out. 'What's happened? I left it on sleep.'

'Always shut down when ye louse. S'that no how it's done at the Military Base?' I shook my head.

'Well here when power goes out at night things switch tae a generator wi limited capacity. Your 'sleeping' station drains that power and risks further cuts. And we don't want generator power cuts do we?'

What was he babbling on about?

'No we don't want that. If the generator goes down they lock us aw in the main hall an' leave us there in the dark. This is an aw male unit. Horrible. Horrible. People get hurt, killed, diseases spread. Power cuts equals misery.' He clamped his mouth shut. So much said in those few sentences and still no zap. If this was normal acceptable banter, what horrors was he omitting?

'OK, hold your rant. Power cuts equal misery, message received. I'll try to remember. Anyway look at this.' I showed him the nature project. 'I need to get out of here.'

'Don't we all,' Scud said behind his teeth.

'Yes, but I haven't committed a crime.' I couldn't help myself.

'Maybe you should remind yer grandfather o' that,' he whispered behind a soft cough, his hand to his mouth, and then to the dot he said, 'Crimes have different definitions for different regimes, different cultures.' The nose was tapped, then 'Enough chatter – work.'

'I need to collect sea and soil samples and vegetation. We have a choice of habitat and seashore is one.'

'Ye'll need tae ask Davie.'

'I already have. He said no.'

'Maybe ye asked him too soon. Maybe ye didn't gie him a good enough reason tae let ye out. Like a corncrake fur instance.'

'I said to do a project and he said no.'

'Well if he won't let ye out he'll need tae answer yer questions for ye, won't he? Ah cannae. Ah'm just a humble historian, ah cannae help ye on this one and ah doubt if he would like another prisoner in here tae help. But he's a busy man, has a prison tae run.' Scud scrolled down the text. 'How's yer projects presented?'

'Hologram,' I said.

'Can ye write on paper, spools, that sort of thing?'

I shook my head. 'Don't be such a crunk, that's obsolete.' This paper thing again. Natives can be so primitive.

'Can ye read and write handwriting?'

'Of course.' What had this to do with getting outside? 'Ancient art is still taught in Academy, you know.'

'Ah see.' He looked down at his pale and barnacled skin but seemed to concentrate on some far-off world. Then he clapped his hands together and rubbed them so fiercely I ducked from the flying skin particles. Someone would have to sweep up.

'Right, let's be havin ye. Get on with this nature project why don't we? We'll see if our wee pal the corncrake is mentioned.'

Despite his enthusiasm, as we worked through the morning Scud kept drifting into sleep, falling off his chair. At first I left him. Then a humming sounded and he jolted upright. It was like watching a Snap TV Roadrunner cartoon when Wile E Coyote hit an electric wire; sparks flew, his skeleton juddered, eyes bulged and spiralled, teeth rattled, before he was released to the ground, smoking like a doused campfire. Except this wasn't funny and cartoons don't smell of burning flesh and pisshap. The jolt came after ten minutes of inactivity, so I began to wake him after eight minutes. This was disruptive and the planned work fell out of the allotted time. I don't know why this bothered me so much; it wasn't as if the work would be submitted to Academy for scores. Officially I didn't exist, like those boys in my year that disappeared before me.

'Is there an Infirmary here?' I asked on the way to the library.

He nodded.

'Then, I think you should go.'

'Oh ah don't think there's much use in that.'

'Well go to your cell and sleep.'

This was a joke it seemed. 'It's no as easy as that. Ah won't be taken off ten minute activity watch until ah've finished ma chores fur the day. Ah still have the duty roster for next week tae finish and ah huv a new bunch o' young detainees tae brief on the principles o' the Land Reclaimist Party manifesto.'

'Why do you have to do that?'

He shrugged. 'Someone has tae dae it. – "No rest for the wicked," as the ancestors used tae say.'

• • •

The library was as I left it, minus the tyrant. A slim book, almost a pamphlet, lay on the table beside the skin chair. Its pages were ragged, the binding rough as if it had been home-made in a native shantytown. It was entitled *History of the Clearances (2064-2066)*. It was planted but I played along even though it was sure to be propaganda of one side or the other. Most of its text was humdrum, stats, charts, boring. So what if the ethnos from the Eastern Zone and Desert States willingly lived on these shores? They weren't here now. The Purists got rid of them, sent them back to their origins, everyone knew that. No one ever challenged how ethnic origins were established though and this propaganda claimed a DNA test was devised – if the ethnos failed to show the desirable mix of alleles they were deported. There was a footnote: early natives had welcomed and assisted in the clearance of the ethnos, but in a land of diminished resources and ever expanding populations, who would be next? I reread the stats – there were tens of millions deported back to Desert States. Some never arrived due to something called genocide. The old raggedy dictionary drew a blank on this word as did my reader. It's funny though, how some words carry their own meaning in their roots. *Geno* = race, and the meaning of *cide* is a no-brainer. Put them together and you reach hell. It made my skin crawl, the histories of millions of lost souls prickling at each of my pores. I could see now there were clues and remnants of this history all around the Base even after all the decades. Some families must have cheated the system.

Once there was a doctor who came to Academy to inoculate us against some new virus or other. It was a bright day. As we lined up in the drill hall the sun streaked through the window onto the area where the doctor stood sticking inoculation patches on each arm bared to him. His colour was Caucasian and his hair light brown. The heat in the hall became intense, cranking the joules to red. I don't remember why, maybe the air-con broke or maybe the power was out again. The doctor loosened his tie and unbuttoned his shirt at the neck. It was possible to see tight curly black hairs on his chest. Whispers trickled through the line like rubble through a riddle. He dyed his hair, what a dolt. There was a scuffle as everyone in the line tried to swatchie a look, but before it was my turn to receive the patch a guard appeared at the door. Sweat now buttered the doctor's face. The clamminess of his touch when he put the patch on my arm smeared so much the patch wouldn't stick. This was the first time I ever smelled the fetid reek of fear. The doctor's car remained in the parking bay for days until it was eventually carted off on the back of a truck.

Davie owed me an explanation; he had left this history here for me to read. Why?

A sepia, blue and green globe that looked as though it belonged to the Romans was shoved in a corner behind the desk. On closer inspection different hues of colour emerged showing borders, individual countries and states. It was inconceivable that so many countries once existed within the land mass that is now Esperaneo. I spun the globe hard and these borders fused into a conglomerate, each country becoming as indistinguishable as greasy handprints on a prefab food-chain door. Was this how the world became carved up into three slices – some power took a globe and spun it off its hinges to reach the desired mix, throwing populations into turmoil, until it slowed and settled? The only problem was the turmoil still existed and the globe continued to spin.

Twenty-one hundred hours and Davie was a no show. The old crumbly must have guessed I'd be waiting for him. No use asking Scud about the pamphlet; disclosing that sort of information would zap him into orbit.

. . .

A meal of the usual synthetic nondescript muck was laid beside Beastie. The grey broth was cold and had a film on it thick enough to plaster the cracks on Scud's skin. It heated in minutes by thermo-rod and filled a hole. There was too much time to think in this place. Images of peoples cast out from their homes, murdered and banished to foreign lands crowded my pea-brain. How could the world have changed so much in half a century? If all this happened during my grandfather's lifetime then how many more oldies like him were involved? Of course there weren't too many oldies of his generation around now since that nasty little silversurf virus wiped them out. How convenient.

Scud said his condition wasn't a virus, but how could he be sure? My stats were reading normalish for someone my age with no access to daylight but that didn't stop a cold shudder raking my spine. What was happening to Scud and when would it start to infect me? I once read a text called *The Count of Monte Cristo* about a man falsely imprisoned on an island for years. Was that my fate?

The erratic lighthouse beacon flashed across the floor. 'Please come back for me,' I willed to the distant Ishbel, but there was no sound of an approaching Transport. I listened above the sounds of the sea and gulls and that stupid non-existent corncrake until my ears almost bled but no amount of wishing and listening made her come.

. . .

Breakfast was served next morning by a small man with spiky white hair and pink eyes – a goblin of the kind found in fairy tales. The sight of him was enough to put you off the rest of your life.

'Where's Scud?' I asked. His watery pink eyes blinked in fear.

He shook his head before scuttling from the room backwards

and knocking his Neanderthal knuckles on the door jamb. There was a crunch and whimper and he vanished, no doubt muddying the corridors with his blood as he dragged his knuckles after him.

Where was Scud?

The morning hush deafened. It was almost a relief when rain splattered the window and the wind rose to whip up the waves into their fury again.

The goblin was back with lunch.

'Where's Scud?' Even though Scud said the prisoners had messaging access, Beastie gave as many answers as this gobo. There was an even bigger catastrophe when I found the library closed during opening hours. I hammered and kicked on the door to no effect. I thumped it one last time just to let the corridor police see how this hurt before I dragged my beaten ass back to the cell and shut myself in a world of learning.

Several listings of corncrake calls were available on FuB with links to articles about the shy wee creature. What else could I find? Not enough to keep me sane. The Count of Monte Cristo dug a tunnel into an abbé's cell and learned everything the abbé had to teach him. This had taken aeons, but I didn't want aeons. My brain would rot into madness before that.

· · ·

The daytime was growing longer and the light was changing. Torrents of black rain gave way to the gusty squalls of the pre-equinox. Sudden portals of sky appeared between grudgingly parted clouds. Insipid daylight often crept across the floor before morning wakeup. My room faced south-east and caught most of the day's sunlight, whenever it chose to shine that was.

The changing daylight hours bothered me. If I was to get out of this prison and get a message to Ishbel it would need to be before second quarter. Darkness was used to bring me here. Darkness worked.

After three days of silence from my grandfather, the non-appearance of Scud and a locked library door, I settled into a life of solitary captivity and began to tap the walls with a spoon, à la Monte Cristo. My nails were bleeding from the gnawing I inflicted on them. When I was about to start on my toenails Scud reappeared. His pale scabby face was not a pretty sight, but prettier than the silent gobo.

'Where have you been?' The urge to hug him passed the moment his putrid aroma followed him into the room.

He held his finger up to his nose for silence and I obeyed. No way was he being zapped from me again.

Scud was morphing. Hair normally falls out, or turns grey as humans move from prime to senior then oldie when the whole body starts to disintegrate to dust. Scud's hair was fading as if all the pigment was being rinsed out. It was pointless asking him about this phenomenon. The only reply he could chance was a tap on his nose or a roll of his eyes in the direction of the dot.

It had been over a week since I last saw Davie; not since he had left that propaganda pamphlet out for me to read. His reasoning for this mystified me and maybe he was regretting the whole thing. At least I might now have access to the library again. I would be seriously cooked if that privilege was taken. So corncrake project it was, but all the evidence stated it was extinct. Scud however rubbished that claim.

'Just listen,' he said. 'It's best heard at dusk.

'What dusk? Dusk is linked with the sunshine and that's practically an extinct species. Anyway I have been listening.' The pillow I threw across the room settled on Beastie like a marshmallow fedora. 'I'm sick of listening. I've nothing else to do but listen.' Despite Scud looking like a biblical leper and the risk his arm might break off in my hand, I dared to grab him and drag him to the window.

'Go on, you listen. That's it, all it is, the overpowering noise of the sea. How could an inland bird-call penetrate that sound?'

Scud pursed his lips like an old woman. 'It might be your only way out,' he whispered.

Chapter Thirteen

Ever since my arrival on this island my body mass reduced daily, despite the vitamin enriched food stuffs in my diet. I'd been unable to partake in physical exercise apart from my daily tutorial work-out Scud programmed into the system, but that was worse than useless. A sprint up and down the corridor took milliseconds, sink press ups gave me white blindness and after I'd retrieved the pillow from Beastie's crown the pillow thumps left me despondent. My legs grew scrawny and my muscle wasted. If my fitness instructor at the Base saw me she would banish me into the 'weeny' team.

Some nights as I lay listening to the blood rushing through my brain, I'd hear alarm sounds in the distance, from the main block. Seconds later the searchlights punched the night. I knew what was coming next; a louder alarm blared, inside lights dimmed to energy saving mode and guns blasted. The first time this happened was a real shituation. I imagined a mass breakout: hundreds of angry men coming to spoil and riddle rap a minted young boy. Now it's typical; the alarm sounds every few days. What puzzled me was why someone would attempt to escape this shit hole. There was nowhere to go. Even with an accomplice the odds of success must be pretty slim. The thought depressed me. Often on these breakout nights I'd count off the seconds of the beacon and dream of Ishbel flying to me in her Transport, coming to carry me to freedom. But that was childish fantasy land and the options left to me were to wise up or decay.

• • •

Routine – or was it rot? – set in. Scud and I worked on modern history most mornings because this was his FAV and gave him the opportunity of much head scratching and mumblings, like it was his duty to give me the gen on what was what. Pa had already debunked some myths; Davie's library was rubbishing the rest. What more was there to spill? Message received – world history according to FuB was an elaborate fabrication devised by three corrupt global regimes and their arrogant media machines. Even though it was serious stuff it was also hilarious to watch Scud work himself into a tizz. A zapping was in the offing but like a drunk with a bottle he couldn't help himself.

We studied the media of fifty years ago and creased at the lies told then. Even the history books made fun of some of the ridiculous publications. There was a point in history when two media moguls had the world in their pockets but the great god of greed blinded and deluded them; their empires imploded and like some Greek tragedy they tore each other apart.

'Serves them right,' Scud said. 'Only problem is aw we huv now is that duffer, FuB.'

We were working on an example of mass media manipulation when apropos of nothing Scud asked, 'Thought any more about your art project?'

We both knew I didn't have an art project. What was it with this native and his obsession with art? The art module was not due until third quarter. Maybe it was more than his skin that was faded; he should make up his mind – art or corncrakes.

The ubiquitous dot on the wall glazed over like a fish eye. No doubt the surveillance trogs were ambivalent to my studies. Losers. Most of the recruits in the security services at the Base were burly blocks with necks thicker than heads and heads denser than a carnivore's turd. Here the creeps behind the dot may even be natives who probably couldn't even read. And yet Scud was a scholar, and he didn't waste words. Art was important to him so I played along.

'Art. Yes I need to start it,' I said, 'and I want to tie it into my nature project. Maps, illustrations, that sort of thing?'

Scud nodded and smiled.

• • •

Routine; library PM. Opening the door was like breaking into a sealed tomb; air sucked in from the corridor and the overpowering perfume of vanilla and paper mix clawed and filled my mouth with spit. The wait for Davie would be painful but my resolve was firm even if I had to stew in this sickly smell for the rest of my life.

Some of the shelves were arranged by style. Hard leather-bound tomes hogged one wall while another held a strange rainbow collection called Penguin Classics. The brand was legendary and forbidden. Some of the covers were gaudy; all had creamy paper that yellowed to a musty crust at the edges. Most of the books were medium in thickness and I calculated, even skim reading, it would take many years to devour them all. There was no point in beginning at A and working alphabetically through the titles, so I picked *Brighton Rock* at random because the cover show a boy who looked like me. The sensational blurb declared the book as an underworld thriller, but the lives depicted in the olden days seemed drab. I curled into a foetal ball in my usual chair positioned behind a large table lamp. The surveillance in this room remained a mystery to me, but this chair seemed like a blind spot from any angle. The conclusion to the book happened quicker than I expected. The text ended with some pages spare before the back cover. Three blank pages. Paper was the most forbidden substance in the universe. Books had been banned in the first Purist Years and a paper ban followed years later when the Reclaimists took power. Yet here, hanging in their bindings at the end of this book, waiting for someone in trouble to claim them, were three unblemished blank pages. My foetal ball curled tighter with the book at its nucleus. I pincered the middle blank page and gently tore it out close to the binding. The sound of the ripping paper shuddered through the air like an approaching ground tank. I waited for an alarm to sound and then for the even greater catastrophe of the book falling apart – neither happened. The book survived, with hardly even a ragged edge to show where the atrocity had taken place. Greed egged me to take a second page but the worrywart gene won as usual.

There must have been at least two hundred Penguin Classics lining the wall. It was incredible, if there were blank pages in one there might be in others. My fingers trembled as I folded the page into the smallest square imaginable and tucked it into the top of my overall. My stomach grumbled too but that might have been the dodgy-looking grain bar I ate after lunch. It was easy enough to check the other books. I sauntered back over to the classics wall, replaced *Brighton Rock* in its slot and ran my finger along the other titles. Random selection chose *The Day of the Triffids* by John Wyndham. I read the back blurb, I read the introduction, I flicked through the pages and had to stop myself tripping when I came to the back. Three blank sheets of paper. *Madame Bovary*, same format, four blank pages this time. *Destruction.Com*, the same. Here was a vast supply of blank paper right under Davie's nose; all I had to figure out was how to use it. The plan to wait for Davie dissolved into the euphoria of the find; the prize must be stowed along with my passport.

Everything remained the same in my quarters; no armed guard was waiting to cart me off to the paper police. As I suspected, there was nothing I could use as a writing implement. Everything was solid and made of bio-plastics or glass. The chairs were moulded from that sustainable organic material developed in another bid to save the planet. In the washroom all the washing implements were integrated; even the tooth cleaner dissolved into a biodegradable mush within two minutes of moisture contact. My search proved futile. I had only just begun to look at the material on the walls when the lights went out. An early evening power shutdown. From the window I saw that the large perimeter lights had even failed. The ventilation and heating system seemed dormant. The sky was partially overcast, the shadow of a full moon hinting at a curtain call took the edge off what could have been a total black-out. I groped my way to the slugbag, lay on top and listened. There was nothing but the sloshing of the sea. Somewhere on the other side of the penitentiary chaos was sure to reign with men being corralled into a holding hall. I felt sick.

I fumbled my way to the door to check for the red emergency lights that ran along the corridor. There was nothing; it was a black hole. The door lock failed so I pulled the chair over to bar it.

A volley of shots clattered in the air. Distant shouts, a single shot, a scream and then a primal baying that made my teeth grind. A sharp pain exploded in my mouth, I tasted blood, I'd bitten my tongue. The thrumming of an engine rose above the noise of the sea and I stumbled once more to the window. Two Transports jounced towards the island, dodging the heavy artillery that sparked fire into the dark like a medieval dragon. An explosion at close quarters lit up the sky. Flames erupted on a Transport's wing; it veered off, dipping towards the sea and away from the island. As I watched it my heart plummeted. Even though I didn't know who crewed the craft, I felt hope leave my soul. The Transport staggered and lifted momentarily.

'Recover, recover,' I whispered under my breath. At first it seemed to hear my plea, then it nosedived into the water leaving a trailing flare behind and a circle of burning debris glittering on the surface like a floating candle. Embers littered the sea, a carnival of dying fairy lights, snuffed out one by one until only a dread remained.

'Ishbel?' The question always rested on my lips.

The perimeter lights found their power and the ack-ack fire continued. The whirl of the other Transport was only just detectable in-between the sporadic fire, its pitch roaring and shrieking, weaving as if it were manoeuvring around the compound crown, avoiding the weaponry burst.

This situation raged for many minutes. I caught glimpses of the remaining Transport in the artillery light.

'Come on, come on.' I jumped up and down like a daftie. The bold insignia flashed by in a fleeting second, just before it turned and retreated back towards the mainland. My blood was racing. It had only been five minutes since the power shutdown. We had been under attack from a couple of Transports bearing the same insignia as Ishbel's craft. When she brought me here Davie had permitted her to land, why not now? And if we were at war, who was our enemy and what side was I supposed to be on?

Something woke me with a jolt. It might have been my brain, which was scouring every interior surface of my skull. Or it might have been the ten-ton slab on my chest. I hauled myself upright and filtered a puny breath into my burning lungs. What the snaf had happened? The ventilation system and the lights were still off in my quarters. Everything was quiet – no marauding of the hordes, no more gunfire or screaming. Why hadn't the surveillance detected my lack of air? What if everyone had died? Was this my chance to escape? Was that Ishbel's plan? No, snap out of fantasy land Sorlie, this was serious shit.

The lack of air wiped me off my feet when I tried to stand. I crawled and used the chair to drag myself up before pulling it from the door. If possible, the air in the corridor felt thinner than in the room. My communicator pinlight shone only centimetres ahead as I made my way to the shutter door. All the other doors I tried along the way were locked. There was no sign of life. The shutter door was locked too; what did I expect, a free passage? Silence trembled like an angry god sucking at the ends of my nerves. Not even the sound of the sea penetrated this corridor. I edged towards the library door. A gunshot sounded nearby. I dropped to the ground, breathing hard, trying to slow the drumming of my heart and the whooshing of blood in my temples. Silence returned. The dark corridor was endless, pierced only by the pinprick of my inadequate torch. It took twice as long as usual to reach the library, or at least it seemed like that.

I cracked the door a millimetre, not knowing what lay behind. The smell of vanilla was replaced by the choking stench of death like that of the burning carcasses that clung to the countryside after the last big Land Reclaimist domestic animal purge. It clawed at my throat and robbed me of my last few grams of O_2. If the ventilation system remained dormant, suffocation was a real threat. The mainland search parties deployed to investigate the unresponsive Black Rock would soon be entering a tomb where all the inhabitants had suffocated. It would be just like the last magma eruption to consume part of the Northwest Territories in the Forties. When rescuers eventually entered the area, whole towns and cities were encapsulated for all time under a super-highway of ash.

I half expected Davie to be in the library, cowering in terror from what could be raging in the prison, but that was an absur-dity: Davie cowered from no one. The room was deserted and the heavy ornate door to the other side stood solid. Even as I walked towards it I knew the action was dumb; nothing could penetrate that locked door. I had to find air. There was no window in this room. The window in my sleeping quarters was thick; if only I could smash it I could at least get some air. I might even be able to escape, like the Count of Monte Cristo, if the drop into the sea didn't kill me. A weighty brass lamp on one of the tables looked like it might do the job. The effort of lugging the thing was crip-pling. I fell to the floor, like in survival training during a fire drill, and crawled commando style dragging the lamp behind.

When I reached the window I heaved the lamp to my chest and tried to batter the glass with it. The first strike ricocheted back at me. I staggered, lost my grip and the lamp clattered to the floor. I groped for it and tried again. There was a dull crack but no smash. The pinlight showed the only damage my efforts made was a starburst pattern on the glass. Each swing took more puff as the oxygen was wrung from my body. Sleep tried to overtake me but Academy training taught me that would be disastrous. I attempted one more swing but made no impact and this time the lamp dragged me with it to the floor. A rest – I only needed a rest. Only a minute then try again. Just one minute, I'll rest here. The thumping in my head was deafening. My face touched the cool floor; I was floating in a pool. Just one minute more then I'll move.

· · ·

The buzz of the air-con drifted in from a far-off place. My head louped and my eyelids were glued tighter than a miser's purse. Even so I could tell I was alive and it was daytime. There was a vague taste of stale garlic salt from lunch on my furred teeth. Under the buzz I sensed another being in the room. I prised my eyes open – right first, then left – and blinked. There he was, sitting in the chair by the door: Davie, my elusive grandfather.

His eyes were closed. There was a pathetic tilt to his head, a dribble of saliva tracked from one side of his mouth into his beard like a glistening slug train. He needed a bib and a wipe. The skin on his face, on his cheeks and below his eyes, sagged like empty salt bags. The tyrant painted by Scud and Ishbel had been sucked out with the stale air and replaced with this fragile old man.

What happened? The heavy lamp from the library now sat upright by the door, waiting to be returned to its rightful place. There was a dent on the side of the base. As quietly and delicately as I could I swivelled my head toward the window. My skull rattled like broken glass, each crunching movement stabbing me in a hundred different places. An opaque star the size of a dinner plate burst from the window's epicentre where I had struck maybe three blows. Not bad considering I could hardly lift the brute. What a clunk I was; it had been pointless trying to break it, but I suppose panic had set in. But even if I dislodged one small piece it would have made a hole large enough to get some air.

I needed to pee. After days of wishing to reach my grandfather I dreaded waking him. And yet something stirred in me when I looked at this old man who once must have held my mother on his knee and taught her to love. My mother had loved so much. He was all I had left of her and he was here in this room with me.

I was on my bed so he must have placed me here; maybe he cared what happened to me after all, but more likely he just didn't want me messing up the floor.

I eased myself to sitting and Davie, with the reflexes of a race-horse, jumped and brandished an old battered gun at me. My hands flew up in front of my face.

'Don't,' I tried to croak, but a small squeak was all I managed.

For all its tired and worn appearance, the gun looked even more lethal than the confused Davie. My head curdled to scrambled tofu; if I fainted I'd be fried. Tears welled in my eyes and my bowels sloshed to water. Was this how my parents felt just before their end? I held my breath as the seconds began to clear his sleeping mind and the recognition of the situation hit him. He rearranged his features from brutal glare to something a fraction softer but not much.

'Don't shoot,' I coughed, my throat bloated dry. He placed the gun back in its holster and rubbed his eyes with his hand.

I reached for a goblet of water by my bedside and almost knocked it over with my shakes. As he took a step towards me, I shrank back. I didn't mean to, it just happened, and he stopped short of holding out his hand. The water gagged me and I only just managed to clasp my mouth to stop a spew.

'What happened?' My voice was stronger this time.

'The power went out,' he rasped, as if sleep blotted his mouth too.

'Why?'

His face tensed but he remained silent.

'There were Transports and shootings,' I said. 'One exploded into the sea.'

'That's no concern of yours.'

Anger simmered in my blood but I tried to remain calm. He had to be kept sweet if I was ever to get out.

'No concern of mine? I have to live here too. I didn't ask to be brought here.'

Still he refused to answer. My resolve broke and my kickshit whiny voice took over. 'I had no air, I could have died. Is that not a concern of mine?' His face clouded and his eyebrows arched over those winter cold eyes.

My rage foamed. 'I am not stupid! We were under attack. I refuse to be treated as a child or a prisoner – there was gunfire and explosions.' I pointed to my attempted breakout as if he were an imbecile. 'I nearly died.' I stopped when he moved past me to the window and ran a finger over the starburst.

'You are a child and an idiot to think you could have broken through this.'

'What was I supposed do, sit on my bed and suffocate?'

He snorted but had no answer for this question.

'You have damaged a very rare lamp.' Typical Privileged statement.

'Why am I being kept a prisoner here? I've committed no crime.'

Davie turned and cast his hardened eyes on me. 'You are not a prisoner, you are my guest.' He stopped then bowed for a moment as if in prayer. When he lifted his head and stared straight through me, he smiled a sweet smile that sent a ripple of rime to my toes. 'You are my family, Sorlie.'

Time to strike. 'If I am your family and I am not a prisoner then let me leave this cell for a time. I want to explore the island.'

'No.'

'Why not?'

He pulled his shoulders back and lowered his voice as if he were a medieval actor playing a monster.

'I said no,' he growled.

'You said I'm not a prisoner and yet I'm held in a prison. I may not be behind that door with the rest of the prisoners but I would be better off there. At least there I would have someone to talk to.'

He laughed. 'You have no idea what you're talking about. These creatures are animals who deserve to die.' He didn't look at me but at some far-off spot hidden within the starburst of the window. I thought of Scud, of his intelligence, his humour. Did Davie really believe they deserved to die? How long does it take a man to live in these conditions before he becomes an animal or as twisted and mad as my grandfather surely was? When he turned back to the room there was confusion in his face.

'I need fresh air,' I said in my calmest voice. 'I should still be growing physically, but my daily blood readings suggest defects. Do you want to stunt my growth? When I was at the Base I trained every day.' I plucked my puny arm. 'Your food supplements are limited in their effectiveness. Do you want me to end up looking like a native?'

His head snapped up at this, the confusion still lingered. He racked my face with his eyes the way he did when I first arrived here.

'Never compare yourself to a native. You are Privileged,' he hissed. 'Never forget that.' He turned for the door, picked up the brass lamp, then swung round to face me.

'I will think about it – you going outside.' His back straightened, he adjusted the holster on his hip. Commander of the Penitentiary was back on duty, while the old man scuttled back under the cloak of the tyrant. I should learn to tell the difference.

Chapter Fourteen

Scud failed to show the day after the raid. A toad of a man with greenish tinged skin, hooded eyes and thick lips showed up in his place. He was pretty disgusting. His eyes avoided mine as he manoeuvred the tray through the door and even when spoken to he deferred his gaze, preferring the floor to my adolescent mug.

'Where's Scud?' There wasn't much hope of a sensible answer but it was worth asking.

He looked to my left shoulder.

'Doh no,' he said in a strange slang I couldn't quite place.

'What happened here last night?'

His gaze flickered to the damaged window then returned to a spot past my ear.

'Doh no. Power failure – maybe.'

'And the firing?'

He backed from the room, a frightened reptile.

'Doh no,' he said to the window and hopped off back to his pond.

• • •

My head still grated like a newly filled peppermill. The food the toad left wasn't worth picking. Maybe sleep would wash away the pain, but the worry of the attack put paid to that plan. The State of Esperaneo hadn't been involved in direct conflict on their own soil for many years, apart from the reported sporadic insurgent attacks, occasional civil unrest that flashed but was quickly quashed. Was that what this was? But then how was Ishbel mixed up in it? I hadn't imagined seeing her insignia on the craft. The attack was small scale – a bungled prison escape perhaps. What was puzzling was that the air-con had shut down – why had it not affected Davie or Toad?

Later that evening, when the toad brought my meal, I discovered the truth of my near suffocation. There was an air of jobsworth authority on him as he laid the tray down and walked to the small trip box panel beside the door. He thumped the panel with the heel of his hand and the cover popped. It wasn't a trip box. He pulled out a mask and a small cylinder and held it up.

'Eh, yewar grandfather told me to instruct you on this,' he drawled. 'Didn't know did you? About this heh?' He was a cymry, one of those strange natives from the south vallees. Why do natives always take such pleasure in Privileged ignorance? 'Scud nevar told you.' He slurped his big lips, even more pleased with this.' In a power failure see, yewar to put this on,' he said to my left shoulder. 'See, like this,' demonstrating the action of donning the mask as if I were a dolt. He stuffed the mask back in the panel and closed the hatch before tapping it with purpose.

'It's beside the door, see, for a reesun,' he stressed with a sinister air and slow deliberate words. 'So it's eazy – to find in the dark, see?' With this final speech delivered to my desk, he turned and left the room a taller man than when he entered.

Jupe sake, what a tard.

• • •

The shakes and thick head had almost vanished when I rose next day. Scud was still missing so I was left to the mercy of Toad of the Wandering Eyes. His bullishness had deflated back down to his normal puny size.

'Where's Scud?'

'Doh no.'

'So will you help me with my work then?'

'Oh no, not me. Can't do that.'

'Why not?'

'Nevar learned to read see.'

'Right.' It appeared the supply of intelligent natives had dried up.

It was back to the routine rut, but a solitary one. The library had a whiff of neglect, the stale air of the shutdown lingered as if a dead rat lay in a corner somewhere. I searched the room for clues to the attack but had no idea what I was looking for. I launched Davie's workstation and after a couple of attempts at access codes it shut me out.

I picked up a book that lay on a corner table. Kilm's *The Destruction of the Modern World*. More propaganda – what was his game?

The trauma of the past few days cast a great weariness over me, so I curled in the familiar chair and allowed myself to drift into the delicious world of half sleep – naptime. A movement in the room snapped me alert. It was him. My heavy eyelids protected me until I was ready to face him. I waited for his bellow, like the last time he caught me napping here, but it didn't come. Maybe my near death experience had softened him. Had I perhaps pared a sliver off that rock-hard heart?

I gathered my thoughts into neat order before I uncurled my limbs and stretched. Groans and moans escaped my lips, some of which were by no means a put-on.

Something between my shoulders twanged. My physical age had doubled overnight and I would be carted off to an oldies' refuge soon if this trend continued.

The old man of yesterday had vanished. In his place, standing in front of the dormant hearth was the warden of Black Rock. His mane of hair was brushed back and banded at the nape of his neck. In his hand was a cut-glass tumbler quarter filled with a golden liquid.

'Well Sorlie, how are you today?' The gravel in his voice had smoothed with a mix of sand.

'My head and throat still ache a bit.' This was a half-truth. 'The native showed me the air mask. But I still don't know what happened?'

'We had a power failure. I told you, as has the native who tends you.' He held the glass to the overhead lights and peered at the swirling contents. What was he looking for? 'It was remiss of your first native not to instruct you to the safety features of your quarters. He has been punished.'

'Scud? He's alright? Where is he?'

His eyebrow arched. It sounded as though I cared. 'He's been replaced.'

'But I want him back. He helps me with my studies. The replacement can't even read.'

My grandfather snapped his fingers. 'I will find you another scholar.'

'I don't want another scholar. I want Scud, he's useful to me.'

'You say a native is useful? You have expensive superior learning packages. How can a native be useful?'

'I don't know, he adds something … I don't know, an extra dimension the courses don't give me. I've already achieved top quarter marks for original content in my last self-assignment. That's never happened before.'

The eyebrows relaxed. Obviously my achieving top marks pleased Davie.

'He adds texture,' I persisted.

Was that a quiver of a smile on his lips?

'Texture you say?'

'Yes, something only experience can give.' I picked my words carefully. 'I will gain a great advantage over my peers, when it's needed.' What I meant was 'if I ever get out of here,' but clipped my tongue on that quip. 'Texture helps.' I could see he liked this word so rubbed it a little harder. 'Texture gets results.'

'Texture,' he said to himself, as if he enjoyed the sound of a new word in his mouth. 'Well, we'll see. He has other duties, this past native of yours.'

I wobbled a little as I stood and my grandfather stepped towards me as he had done in my room. At first I thought he was going to steady me, but as he put out his hand it froze in mid-air and he stared at it as if it didn't belong to his body. I sank back in the chair as my grandfather turned his attention to his drink. Then he pressed the call button on his communicator.

'Go to your room and rest, you are still not recovered.'

'I want to go outside to explore the island.'

His grasp tightened on his glass as he looked to the ceiling in exasperation.

'You said I wasn't a prisoner.'

'You said, you said,' he mocked me.

I coughed feebly. 'I've not breathed fresh air since entering these prison walls. My head thumps constantly. I'm ill.' His eyes narrowed again and I could see I was starting to get through to him. 'Confinement is not healthy for me and is probably hampering my recovery.'

'It does not seem to be hampering your insolence in persisting with this line of request.'

I pulled up the sleeve of my tunic. 'My white blood cell count is dropping.' He would know this was true because my body's activities were monitored hourly.

'I have been brought up on a daily dose of daylight, your daughter saw to that. If I remain indoors much longer I will turn into an awful gobo.' I heard a gasp from the corner of the room. The toad had arrived at Grandfather's bidding and cowered in the periphery of the scene, failing to perfect the native invisibility.

I would not be deterred. What was the worst he could do to me? Kill me? I was slowly dying anyway.

'Send one of the guards with me if you must keep me prisoner.' And then I remembered my project and pulled my ace card.

'Have you ever heard the corncrake?'

'What?' He puzzled at the change of subject. Confusion crossed his brows then settled into a frown. Fear entered his eyes again. His gaze searched the bookshelves as if seeking an answer there.

'You know – the corncrake? The fabled bird?'

'Corncrake, yes, yes of course. A fabled bird, the corncrake.' But

I could see he was bluffing. 'I have a book on them somewhere.' The fear was still there.

Easy does it. It was like cradling a cup of nitro-glycerine in my hand while trying to gyrocycle. 'Well, you'll remember a corncrake was a rare bird that in the last century lived on the islands and it is believed to have become extinct fifty years ago.' His face relaxed an inch; he was interested. 'It had a very distinctive call, like a creaking piece of metal.' I paused for effect.

'Yes, yes I know what a corncrake is,' he said. Who was he trying to convince, him or me?

'I think I heard one the other night,' I announced.

He shook his head. 'That's impossible; from your side of the installation the sea dominates the noise. And as you have said they are extinct.'

I shook my head. 'No they aren't. I'm sure. The other night it was calm, maybe the tide was out, I don't know, but I heard something different, something weird, ghostly, something rare.' I was hamming it so changed tactic. 'Imagine what this would do to your profile with the LRP if we,' I stressed the word we, 'if we discovered a bird believed to be extinct.' I showed him the download stored on my communicator. 'Look at the habitat it prefers, it is a scene from right here. Black Rock.'

He snapped his fingers and I handed him the device. He read the detail then signalled for the native to leave us.

Davie moved to his screen and blinked when he found it already powered up. He flopped down wearily and glanced to me but said no words. He turned his back on me as he keyed in his access pin. Seven characters, all on the left-hand side of the keypad.

A list of names and times dotted onto the screen and he took a few minutes to scrawl through them.

'Go to your room,' he said without turning round. 'You seem to have miraculously regained your strength. And I need time to think.'

'Can I go outside then?'

He spun in his seat to face me. 'I said go to your room.'

· · ·

'Textured – nice one, wee man.' Scud, the old Scud, returned after more days of routine. His infliction seemed cured although he was more fidgety, shifty even. He placed a tray on the table and chuckled to himself. Even though I was rapt to see him back his constant trips to the window were as irritating as ever.

'Don't you have a window?'

'Just a wee crack below the ceiling, just enough tae let daylight in.' He stopped and tapped his nose, 'And the beacon of course. We couldnae sleep without that wee comfort blanket.' It was a strange thing to say but he was a strange sort of guy.

For aeons I had waited to give him the stolen paper, still tucked in my tunic, but now he was here I almost forgot.

'Art project,' I blurted out as he opened the door to leave. He pulled up, closed the door again and slowly turned back to the room, his broken top teeth biting his bottom lip.

'Aye?'

'Remind me. Why is it so important to do?'

'It's fur yer education. Huv ye no sussed that yet?'

This was getting us nowhere. 'You know that I don't have access to paper?'

'Aye.' He laid the tray down next to Beastie and stood with his arms folded. For once he had all day to waste.

'Yes it is a pity with all the books lying around.' I said. His brows pringled. As I moved towards the tray Scud stepped sideways and positioned himself between me and the dot. It was a fleeting move, no more than a native getting out of the way of a Privileged, but it gave me enough space to slide the contraband under the plate and for Scud to see me do it.

'Aye well mebaes we should forget the art project and focus on the nature project.' He tapped his nose with his finger. 'Ah think that wid be much mair productive, don't you?' He smiled and I couldn't help my grin. We understood each other perfectly.

'Be careful with that plate, it has a crack in it.'

'Aw, hus it now, ah've got jist the thing tae sort it.'

'Yes, I'm sure you have.' Even though I had no writing implement, there was no doubt Scud was resourceful enough to find something suitable.

'Do you think I'll be allowed outdoors to search for the corncrake?' I asked.

The weariness of an oldie passed over Scud's face. 'Ah don't know. Huv ye asked him again like?'

The last conversation with Davie had been days before, or maybe weeks – each solitary day broken only by meal breaks had merged into one monotonous blur – but there was no word from him.

I relayed that conversation to Scud. 'Aye, ah see, and did yer grandfather say whit he wid dae if ye were allowed out and ye didnae find the bird?'

'No – why would he do anything?'

He began plumping up my pillows. 'Mony's a time ah've seen him displeased. It's no a pretty sight. You dae realise ye might no find wan.'

'Wait a minute, you were the one who said you heard one, are you now saying you didn't?' Scud punched the pillow and threw it on the bed but stayed silent. 'Anyway, I think I heard it too.' This was a lie and he knew it but the surveillance didn't.

Scud stopped fussing. 'Did ye now? That's interesting.' He could be so maddening sometimes.

'Well jist as long as ye know where tae look and remember not tae make Davie boy appear a fool if he does let ye out. That is an unbearable thing fur a man such as he.'

'You've changed your tune.' He seemed almost to be warning me against going outside now. Or was it just an act for surveillance? Or maybe he didn't care now he had the paper.

'Tunes that urnae written in stone are there fur the changing.' He said picking up the tray. 'Now ah'll away and synd these dishes and leave ye tae yer lessons. Yer Modern Languages need nae texture fae the likes o' a native like me. Ah'll be back in a wee while fur yer history lesson.'

Scud's fidgeting was infectious. I foutered through the syllabus, tinkered with languages, picked at maths and settled to neither. FuB's News Channel spouted the usual dross. Our Esteemed President, acting on behalf of the Esperaneo Energy Company, was in talks with the Emperor of the Eastern Republic. Both men shook hands but did not smile. Since one of the Eastern partition countries had launched a missile strike on the Antipodes, killing no one directly but creating an earthquake, the tension for war had heightened. The footage showed towers of red dust clouds trundling across a desert. A fracking installation crumbled like a giant reptile cut off at the knees then exploded into an inferno, hurling a black plume into the cosmos.

Here in Esperaneo, the Purist opposition party accused the Land Reclaimists of taking a U-turn on their threats of sanctions against the East. The Purist's claimed the LRP were more interested in saving the planet than saving the human race and if they let things carry on in the same vein then neither planet nor humans would survive.

The news reporter, a woman with cropped grey hair and sapphire blue eyes, reported that the Purists wanted pointless international and stellar embargos placed on all goods, services and communications going in and out of the Eastern Zone. 'Everyone knows,' said the reporter, 'that the Eastern Zone had achieved self-sufficiency even way back when it was classed a third-world economy. Esperaneo is in no position to starve them out.'

There was a real fear in Esperaneo that if the Purists gained power again as they had in the strict regime of the 2060s, it would be unbearable for the Privileged and disastrous for the natives. This reporter was taking a risk. Her obvious Reclaimist views would be deadly if power switched. People had short memories when it came to voting, especially if the opposition promised to put more credit in their pockets. But governments' memories were long and vengeful.

Nothing changed. The same news had been playing since I was a toddler. There must be a library of footage somewhere with a scheduler set to run these regulation clips at prescribed intervals, but in a different sequence. Only the reporters changed to reflect fashions and trends.

• • •

Scud returned in less than an hour, agitated and distracted. He slumped in the chair. Beastie had been crashing all morning and had only just decided to crank its way through some of my earlier equations. Scud crowded me out – too close, too close; his rankness clung to me like a witch's embrace. I was on the verge of telling him to quit my personal space when he slid the paper under the desktop and moved to take up his usual stance at the window. The rapid whoosh of my blood pressure was sure to register in the health readings. I hadn't expected a message back so soon. What was so urgent? Something worth risking his life for, that was for sure.

Now the deed was done I was anxious for him to scuttle back to where he had come from, but he didn't move. He scratched at the starburst that muddied his ocean view.

'This'll never be fixed you know.' When he spoke his voice was deeper. There was a new change in him, even in the short time since breakfast. When he turned I saw a milky film form over his eyes. The transformation was happening real-time. His eyes, when the film cleared, were the colour of walnut, deep and searching.

It was the classic text of Stevenson's *The Strange Case of Dr Jekyll and Mr Hyde* taking place before my eyes with this poor native prisoner as the protagonist.

'What's wrong with you?' I whispered.

'Nothing,' he said in a deep voice, then snorted. 'Well, nothing a spell away fae here wouldnae cure.'

He held up trembling hands, clenched his fists and shoved them under his oxters.

'Just go,' I said. 'You don't need to be here.'

'Ah cannae.' He shuddered at his own voice. 'Ah have tae stay.' He tapped his command band. As he moved towards me his stink beat him to it.

'Well go and lie on the floor over there, I'll wake you before the zap.'

He moved his chair from my space and slumped down. The way he glared at me with walnut eyes gave me goose bumps.

When his allotted time had passed he left.

'Leave the door open, I need some air.' But he chose to ignore the slight and the request, closing the door behind him.

The message was still under the tabletop, all I had to do was work out how to retrieve it. I lay on the bed and stared at Beastie willing a gift of telepathy to magic the image to my mind.

A small sneeze caught the back of my throat, damn that native and his viruses. Black linen nose sheets were stored in the locker by the bed. I snatched one and dabbed my nose. The sneeze vanished but I forced the noise just the same. Serendipity is a word and notion I always loathed but it was the only one to spring to mind now as I held the nose sheet to my face. I rolled off the bed and sauntered to the desk still dabbing my nose. Ham acting should be part of Scud's curriculum. I acted out several sneezes into the linen, throwing my head forward, handkerchief to nose; I flipped the paper from under the desktop into the linen then looked, as everyone does after a sneeze, just to check the colour and density of the bogey.

I dizzied back to the bed, making a big show of feeling unwell, sipped some water and dimmed the lights. I had no idea how the surveillance worked, but hoped, with a bit of luck, those guys would grow bored watching a sick boy.

Cooried under the bed cover, I fumbled to unravel the paper from the hankie. My whoosh of blood earlier was replaced by a deep pounding powerful enough to set off the earthquake alarm. The paper was neatly folded. The page had been torn in two.

Clever man, he had kept the other half for another time. With the pinlight from my communicator I picked out small marks, dotted like music notation. Words emerged from the dots like pixels on a scan. I don't know what he used as a writing tool, it looked like charcoal, something dark, drops of blood or shit? I breathed the sour smell – no, not shit. I was rusty in the practice of the ancient art of handwriting but this erratic scrawl was clear and the urgency in his words was frightening in its vitality.

help us we are experiments DNA mutants many have died
ALL soon diluted help us help yourself find Him

It was fantastical and horrific but explained Scud's changing form. *Find Him* – find who? Was it Him who attacked the other night? And was Ishbel somehow mixed up in this? What did Scud mean when he wrote *help us help yourself*? The chill that ran through me rattled my teeth. I hugged the covers tighter. *DNA mutants*. What was in my DNA passport for Ishbel to hide, to lie for? What needed to be protected?

• • •

Toad brought my evening meal with some medicine for my cold. They know everything here. This time I did not ask where Scud was. And I was relieved he was absent; I don't think I could have trusted myself with the information I now had. The medicine tasted of herbs and must have conked me out because before I knew it, morning greyness sulked into the room and there was a ping pong match being played behind my eyeballs.

Toad looked lighter in colour when he brought breakfast, but I abstained from commenting because he was accompanied by a uniformed guard. The guard was overweight and much taller than me. His thick brown hair shone in the artificial light and by the olive colour of his skin and the blackness of his eyes I could see he was neither Privileged nor native, but a Bas – that strange breed of lowlander who had made their home in Northern Esperaneo. They were often found in civil servant roles. A generally sullen lot who rarely smiled, this guard was no exception. He loitered in the corridor as if afraid to enter my quarters. What was he doing here? Since I had arrived I had encountered only native prisoners.

'How are you? How's your cold?' he called through the door.

My sniffles had gone but my head thumped – what was in that medicine?

'I'm well.' I looked at the fading Toad. 'Where's Scud?'

'Scud's too sick to come,' Toad said.

'You don't look too well yourself,' I told him. What if Scud had been discovered with the extra piece of paper? 'Is Scud being taken care of?'

'He's too sick.' Was that all he would say?

All soon diluted. The written words flashed behind my eyes – how much more could Scud's body take? I thought of his hair and the way it sometimes looked translucent, the pigment missing. And his freckles, the freckles he told me were not his to miss, the dreadful pallor of his skin. *Many have died.* And after all, who would miss a bunch of native prisoners? Davie said they deserved to die. I had to get out of here to see my passport. The guard lurked as Toad tidied my room.

'Why are you here?' I asked him.

'I have come to assess your health.'

'Are you a doctor then?'

'No. Your grandfather asked me to assess your health.'

I brushed his bland comment away. I wanted to sleep; I was tired of this intrusion.

'Tell him I'm fine, I just need some peace from natives and lowlanders.' I dismissed them with a wave of my hand before I noticed the guard carried an outdoor jacket.

'Why are you…?' But the words were broken.

The guard's communicator screamed alarm, flashing red. He spun his hefty bulk on his toes and bolted to deal with whatever situation summoned him.

'What's going on?' I asked, but Toad had already hopped off in the guard's wake.

Chapter Fifteen

The mirror never lies. Oh really? Well where were the lines of evil? Where were the traces of Davie on my face? He's the one in charge here. If Scud's note was to be believed, then my grandfather was responsible for the horrors in this place.

The tally of my juvenile evil seeped into my memory right on cue. The time I pulled the wings off a dragonfly and watched it squirm; the time I wouldn't let Jake borrow my express gyrocycle; the multitude of times I watched *Death Match* on Snap TV; the time I was too busy wrestling to say a last goodbye to Ma. I searched in my eyes, my blue eyes, almost the same colour and tone as Davie's. The same hardness?

'Wise up, harden up or fall.' The mantra of Academy boot camp. Was I capable of the level of evil this man Davie seemed to have no issue with?

Help us help yourself.

The sea pounded the shore below; guards manned the inside surveillance and perimeters. Screams and shots still rang every other night, but now I understood. What had they to lose? My reflection told me I had no choice.

Find Him.

• • •

The illness ruse continued and meant instead of smuggled notes, the smuggled passport cooried under the covers with me. The soft material of the primitive binding was warm to touch, the stitching spiderweb fine, better than the average passport cover. From the pitiful pinlight cast by my communicator I could barely make out the pictures of my ancestors. The holograms were functioning but to scan them within the prison walls under the vigilant eye of the Internal Monitors would be ludicrous.

Suddenly, as if someone guessed my purpose, the power shut down and with it the air-con. Leaving the passport under the covers I fumbled my way to the door, thumped the panel, pulled the mask over my face and scrambled back to bed where I lay listening to the waves, waiting for another attack. Blood whooshed round my brain like a gyrocycle in a velodrome, wobbling with every turn of thought. Maybe this time they'll succeed in breaking in. Maybe this time they'll stop what's happening to the prisoners and my help won't be needed. Within my cocoon of manufactured air I bent back to the task.

Beside each DNA code was the hologram chip and beside that, for some antiquated reason, the old-fashioned images were left where they had been pasted long ago. When I was small I often built tents with my bed covers and pretended I was an explorer in the Southern Deserts, hunkered in against raging sand storms while I plotted my search for hidden treasure in the earthquake zones. This time the tent I built was to create more space to explore my heritage. The pixelated faces of my ancestors emerged, almost reluctantly, under the pinlight. My grandmother Vanora, Davie's wife, stepped out of the past and challenged me with her smile. The air mask clamped my face as I gasped and my bowels rumbled distant drums to my demise. OMG. Red hair, green eyes and freckles all spelled one word – native. It didn't take an IQ of twenty to work out that if she was native then I carried some of that shit, and Davie had me sitting with my feet dangling in the piranha pool of experiments with the rest of the inhabitants here.

Aeons slipped by in my new terror zone but by the time I grew accustomed to the face mask and breathed normally I'd convinced myself I'd been hallucinating, or that she had dressed up as a native for a bet. There was a wicked twinkle in those green eyes, but I couldn't be certain until I viewed the hologram.

Oh how easily delusion creeps in, but the ancestors were having none of it. As I prepared to take one last look at Ma's image my thumb caught on a rough edge of the passport's back cover. There was a three cornered flap as if someone had sliced the material then stuck it back in place. The puny pinlight was fading so I extinguished it to save power and worked by feel alone.

There was a bump, something hidden the size of my communicator face, under the flap. With my thumbnail I sawed at a loose corner, careful not to damage what lay beneath, unpicking the lock of some secret I dreaded to find. Hadn't this passport revealed enough in this one sitting? When the opening was the size of a maize chip I wiggled my thumb inside and began to extract what felt like a crinkled piece of paper. It emerged slowly, resisting like a worm being pecked from the earth by a blackbird. One last tug and it rested in the palm of my hand. With the delicacy of a bomb disposal sapper I unravelled the pleated paper, pressing and smoothing as I went until it was the size of the paperback page I had given to Scud. Before I shone the pinlight I took several deep breaths within the mask and wished I could have wiped the sweat that drenched my face and used it to quench my parched mouth. The terrible secret of Vanora was held within the pages. What could be so horrific to have required this covert treatment? When I at last shone the pathetic light on the truth I almost choked with horror and shame.

It was an old-style birth certificate with no DNA listing. The paper was cheap and dry with a crude printing of the crest of a lesser colony of the United States of the West. The ink was faded but I could still make out the terror scribe.

Name: Ishbel Pringle
Born: 17th day of the strawberry moon 2068
Father: David Pringle
Mother: Vanora MacLeod

. . .

My mind hurtled through the possible explanations, even though there was only ever one. All those years she had cared for me she was actually in the protection of her big sister, Ma. She must have been a child when she came. I had thought she was ancient, but she was only twenty-one.

Why hadn't I noticed before how alike Ma and Ishbel were? The shape of Ishbel's hands – long slender, pianist fingers like my mother had. I looked at my own hands now in the dim light and could not deny what I saw. It was true Ishbel was taller and stronger than Ma, but piece by piece I thought of their features, their round faces with the raised cheekbones as if plumped by Botox enhancement. Their hands. No, I couldn't think of my mother's hands, blown, blown apart. But now there was no doubt of Vanora's nativeness.

· · ·

Three hours had passed since the shutdown and no Transports came. When I'd packed the air mask back in place and returned to bed, I tucked the secret back in its womb and took a last look at my Ma's image. 'Why didn't you tell me?' I wanted to ask, but of course it was much too late for that.

Did Davie know Ishbel was his daughter? Possibly not – he called her a whore. Ma had told her to give Davie the passport, and Ishbel defied that instruction. Ishbel must have been the one to hide the paper. But why?

Part Three

Chapter Sixteen

When a rather chirpy Scud swung by next morning I asked what had happened with the power but he just tapped his nose. Although he looked healthier, he retained the walnut eyes. He looked almost Privileged and even though he could never have suspected, for once our roles seemed reversed.

It monsoon rained all that week. Scud's colouring and skin tone plateaued. He of the Walnut Eyes gravitated to the window every once in a while and even declared rain 'quite beautiful'. He was like one of those mad arty-farties who maintained a lump of concrete was a huge contribution to modern architecture – clueless. There was nothing to see out there except gloomy skies and rain-streaked glass. Even the perimeter lights were dimmed by the constant haar. My concentration for work dissolved in a pitcher of diluting nativeness. Scud was raging with me. He said that if I didn't buck up I would fail my exams.

'What exam?' I said. 'The whole thing is pointless.'

Scud rubbed his scraggy chin. 'Ah, the tantrums of Privilege – so last year.'

What the snaf did that mean?

• • •

Then one day an unusually strong sunlight stroked my face as I woke. With my hands behind my head, I stretched in bed and bathed in it. Scud dragged into the room, almost dropping the tray before reaching the desk. It seemed as if the weight was three times the normal capacity of his capabilities. Without saying a word he left and returned seconds later with a bag, which he dumped on the floor.

'A present for ye,' he grinned. 'Looks like ye've done yer prison stint, young Sorlie.'

'What is it?'

'Well now, let's see.' He knelt down, ripped open the bag and pulled out a waterproof jacket, trousers and boots. 'It seems that perseverance pays off,' he chirped. 'Ye don't need these in yer cosy wee cell. So you must be going outside.'

• • •

Scud said Davie had given him instructions to leave me after he'd delivered my breakfast and clothes. His grin cracked so wide I was sure his face would shatter like porcelain. As he left the room, he tapped his stupid nose and creaked a corncrake call – a very realistic corncrake call based on the recordings I had heard on FuB. I couldn't believe I was finally being let out, but before the fact fully sank in a dull knock sounded at the door. It was the Bas guard, the one who checked on my health many days ago. He hulked in the doorway, taller than me but not as tall as most of the Privileged, though what he lacked in height he made up for in girth. The parcel Scud had dropped spewed garments over the floor like a badly constructed soya kebab. And judging the screwed up nose on the guard's face it could have smelt like one. He didn't smile as he toed the mess on the floor, then signalled to the door with his head. 'Better get kitted out sir, it's pretty wild out there.'

'So, I'm being allowed to leave the compound.' Stupid statement but it was better than hugging him which is what I almost did when he arrived.

'That's right sir.' His voice was strange, clipped, neither that of a native nor of a Privileged. The way he pronounced his R's was weird. I wondered how he ended up here. He wore his uniform with misplaced pride and carried red waterproofs. On his belt was slung the regulation baton and gun.

I pointed to them. 'So I'm still to be treated as a prisoner.' He shrugged, the usual response in this place.

• • •

The yellow jacket drowned me. I rolled up the sleeves and hoped for the best. The trousers hung long but I tucked them into socks I found in the bag. The boots were also too big so I dug around and found another pair of thick socks which padded the space; a purple hat and matching mitts had been stuffed into the pockets of the yellow jacket. We looked like the united colours of Black Rock. With his red and my yellow, even in the heavy rain and mist we'd be hard to miss. I peeked a look at the guard for any sign of impatience at my faffing but saw only boredom. Probably some human traits had been trained out of him. He stared straight ahead and waited until I was ready. His indifference gave me the opportunity to tuck my passport into the oversized jacket without his noticing. As we left the room I intuitively turned towards the library but the guard strode the other way, towards the shutter door. I followed along the short corridor past what looked like a cooking area where Scud bustled and crashed. It was strange to see him in there, so close to my quarters. I had assumed the meals came from the main building.

Scud nodded sagely as he handed a package to the guard. 'Just a wee something for the young master, in case ye're not back in time fur a meal.' The formality could have been some sort of code, but there was no follow through with the nose tap.

'He'll be back in plenty time,' the guard grumbled as he stowed the food in his sac. Scud smiled nervously even though he looked fit to fall in a heap on the floor.

When we reached the shutter at the end of the passage the guard drew his gun and pointed it at Scud.

'You know the drill. Don't move a muscle.'

'I don't think that's necessary,' I said.

My communicator buzzed with a one word message from Davie. SILENCE. Of course he was watching. And Scud was a prisoner.

The guard looked uncertain for a split second, but Scud's mournful eyes were not on the gun but on me. He had a pleading

119

look of a fighting bear whose nerve had left it and knew it was about to enter the ring for the last time. I don't think he could quite believe this was at last happening. My shoulders sagged with the weight his look placed on me and the opposing pressure of the passport in my pocket. Failure wasn't an option.

While the gun stayed trained on Scud the door shuddered upwards, grating and grinding, setting my teeth to water. I was relieved for Scud's sake that the door did not open to the outside. I was sure with his window obsession, gun or no gun he would have bolted just to catch a moment of outside freedom before he was gunned down. As we entered the brightly lit ante-chamber I took one last look at those beseeching eyes before the shutter cranked down, erasing the frozen image of Scud piece by piece from head to toe. My palms were sweating. I still couldn't believe I was leaving the prison after all these weeks.

The guard lifted some walking poles propped against the other door and handed a pair to me. He drew in his breath and his chest as if to make himself even taller.

'Right Master Sorlie, we are to venture outside,' he said. 'I will walk with you at all times. There will be sections where we cannot walk side by side, at these times you will walk in front of me. Do you understand?'

My skin bristled – how dare he speak to me like that? I squared my shoulders to tell him so, but before I had a chance his head drooped and he continued.

'These are the instructions of your grandfather; to disobey would mean deep trouble for you and even deeper trouble for me.' He peered at me and there was something indiscernible in his eyes. 'Do you understand?'

I nodded even though I didn't really understand. Did he hate Davie, or fear him?

From his pocket he pulled a map reader and held it out for me to see.

'We are to go to the other side of the island and back, nothing more today.' He traced a line on the map with a stylus which showed the journey as the crow flies. This man hadn't a clue how to read a map or how to use a map reader. His route would take us across wide unbridged rivers and over sheer cliffs. There was a natural contour that meandered cross-country with dotted markings of old drove roads. The other side of the island was a good couple of hours walk away following the path marked on the map and I knew that once outside the guard would blindly follow this.

'Can I have a copy of the map? I love orienteering.'

He thought for a moment, obvious of his own shortcomings no doubt.

'Your grandfather didn't forbid it,' was all he said as he beamed the map to my communicator. It was that easy. This guy was a cretin.

Escape was in my grasp and I could see many possibilities, but first I needed to quell the panic in my belly and keep calm. We climbed a spiral stairwell that narrowed with each step and, as if we were being squeezed out of a tube, the higher we climbed the tighter the turn, wringing the breath out of me like a wash rag. When we reached the top and the guard opened the door a rush of air hit me with a force that almost sent me spiralling downwards again. I inhaled fresh salt air for the first time since arriving here.

I had expected us to come out on some high Transport platform but the door led onto a podium projecting over the clifftop, protected only by a rusting metal rail. My ears whistled with the exposure. My eyes teared with the light and breadth of the sky. When I grasped the rail it wobbled and I fell towards the guard, snatching his sleeve to stop me tumbling over the edge. He stood rigid and stared straight ahead. I tried to protest at the dangers but the words whipped from my mouth. The guard took hold of my shoulders, easing me forward towards uneven steps cut into the cliff edge, but my feet were glued. My knuckles, white and cold, tightened on the material of his jacket. I sensed rather than saw the horrific drop to the rocks below, long and deadly. I wanted to retreat back through the door. The guard said something I couldn't hear. He slapped his hand on the rock of the prison wall. He prised my fingers from his jacket and placed it on a metal wire. The wire threaded through iron rings bolted to the wall to provide an inadequate make-shift hand rail down the cliff face. Despite his earlier instruction for me to stay in front he squeezed past me to relieve me of my poles and with one step behind the other he descended backward, his free hand held out to me for support. Like a fledgling I was led down the precarious steps to a broad path on a mound twenty metres below.

When we reached level ground my panic flew into the wind and my legs at last supported me. I shook my shoulders back and stood straight, but my cover was blown; me and heights went together like salt and slugs.

Bored was the only word to describe the expression on the guard's face. He obviously would have preferred to be back inside in the warm, slumped in front of surveillance monitors.

'Right come on then,' I blustered, 'show me your island.'

• • •

The path was composed of ash and shale with culverts that ran with water, some of which disappeared into the manmade mound we stood on. This mound must be within the grounds of the penitentiary but it was almost unrecognisable as such. Any invaders would be hard put to find this hidden bunker in daylight, but lights from quarters such as mine with windows out to the cliffs must give the game away in the dark. There could be a barrier deflecting the light back into the installation, but it was impossible to tell from this position.

We walked from the mound along another cliff edge that dropped sheer into the sea a hundred metres or so below. Weird rock sea stacks, like chess pieces, thrust their heads from the foaming waters as if they had once been attached to the island, but constant pounding of the sea had eroded the rock to form small channels and a new coastline. I had a strange notion to lie on the ground and edge my way to stretch over and see if I could locate my window; my phobia would hold if my whole body was anchored. Soon the path veered from the cliff and the iron fence that protected us from the crumbling edge. The sound of the sea was constant and the rivers that ran into it threw up white flags of surrender on impact. The booming sea meant I had to shout to be heard. The topography of the ground changed, which signalled the boundary of the building perimeter. Looking back I saw the ancient crown of the old fortress with no visible lights showing. They must only emerge after dark. From here the prison looked as innocent as a ruined castle. The guard ignored my dallying and strode on ahead despite his earlier reluctance and instructions. He seemed eager to move into open ground and away from the compound, as if he too felt a prisoner. As we cornered the last bastion of my grandfather's dominion I stopped. A few times I had been to the High Lands where military manoeuvres took place but islands have always been forbidden territories. It's strange to think until only a few months ago I had never seen the sea and now, standing on a small hillock on Black Rock, I embraced the surrounding aspect of the wild and vast Western Sea. The changing government regimes may try to stifle and tame many things in the world but they will never tame the sea.

We followed a path into a dip and through a patch of invasive dying bracken. The path was overgrown but every now and then the guard stopped, looked at the ground and then towards the sea. What was he doing? I followed his example and found trampled vegetation and evidence of recent boot prints, not his, which were large and broad; these were smaller, narrower boots. Some other inhabitant? Every now and then the guard looked over his shoulder to check I was keeping up but he never mentioned the marks.

Find Him

But I had other nests to raid.

Terraces of slanting crags bearded the slopes to our left. Water ran over the rock forming green fluorescent sludge. I wanted to stop and taste this water that was rumoured to still be pure, hard to believe in a world where all water was routinely purified before consumption. But I had no chance, for the guard sped on and grunted that I do the same. Acquiescence to minions didn't sit well with me but I was loath to displease my grandfather on my first outing. The pounding of feet on the path summoned images to my mind, like that of my father standing straight against a wall followed by the sound of a shot, so loud and clear I almost ducked. Why hadn't he told me about Ishbel on the camping trip? No. No more thoughts of my father.

The sight of any manmade forms disappeared behind us. Even without the map I knew we were moving northwards just by the position of the weak sun behind the clouds. We banked a rise and I could see the path stretch forward, a watery trail weaving straight through the heather and bracken like a fine silver thread through tartan. There were no trees apart from the occasional mountain ash, the one with the red berries: the tree my father said everyone should have in their backyard for luck. And yet each tree he tried to plant in our yard died. Sakes! Stop it Sorlie!

The western shore had looked far away from our start point and yet we reached it in no time and were soon standing on a headland. The guard consulted his communicator, no doubt checking the time. I was surprised his belly didn't tell him that. He looked as though he couldn't go for much longer than a couple of hours without a good feed. The view from the headland was sea, but as I breathed deeply I imagined land. The other side of this water was the United States of the West with no stopping points between here and there except a few floating islands constructed for deep sea mineral mining and gas storage. The guard sat on a rock and began to unhook the laces of a boot. He took it off, shook it upside down and rubbed his toe.

'Do you live here?' I asked him. 'All the time I mean.'

He glowered at me. 'I am not permitted to converse with you,' he said and returned his concentration back to his boot.

To the south of us a small cairn marked a path junction: one path led towards a peat moor while the other disappeared down a couloir to the sea. The guard started to retrace our steps from the headland, but before I moved I consulted the map. It showed the junction and its branches. The path to the sea led not just to the shore but to a sandy beach and cove.

'Can we stop for some food? I'm starving.'

The guard checked his communicator again.

'We should go back.'

I plonked myself down on a boulder. 'Well I'm stopping here for a bit. I'm starving.'

'I was instructed to bring you back before fifteen hundred hours,' he grumbled.

'We've plenty time then.'

He sighed, sat back on his rock and unzipped the sac, handed me a grain bar and a piece of synthetic fruit. I took a bite of the fruit then doubled over clutching my belly.

'Ooh I've such a pain. I need to go drop some.'

The guard clocked around him in shock. 'Didn't you perform your body waste management today?'

'Yes but this is extra, unexpected. Something's wrong with my gut.'

I watched indecision cross his face. 'You can't go here, you have no cleansing unit.'

'I need to go – I can go in the wild, I've been taught, I can use moss. OOH!'

Panic flashed his eyes. He didn't want a mess on his hands. 'Alright, but be quick.'

'I'll just nip down here.' I pointed to the couloir leading to the shore. He began to shake his head, but I was already on my way.

'It's alright, there is nowhere for me to go.'

He nodded. 'OK, but hurry. And don't go near the beach, it's mined.'

The path was steep and narrow, at times slippery. I fell and skittered down the last few metres on my bottom. I would need to be quick to view the passport. But fate had other plans for me. When I stopped scarting down the path, I brushed my pants and then froze. A small fishing boat was anchored in the bay, one of the trawlers broken free from its pack. I looked back up the couloir – was it far enough inland to be hidden from the high path? It seemed to be deserted. How to make contact? The only thing I had apart from the dazzling yellow jacket was the lens on my communicator, which I tried to catch in the light but the sky as usual was dull and the light dimming. Nothing flashed but just as I'd waited as long as I dared a light winked in the corner of the boat – a signal. My heart crash dived. Was it intended for me or *for Him*? Or was He on the boat? Beads of sweat blistered my brow. Was there a chance I could escape? Just then a rock tumbled down the slope and I scrambled up the path before the guard spied the boat. He narrowed his eyes at my approach as if my secret was plastered over my sweaty face.

'Are you all right?'

'Yes, fine now, thanks.'

• • •

Despite the guard's grumblings I insisted we travel back along the south side of the island. I needed time to think about the boat. Had I blown a chance of escape? What a moron. When will I learn that standing still, staring like an idiot, never helped anyone? How could I face Scud? The guard said the beach was mined, what could I have done?

The guard was deliberately slow. He kept stopping and coughing and taking slugs of water from his bottle. After another hour of tramping he stopped and said, 'Look, we must go back.'

A few hundred metres ahead the path rose up and over a shoulder and I knew once we reached that rise the distance to the sea was a short yomp.

'But we're almost there.' I pointed. 'The other shore.'

'Remember my orders. You don't want to disobey your grandfather, do you?'

'But it's not fair. You're too slow. We could have been there if you had hurried.' I saw his expression shift but he still showed no real emotion.

'I'm not fit. I can't keep up with a young master like you.' He could have reminded me of my toilet stop but he didn't. He walked behind me and herded me back along the path.

My head hung low as I tried to tell myself I had won something today. A sighting, some hope. Even if I failed to see the passport – next time would be different.

'Can we come again tomorrow?' I asked.

His words said, 'If your grandfather allows.' His expression said, 'I hope not.'

'Don't you think it would be good for you to get out of there too?'

He ranged round as if checking for surveillance, but there was none. His face brightened. 'That's not for me to say. Come, we must go.'

The landscape shifted as we trudged. Colours changed on the sea water from greens to greys, slate, hammered pewter and back again, depending on how fast the clouds travelled. Bands of rain slashed the sky just off the coast and I calculated that if we weren't back soon we would be caught in a downpour. Despite this, I deliberately slowed.

The path climbed and dipped and at one point descended to another cove, which was broader than the one with the boat. Small shingles and broken shells constituted the lower beach progressing to a litter of pebbles, round and smooth along the tide line. I picked a pebble of similar size, shape and colour to the one Ishbel treasured and thought of that incriminating certificate stamped with the crest of the colony where she had been born. She should have had the same life as Ma, but something pretty serious must have happened to make Vanora leave when she was pregnant. I almost placed this new stone in my pocket but turned and threw it far into the sea. Where did I belong? Certainly not here. If I ever escaped this island I wanted no reminder to carry in my pocket, weighing me down. I already had my extra baggage of grief and uncertainty.

There were larger blocks of stones lying further back from the shore, on the grass. These I had noticed as symmetrical shapes from the path above. I walked over to them and saw among the overgrown bracken and briar a cut out square with a flagstone below. It was where a door had once hung. These must have been dwellings, abandoned decades before by the miserable looking folk in the photos.

My eyes were drawn to the sea, to the waves slapping the shore, to the small beach and the high cliffs surrounding this cove, now reclaimed by thousands of seabirds. I felt ghosts brush past my shoulders on their way to their boats. And I envied their luxury of taking one last look at the homes they left behind. I had been whisked from my home in the dead of night not realising I would never see it again, but now Ishbel's urgency was clear – we were both outlaws.

The rain caught up with us and before I drew my hood over my head I let it soak my upturned face. It had been many months since soft rain touched my skin. The guard negotiated his heavy bulk up the path without waiting and I wondered what I would have done if the small boat came round the headland now. Would I run into the sea, dodging mines to swim for it? The signal from the boat had been clear. I had been meant to see it and yet the boat people had made no attempt to rescue me. What were they there for? How did they even know I would be on that beach?

I stopped to catch my breath as I breached the cliff above the cove. There was a grand view of the island from here. Then it dawned on me something was wrong. There was the crown and the mound of the penitentiary and the path that led back to the coastline we had just left, but where was the lighthouse? I scanned a three sixty – nope, nothing. The view of the installation looked no different from this angle and yet as I walked towards it I felt the grey imposing walls of the crown begin to close around me even before I stepped into its shadow. For the first time I noticed the guards on top of the walls watching our approach with rifles poised. If they failed to recognise us in our heavy yellow and red jackets what would they do?

The climb up the stone steps to the door was not as bad as the scary descent. I even braved a pause at the top to take one last gulp of air before re-entering my next period of incarceration. Back inside, the guard waited until I crossed the threshold before bolting the door behind me. That bolt snipping hard into its place sent a shudder through me and I'm sure I felt the guard bristle too – we were both prisoners again.

He led me down the spiral stairs to the ante-chamber and instructed me to hang my heavy dripping coat on the pegs that ran along the wall. I removed my soaking boots and socks and pulled on the warm pair of slipper-ons that were lying by the inner door. They were my size and seemed to have my name on them.

'What's your name?' I asked the guard as I watched him struggle with the bindings of his boots.

Judging from the horrified look that passed his face, this was not something he'd been expecting.

'That is not required information, sir.'

'It will be if we're going out tomorrow. I can't tramp this island thinking of you as "the guard". We will be going out tomorrow you know.'

His face was inscrutable. 'As I say, that is for you and your grandfather to decide.'

'Well I wish to go out tomorrow and the next day and the next.'

The guard's shoulders sagged. 'Very well sir.' When he removed his coat it exposed the extent of his rotund shape. Maybe his reluctance to go outside was because of this. It must be difficult for him to breathe carrying that weight. Perhaps a few trips across the island would be good for the man, make him healthier, faster on his feet. I handed him my uneaten snack.

'Here, you take this; you look as though you're hungry.' I didn't want him to be too fast. The man looked at it greedily but shook his head.

'Go on, I want you to have it and I can see you want it.' He took it and put it in his pocket but I bet he'd have it devoured before he made it back to the main block.

'So if we are to go out together again you'd better tell me your name.'

'Ridgeway, sir.'

'Is that your surname or your first name?'

'That is my only name, sir.'

'OK Ridgeway, when you come back for me tomorrow, come an hour earlier. I want to spend more time out there.' I pretended to consult my communicator to let him see I had other tasks to be getting on with. 'And bring more food,' I snapped. 'It is not yet dark, we could have stayed out longer.'

'It was raining, sir.'

'When does it not rain? And rain does little damage these days.' I tapped the communicator. 'Anyway, MetO says it'll be fair tomorrow.' He looked at his own device and nodded.

'Remember, an hour earlier.'

'Very well, sir,' he said as he cranked the shutter door closed, snapping the lock and rattling it for good measure. He led me down the corridor towards the living quarters. We passed the galley where I looked for Scud but there was no sign of him. The surfaces were clean and free from clutter, his work there done for the day.

There was no question of going to the library on my return. The thought of facing my grandfather made me feel physically sick. Anyway I was cold even though my heart still raced from the exhilarating walk back along the coast.

When we reached my quarters I felt an uneasy sense of safety. I wanted to escape this guard who had been with me all afternoon and spend some time with my own thoughts.

'Goodbye Ridgeway.'

Ridgeway merely nodded and walked away.

I enjoyed the warmth that enveloped me when the door slid open. Someone had turned the heating on. Even though I had showered the previous day, a green light shone from the wash unit so I wasted no time jumping in before the moment passed. Its hot steam hugged me but my feet stung for the first few seconds. I looked at them and saw that they were rubbed red at the heels. After a couple of minutes the water turned cold then stopped; my allotted time was up. Hot towels hung from the rail. I felt pampered by the conscious effort to make my return as luxurious as possible. Was it Scud's doing or Grandfather's?

When I moved back to my sleep quarters a tray of hot broth and rice stew had materialised. Eating it filled me with joyous warmth I had not experienced since the day Pa drove us to the coast, but that thought was squashed. I spun out the meal as long as I could to savour the joy and tried to ignore the gnawing thoughts of my DNA discovery and my failure to unearth the whole truth. The picture of my grandmother flashed in my brain, her brazen name Vanora MacLeod on Ishbel's certificate, and my joy evaporated in a double dash of negatives. As I scraped the last grains from the bowl I noticed my right hand. There was a freckle I had never seen before. Had that always been there? I rubbed it to see if it was perhaps a splash of food. It remained. The bowl had a residue smeared on the base and yet the food had tasted normal. My bowels grumbled with fear. What if? No, impossible. I was his grandson after all. I rushed to the mirror and examined my face, but everything was as it should have been. My teeth shone white as I laughed at my idiocy. The fresh air and the boat sighting had gone to my head. I needed to settle down.

There was still some time before lights out so I picked up the latest library novel from the locker: *Brave New World* by Aldous Huxley. This was an ancient work and quite fanciful. As I turned the page I became aware of a ragged edge as if one of the pages had come loose. I rifled through and found the culprit. It was not a printed page but one filled with small writing. Scud had left me another note. Was he mad? How could he have been so careless? The paper could have fallen out as soon as I lifted the book. He must be desperate to try such a trick. I crawled into bed and I pulled the covers over my head and could just make out the handwriting:

did you contact   get them in here   only you can

• • •

Those last few words punched at my conscience and made me feel cold in this overly warm room.

Only you can

It was as if my presence on this island had been planned long ago and Scud knew it. But how? He had been locked up in here all of my life and longer, and in that time he would have had no contact with the outside world. How could he know that my parents would be killed and that Ishbel would bring me here after their death?

Only you can

• • •

Grandfather came to my room while I napped. He tossed the cereal bar on the bed from where he stood by the door, almost hitting me with it. When he entered his presence stretched into every corner. He scowled at my licked-clean dinner plates. Thank jupe I'd had the foresight to hide the paper scrap before closing my eyes.

'You would not be so hungry if you did not give your food to the guard.'

My heart beat faster and I hoped Ridgeway hadn't been punished.

'Have you now had enough to eat?'

I picked up the bar. 'I might need something later, but I am fine just now.' My laugh sounded forced. 'Fresh air makes me hungry.' Maybe he would see how good the walk had been for my health.

'Well don't get too greedy. I only have a small food ration for this place and the supply boat isn't due for months. The guards have their own diet,' he said as he walked to the window. It was almost dark and his reflection in the corner glass showed the tired ancient he was when he didn't know he was being observed. 'Did you find the corncrake?'

'No, not yet.' My face flushed because I had forgotten the excuse for being allowed outside. I hadn't even bothered to take a decent recorder with me, I had been too absorbed with the passport. The passport. Sakes! My flush must have turned me purple. It was still in the jacket, behind the shutter door.

Grandfather grunted and waited for me to speak.

'We just walked to the end of the island and back. Stuck to the path. I don't expect such a shy bird will nest next to the path.'

Could I retrieve it? There was surveillance in the corridor, so that would only attract more attention. Shit, what a supreme clunk, major tard.

'What are you babbling on about boy? Those paths are over-grown from disuse. There is no one to disturb the prim bird.'

His naivety comforted me. He must be deluded into thinking his fortress island was impenetrable. Those footprints were fresh and the path was not so overgrown. It told me that he had no idea Scud had passed me notes and he seemed to have no interest in the soaking wet jacket with the incriminating content that hung in the ante-room.

'I feel better though, you'll be glad to hear, and I want to go out tomorrow again. I've told the guard to come earlier.'

I made my voice perky and assertive as I had been taught in Social Tactic classes.

There was a look behind Davie's scowl. Was it approval or rec-ognition? I couldn't tell. He searched my face then pulled a tab from his waistcoat. 'Enter your government password in here to request a duplicate passport. If your mother really did destroy it you must apply for another.' So he had his doubts. He pushed the tab into my hand and signalled me towards the Beastie. 'Go on, apply now.'

His brow was sweating. This was important to him.

'I don't understand why you need this?' I asked. 'If you are to keep me here, hidden from the Military, won't applying for the passport alert them to my whereabouts?'

His bushy eyebrows sprang up at my impudence and then confusion flooded his face. He grabbed the tab from my grasp, almost wrenching my arm out of its socket, and barged from the room.

Chapter Seventeen

Scud gave me the boak next morning as he shoulder-surfed on my nature project. His skin had the translucency of drinking water. Blue veins pulsed visibly and his bone structure was so pronounced I was convinced if he tapped his nose, which he did often, it would break off like an icicle snapped from an overhang.

I took him through the fabrication of what I'd found so far and laid out a plan of what we should expect to discover on the island. As well as the book I'd read we had unearthed a good historical record of these islands; records by the long abolished churches had been saved for posterity as had those recorded by old historical environmental quangos set up to look after the province of North West Caledon. These quangos were pretty ineffective due to the usual reasons – men looking out for their own careers and taking their eye off their conflicting end goals. They were eventually disbanded and merged by the Land Reclaimist Party who in the end had no choice but to implement more extreme measures to save the planet. Time would tell the outcome.

Scud started to yawn as we scrolled through the many old catalogues of animal, bird and plant species. Many of them had been marked as extinct, even then, thirty years ago when the catalogue had been compiled. Goodness knows how many more had disappeared.

'Gowd, this is so boring,' Scud said.

'How can you say it's boring? You were the one who suggested this project,' I snapped then bit my careless tongue.

Scud held up his hands. 'Well now, ah didnae say it wid be boring fur you,' he said. 'You're a lad wi loads o' energy and enthusiasm and this is the type of stuff wee boys love.'

'I'm not a wee boy!'

He tapped his nose and I winced, expecting it to fly off his face and onto my lap.

'But men, now,' he continued and shook his head, 'full grown men, who dae a hard day's work fur a hard day's pay, well they fund this stuff boring, they wid be much happier watching a wolf fight or dealing a game o' cards.'

Then I twigged what he was up to, goading the guards to leave their post to have a game of cards rather than sit and watch a boy make lists of flora and fauna. With the exception of Ridgeway the only guard I had seen up close was the one on duty when I arrived on Black Rock and he looked pretty gormless. But Scud was deluding himself if he thought a guard would fall for his manipulation by unsubtle hints. Although by the look of Scud's smug smirk, it seemed he knew them better.

He fell silent, so I continued to select the species of this island and drag them to my list.

'There are quite a number of unusual things on this island,' I whispered.

He yawned theatrically. 'Oh yeah, like what?'

I chewed my lip trying to play the right words in my mouth and glanced at the dot on the wall before speaking again. 'Well the bracken is quite tall along the paths – mostly overgrown.'

'*Mostly* overgrown,' he drawled.

'Yes, mostly. And even though I was there for only a moment, the sea shore was interesting.'

Yawn. 'Oh yeah, how so? You see anyone get blown up by mines?' He gave a peculiar laugh at this.

'No, no one blown up, just some shingle and shells and debris that winks and blinks.'

He shifted in his seat.

'Lots of debris, I mean. There must be quite a few boats pass by here.'

'Ships you mean, young Sorlie.' He perked up and looked directly at me with his back to the dot.

'No, boats.'

'Passing boats,' Scud murmured into himself.

Then he looked at me and smiled and I smiled back and thought that I liked this new kind of communication. It worked well between us. And it meant that he did not know I had done very little to save him.

'Won't come in too far though. Ah wisnae joking,' he said with his peculiar laugh. 'The coastline is mined and netted.'

I tried to look calm. I scrolled to an image of a curlew, similar to one I had seen on the beach.

'On the beach, I wonder why the birds don't get blown up.'

'You can be really stupid fur such a clever boy.'

'Well, why is it necessary to have such protection? You are only prisoners.' I could feel my face redden, too late to hide my embarrassment.

'Aye as you say young Sorlie, only prisoners, low life some would say. Who cares what happens tae us, we could hardly paddle fur another shore here in the middle o' the Atlantic, oops ah mean the Western Sea.' His voice had changed, low, less nasal, refined or affected, almost Privileged. He laughed again. 'Maybe they're scared someone'll try tae break in tae the prison. Pirates!' he added with wide eyes and jazz hands.

'Pirates, is that who attacked the other week?'

'Probably.' He tapped his nose so I could see he was stretching the truth, only a code for his half-truth. 'There are many pirates out there, hijacking large cargo ships. Ah'm sure they would just be having a bit o' fun wi us. We aren't worth anything tae them.' He paused. 'Well, not that they know of anyway. But maybe one of their numbers is here and they were attempting a breakout the other night. Pretty amateurish attempt though, eh? It would take more than pirates tae take over this island even with its poor defences.' He looked at me with bloodshot eyes. 'Have ye not done yer prison histories?'

I shook my head.

'Many, many years ago there were islands where prisoners were held, but these prisons were close to shore. Sometimes prisoners tried to escape and swam to the mainland. So they added a new defence.'

'What sort of defence? The mines you mean?'

'No, anyone can get past mines. No, every prisoner on these islands has a part of their brain removed disabling their ability tae swim. They sink. Genius really, the best defence the regime has against…' He stopped speaking his eyes rolled back into their sockets and he started to shudder then fell to the ground. As I stepped towards him a voice roared. 'DO NOT TOUCH THE PRISONER, DO NOT TOUCH THE PRISONER.'

• • •

So the guards hadn't gone for a game of cards after all. They probably hadn't taken their attention from us for long. Scud had told me quite a lot in that time but I wished he hadn't gone on. It was a barbaric punishment. Just like the last time, after a few minutes he began to come round, he rolled over on his stomach and moaned. He lay on his face gurning for maybe five minutes, then got to his knees and climbed back into the chair.

'Ask your guard,' he croaked, risking more pain. He was shrivelled, like a dried piece of fruit past its sell by date. Whatever this dilution was Scud couldn't take much more if he persisted in taunting the surveillance and subjecting himself to the additional distress of being zapped.

'Right let's get back tae yer lesson.' He coughed. 'What are ye going out tae find this afternoon?' he said with an even voice, but as he reached for some water his hands trembled. After ten or so minutes he slid from the seat to the floor and crawled to the corner of the room by the window. His back arched like a cat ready for a fight but his head hung low between his shoulders and painful sounding rasps of breath snuck out from under him. As I rose from my seat to help, he lifted an arm and held his dry flaking hand up to halt me. When the breaths eased he straightened his spine, rolled off his knees and leaned against the wall. The urgency in his wide-eyed stare was more potent than his paper scrawl.

• • •

As I prepared for the arrival of Ridgeway to take me on my afternoon trip I couldn't help replaying Scud's words about the prisoners having their swimming function disabled. That was the moment of the zap, but he risked more to tell me to ask the guard. But ask him what? About the operation or about the pirates?

Ridgeway arrived at my door just as I was sliding the small utility tool in my trouser pocket. I'd found it in the bottom of the holdall Ishbel had packed for me. It was an incongruous looking thing, shaped like an old-style phone some oldies still preferred in place of communicators, but I knew this multi-tool had scissors and a small pen knife as well as screwdriver and toothpick. It had lain in a drawer in our kitchen for as long as Ishbel had been with us and she had used it for small household chores. The reminder of home tugged my senses but I couldn't deny it was a real prize.

Ridgeway looked different today, not physically changed like Scud but in presence. It was as if he decided that he was in charge and that his status on the island was greater than it had been. His shoulders looked broader, his stomach less podgy. He almost carried a military air. I couldn't help smiling at his pomp; he'd been taking lessons from Davie. I studied his face for any give away that my passport had been discovered, but there was none. When we entered the ante-room I was stunned to see the coat hanging, untouched, despite the telltale sign of the pocket dragged down with the weight of the passport. Ridgeway must be blind.

Before he opened the door to the platform he said, 'Are you ready for this? No swooning now.'

'What do you mean?'

'Well you almost had us both over the edge yesterday.'

'It was the shock of the exposure,' I blundered on. 'I'm psyched up for it this time.' And I was. There was no way this guard would have the pleasure of seeing me freak out again. 'I'll be fine,' I said as I took in a lungful to prepare.

We followed the coast in the opposite direction, but soon joined a familiar path. Despite his change in posture, Ridgeway was even slower than before. He winced as he climbed over a huge boulder on the path and I suspected this was his muscles telling him that they had other uses than sitting in front of a monitor. I took the opportunity to race ahead. He called out for me to wait but I shouted back, 'It's OK. I'll wait for you at the junction.'

I knew he would probably be a good bit behind me so once I was out of his sights I started to sprint. Despite everything I'd learned in the past few days I wanted to bounce. I leaped over culverts with more spring than was needed. I squealed at the chill when I splashed through mud puddles. I held my face up to taste the moisture in the air even though this was probably not the best thing for my future health. By the time I reached the junction I was grinning like a chimpanzee. I calculated I had a stretch of at least one hour over Ridgeway. Hunkered down between two boulders, it afforded me a good view of the path. The weather was damp but the rain compared to yesterday was lighter and travelling west. Even through my waterproof trousers I could feel the cold damp of the stones. As I pulled the packet from my pocket my heart jumped with more than the exertion of the run. It refused to slow. My hands shook as I pulled on the brown leaf booklet which had been placed in this biobag by my dead mother's hand all those years ago. The hand that in my imagination had blown from her body, her ring spotted with blood. No, I blinked back the tears that stood in my eyes; there was no time for tears. They could wait for later.

My grandmother Vanora's hologram was top priority. I ruffled through the pages until I found that awful native image again. Without dwelling on this unreliable technology I peeled off my glove and with my thumbnail booted the passport to life. A menu flashed a map of names starting with my own, fanning out in chronological order through the generations of my ancestors. Despite my resolve I selected my own first. A hologram appeared on the slab of stone before me. It was me as I was one year ago; until coming of age all passport holograms are taken annually. I was small and puny; my hair had a faint tinge of copper but was mostly mousy brown. I took a certain pleasure in seeing how chubby this boy was, but maybe it was an illusion. Natives also had their holograms captured. There were set periods in the year when the under-aged were rounded up and carted off for the day. Ishbel had gone too, until a couple of years ago, so she must have some sort of false ID. Why the pretence? Why did she come back to enter our home as a native and put Ma in danger? Anger flared in me. Life was one humongous lie.

I checked the path: no sign of the guard. The urge to view my parents' holos was strong but time ticked. My grandfather was listed with his wife Vanora. I selected her. When she appeared on the stone, the air was knocked from my lungs. There before me, in my passport, a copy of which could be held in the government's Department of Ethnicity, was the clear image of a native, my grandfather's wife. There was no mistaking it, no blaming old technology. Red hair, green eyes, freckles; her height, one hundred and forty seven centimetres – tiny. I believed such small peoples died out in the last great plague. She turned to face me and smiled as if she knew I would see this. Her teeth were good, small pearls with only a tinge of staining. Her high cheekbones, that telltale feature that dominated in both mother and daughters (plural), were pushed higher by her smile. Smiling was never encouraged during hologram capture. I remember well the technician roaring at me because I couldn't help but smile at my mother as she stood side-stage waiting for my image to be stored. And yet here was my grandmother blatantly smiling and I had the impression that the person capturing her image was enjoying her smile. She may even have been flirting with them. Gallus, my mother would have tagged her. How could it happen? How could a native be permitted to reach such a high position in the now disgraced Capital Broadcasting Corporation? I searched her records but there was no note of her death, nothing to say what happened to her.

She was beautiful – for a native – and even though she was small she stood with great stature as if she were a high-ranking Privileged. It made no sense. I rubbed the DNA code next to her name. It was not possible that I had any of her DNA. She must have been an impostor. It was not possible that my mother had any of her DNA and yet the similarities could not be denied. Her smile was the smile of my mother. My mother's eyes shone through Vanora's eyes; even though Ma's were blue like my grandfather's, there was the same lazy dip of the left eye, the same creases around the corners, the same warmth. How could Ma be half native? She had been permitted to serve in the Military. And yet it was true she never reached the higher ranks she deserved.

I turned to Ma's image despite the pain it caused. Her face and stature were so like Davie's, only a diluted version. Saliva flooded my mouth. Was this the reason my mother was chosen for a Hero in Death status? The word *dilution* took on a new meaning. She must have been tempted to destroy this passport but instead she gave it to Ishbel to give to 'the old bastard'. She wanted me to know the full picture of my heritage but she wanted Davie to tell me.

Why?

Chapter Eighteen

Vanora looked so full of life. What happened to her – dilution? This was becoming an impossible situation. My grandfather knew the truth of my heritage; he would know what happened to my grandmother, but asking him was a no-no because he was mixed up in all this dilution shit. My head was washed out thinking about it. Ma must have had some reason to suspect I was in some sort of danger otherwise she would not have risked exposing Ishbel. The only thing I couldn't work out was whether the danger came from Davie or some other source. One thing I knew for certs – I had to get off this island.

I searched the skyline for Ridgeway and there he was cresting the rise, a good yomp away. His progress down the path was similar to a ground tank on afternoon manoeuvres, howking divots from the soft verge with heavy tread. In a way I was grateful he was so slow, but the military in me couldn't repress the irritation I felt. He was an embarrassment as government servants go. If he had been on our Base he would have been enlisted in the Last Chance Fitness programme, would probably fail, then bye-bye Ridgeway – transferred to Bieberville Border. It's a mystery why Davie permitted such a slovenly approach. Still, who was I to complain? The slack he awarded me was useful.

I stuffed the passport in my pocket and launched the map to trace the route with my fingernail. The track was part of a circular path that hugged the jagged coastline. I tried to match the map to the topography. There, only a few hundred metres away, was the path I took to the shore. What was I waiting for? If the boat was still there I could swim out and they would pick me up

– guaranteed. And then I noticed it: propped on the cairn was a small pile of rocks marked in the form of an arrow pointing to the shore. This was no force of nature but manmade and I was as positive as a plus sign that it hadn't been there the first time I took this path. The arrow was like a starting gun. I catapulted from my hiding place and crashed through the dead bracken. Ridgeway might have seen me but I didn't stop. But what about Scud? What would happen to Scud and the others? Well, so what? Every man for himself, my pistoning arms and legs were telling me. Anyway, once I got to the mainland I could find Ishbel and she would rescue Scud. I was just a boy, how could I be expected to rescue them all?

I scrappled down the scree to the cove. The boat wasn't there. Rocks rubbled under my feet and I skidded to a halt just before I hit the shingle and the possibility of a mine. I dropped to my hunkers and bowed my head. The salt blowing off the waves caused tears to prickle my eyes.

'No,' I whispered into the wind. 'No.' Feeling some release with my words even though I couldn't believe my chance at escape had evaporated within a day. I thumped my fists off my thighs. Should have taken the chance yesterday – idiot.

Despite my despondency, the sea air released some of the pain of my captivity. I felt free yet I wasn't. No way was I going back to that prison. I fingered the utility tool in my pocket and wondered if I could kill Ridgeway with the knife. As my fingers grappled to release the inadequate hilt I imagined the blade sliding into the blubber and being consumed before it hit anything of consequence. The eight centimetre blade would hardly scratch the surface. It would be like trying to harpoon a whale with a knitting needle. By the time it made any impression on him he would have me felled with one blow from his primitive paws. I kicked some shingle towards the sea, taunting it to explode. I trailed my feet on the walk back to a rock by the path and sat down to wait for Ridgeway to come and get me – if he could. With any luck he would break his neck on the way down. I knew I didn't have the heart nor the equipment to kill him, so there I sat, waiting for him or his replacement to drag me back to the prison. Let them come.

The mournful call of a seabird that circled above matched the keening of my soul. A curlew tiptoed on the shingle calling out my pain. It was free. I was not.

. . .

The day had been unusually dry but now a thick rain-band ripped its way towards the island. As I rose to tackle the steep climb back to meet the hapless guard, a hand grasped my mouth and I felt myself bodily lifted off the ground. What was he up to? I kicked and gagged and tried to bite the hand that smelled of putrid fish and a sick feeling hit my stomach. This was not Ridgeway. As my assailant dragged me away from the shore, I bit hard and heard a soft curse. My heels scraped the shingle, carving two deep ruts in my wake. Each time I twisted, fingers dug deep into my cheek and the arm round my body tightened. Daylight was left behind as I was dragged deep into a cave. I felt my bowels churn. Soon I'd be dead meat but the nauseating smell of the hand made me gag and it was this I fought. I worked my jaw free and bit hard again. This time I was released but with the deftness of a ninja I was dumped on the ground, hands and legs bound in twine before I had a chance to find my feet.

The first I saw of him was two ragged skin boots I was sure were poised to kick me if I hollered. I looked up at their owner, a beast of a man. He wore a patchwork coat of small skins fashioned into shape with looping stitches of gut. He groaned on stiff knees as he hunkered down to meet my inspection. Specked black and grey hair covered most of his face and neck, a matted beard framed lips ragged with salt, and a broad broken nose protruded from the mass of hair. The eyes that stared at me below thick unruly brows crinkled around the edges from many days of weather and laughter; they were clear and green, and bright as a thick carpet of forest moss. As they smiled at me a lump formed in my throat, not with the realisation that I was going to live, but with the familiarity of that smile. My planned shout for Ridgeway stuck in my thrapple.

'What…?' I croaked and the apparition held up a grubby finger to his lips, fingernails crusted with muck. My nose ran with the snot of exertion. The bindings cut into my hands as I struggled to free myself. The beast sat back on his heels and grinned at me, shaking his head and chuckling as if he couldn't quite believe what he'd caught.

'Who are…?' The finger came up again.

'No time for questions Somhairle.' The voice was harled but gentle. I sank back against the cave wall. Not only did he use my name but used the Gaelic version.

'How…?'

'Shoosh, we have no time for questions, we must hurry. Ridgeway will be searching for you. He'll be here soon.'

'You know Ridgeway?'

He ignored this question as he leaned forward and gently took the bindings from my feet and hands.

'You don't need these now that you've seen my face and know I mean you no harm.' He smiled then and I could see those laughter lines spread almost to his temples. What could have been dimples appeared in the cheeks concealed under his beard.

'We need your help. That's why you're here.'

'We…?' I didn't understand. He held up his hand

'Unspeakable things are happening on Black Rock. If the experiments succeed, who knows where it will end.'

'What?'

'Didn't Scud contact you? About the dilution?'

'Who are you? How do you know this?' But I already knew. *Find Him.* It seems I had found him.

'I'm Kenneth and I am your kin, Somhairle.'

'Kin? In what way are you my kin?'

'There is no time to explain the whole story now. You must trust me. We need your help – there is no one else. You must go back.'

146

'Why should I trust you? If you are my kin you can help me escape.' I pointed to the cave opening. 'The boat. Did you see the boat? Is that your boat?' I began to stand. At last I could get away. 'I'm not going back. You can't make me.'

'Escape. Why do you need to escape? You're with Davie, your grandfather. He'll not harm you.'

He was too familiar with my life. My hand moved to where my passport was hidden. 'Davie's going to kill me.'

I saw his eyes follow my hand, then recognition passed over his face.

'What do you have there?'

'Nothing.' I folded my arms round my waist.

'Oh, you know, don't you?'

'Know what?' I could hear my voice rising. And where the snaf was Ridgeway?

'About your beginnings.'

I got up to leave, this caveman was freaking me. 'I don't know what you're talking about.'

'Vanora.'

How did he know? No one should ever know. 'It's not true,' I said. 'Vanora is an impostor.'

He put his hands on my shoulders to stop me. 'Listen, Somhairle. You have no trace of a native about your appearance and neither did your mother.'

'My mother? How do you know my mother?'

'You are so like her. How do you think your mother managed to serve in the Military? How have you survived all this time as a Privileged? Your grandfather has manipulated both official passports with the authorities; he has managed somehow to bribe your heritage away from the records. Your grandfather cares for you.'

'Oh yeah? Well how come I have to hide the passport from him?'

'You have two passports. An original true passport was retained by Vanora and passed on to your mother. She would want you to know the truth. Even so your grandfather would never harm you.'

His eyes held the truth, but my heart told me he was misguided and wrong.

'How can you say that? You don't know how he looks at me. Sometimes he looks at me as if he hates me. He's going to kill me.'

'That won't happen. He knows the consequences and Ishbel would have reminded him.'

A shiver that was chillier than the cave ran through me. I remembered Ishbel's words.

'How do you know Ishbel? Where is she? When is she coming back for me?'

He pressed two fingers to his lips as if holding his next words in his mouth for inspection before spilling them. 'Yes I know Ishbel, but she is not coming back. Not yet. You must return to the prison, Somhairle. We need you to help us free the prisoners from the experiments, from their hell. It's almost time.'

'Time for what?'

His nose darkened in a blush.

'I don't know, but it will be soon, I know it will. And we will know when it happens.'

'This is mental, I'm not going back. Why should I do what a crazy caveman tells me when you don't even know what's going on?'

'You must.' He looked panicked now as if it was his life that depended on it. 'Try to access his computer, find the process for the dilution. There is no surveillance in his study. He won't suspect; to him you are only the grandchild he wants to educate. You know you can access that ancient machine. Scud will help you.'

'Scud again. I'm not going anywhere until you tell me how you know all this. How do you know Scud and Ishbel and my mother? Who are you?'

He sighed in reluctance, saying, 'I am your uncle, your mother's brother.'

'No!'

'Yes, I'm Vanora's son – cast out for resembling a native too much.' He touched my head with his hand like he had turned into some ancient prophet with this staggering admission. 'Go now quickly.'

'No!' I screamed. 'Tell me!'

'Shush.' He put a hand on my shoulder and looked me in the eye. 'Soon, I promise, but not now. You must go back until it is time.' He turned me to face the entrance. 'Now go.'

'No!' I was whispering though I don't know why. 'You can't just throw me out after telling me you're my uncle. I want to know what's going on. My mother, she was your sister, Davie, your father. Does he know you're here?'

'No, Davie is not my father, your mother was my half-sister. Vanora gave birth to me when she was very young. Too young to look after me.'

'Who's your father then?' I asked, even though this crazy man was making this up.

'I don't know. She would never tell me. His DNA is missing from my passport, but as you can see from my appearance, I have a fair bit of native in me.

'Vanora met your grandfather while he was at University, but you probably know that. Unfortunately Vanora kept my existence secret from him until after they were married. I can understand why she did that. Davie always had ideas of grandeur and the classes in the old country were well divided. At that time the United Kingdom was going through continued periods of weak government. Davie was a member of the newly formed Nationalist Pure Blood League that would eventually become the Purists.' Kenneth shook his head again. 'Their extremist policies painted a clear line to the way things would turn out.'

'When Davie found out about me he almost murdered my mother. I must have been only about ten, but I remember when she came home to my grandparents' house, beaten and bruised. She was expecting Kathleen.'

I felt my heart leap at the mention of my mother's given name.

'They wanted her to go to the police, but she refused. It probably wouldn't have done any good. In this country the discrimination against folk like my mother was already pretty institutionalised. She stayed with her parents for a while and then went back to him. The gods only know why.

'I was lucky, I suppose. I was a top grade student and because of my mother's senior position in broadcasting I could afford to go to university when I was only sixteen. Wealth then could get past the discrimination.'

'And Ishbel…?'

His smiled through his thatch. 'Ah, so you know about Ishbel – good.' Then his eyes filmed over and there was something like anger in them. 'Look, there is no time for this. You must trust me – I am your kin. I'm one of only a handful of people who care for your well-being.' He pushed me from the cave and screamed a call, almost like that of a corncrake. It would be sure to bring Ridgeway to the cliff edge so I had no option but to leave or reveal his hiding place.

I blinked in surprise at the daylight after the dimness of the cave and as I looked back I saw only a gash in the rock, indiscernible from the unwelcoming cliff face. It was as if I had imagined the whole episode. But of course I hadn't. So much had happened in the last few minutes and out here everything was as it should be. The sea still sifted the shingle, the clouds scuffed the grey sky. It should have been different, felt different, after what I had just learned, but the world was the same. And after a brief sniff at freedom I remained a prisoner on an island full of prisoners. Freedom, that place Pa first told me of, was not for me. I had found an uncle which meant nothing when you were still alone. What would Pa have wanted me to do? He was an honourable man and he too would have wanted the prisoners saved. Kenneth looked much older than Ma, but the resemblance could not be denied. Had he cared for her when they were small? Did she look up to him as I knew younger siblings did? She would have wanted me to help him. And his words – almost the same as Ishbel's. How could I turn my back on one of the handful of folk who cared for my well-being?

My head hung heavy, dragged down by grief. The memory of my parents still as raw as the salt air that nipped and reminded me I was a sixteen-year-old orphan with a newfound dysfunctional family. What could I do that Kenneth couldn't? He was kin and yet no matter how that truth made me feel, he was not my mother or father. Nothing on this earth could replace them.

I started up the steep path conscious of my long absence and yet that call of Kenneth's had not brought the guard crashing down the slope. I feared he had lumbered back to the prison and reported my disappearance. When I found no sign of him at the junction cairn I began to run, to reach him before he got back.

The sea darkened in the afternoon dim. I ran as far as the second cove, then stopped to check the map and determined that at the next bend in the path I should almost be able to see the prison. He might be waiting for me at the ruins, maybe stopped to catch his breath or gobble a grain bar.

The threatened heavy rain of earlier must have passed while I was in the cave, leaving the boulder path slick underfoot, slowing me down. I reached the high point by a standing stone. There was no sign of the bulking guard. The path snaked overland for about three kilometres to the coast before it swung back along the eastern cliffs, towards the penitentiary mound. Seabirds squawked above me – 'Orphan, orphan,' they taunted. I picked up a stone and hurled it at them but missed by a good length. As I scanned the landscape one more time, resigning myself to my loss, he appeared out of a dip in the path like a rabbit from a hole, the gaudy red jacket a paint splodge on an otherwise perfect landscape. I almost cried with relief at the sight of him. His speed had picked up as he headed away from me. How could the fat man have travelled the distance so fast? My call swept behind me in the wind. I roared but it was hopeless. It felt good to run, to have my lungs bursting and my leg muscles stretched. I hurtled over culverts that ran high with torrents from last night's rain. Even though Ridgeway had speeded up I caught him easily – what a lumbering brute he was.

'Ridgeway,' I shouted only a few feet from him.

He jumped and almost fell over as he spun on the spot. I laughed when I saw his stupid face, purple with exertion. He grabbed my jacket in two fists and shook me.

'Where have you been?' The treatment, normally reserved for prisoners, was on me before he remembered who he was addressing.

He released and glowered at his boots, then turned and glanced over his shoulder. He looked close to tears.

'No need to get rough,' I said, trying to steady my voice.

Many struggles were taking place behind his mask of authority. I had put him in an impossible position. He was a man doing his job and I needed his help. I did not need an enemy.

'I'm sorry,' we both said at once and his tortured face relaxed of tension. He held his arms out in helplessness but said nothing.

'I went to the shore,' I said. 'Down the cliff; there was a marker to show you where I left the path. Didn't you see it?' He wasn't to know I hadn't left it there.

Ridgeway squared his shoulders and blew snot from his nostrils one at a time onto the heather beside the path.

'I thought I heard a sound,' I continued. 'The bird, you know? The corncrake. I should have left you a more obvious clue but I was too excited.' The lies flew easily from my lips. It was difficult to judge his mood; he stood like a sulky native examining every crack in his boots.

'I won't tell if you won't.'

He snapped his head up. 'You won't tell?' His voice was rough. 'You ran away from me. Your grandfather will forbid us to go out again.'

'And is that what you want, you big lazy lump?' I shouted. But the 'us' in his statement told me otherwise. 'You lost me.' I lowered my tone. I needed to get things sorted – play cute. 'I won't tell him you lost me. I won't tell him you can't keep up with me. If we always walked at your speed we'd never get to the other side of the island.' I looked at him with exasperation. 'I've a rare bird to find, you know.'

The relaxation had disappeared; his jaw was chewing suppressed anger. Maybe I'd gone too far, but he seemed to be weighing up his options.

'Come on Ridgeway.' I pointed towards the mound. 'You want out of there as much as I do. We can talk without surveillance; we can breathe air that hasn't been recycled through a thousand wasted lungs. Come on, there's no harm done,' I coaxed. 'There's nowhere for me to go. We may as well both enjoy the freedom while we have it.' Was that a small light I saw switch on in his eyes at the mention of the word freedom? He was as much a prisoner here as I was and we both knew it.

I clapped him on the shoulder in a chummy, non-patronising way and tried to ignore his sudden tension.

'I'll tell you what Ridgeway, in future you go at your own pace,' I reasoned with him, 'and I'll skip on ahead and every now and then I'll wait till you catch me up, or you can wait for me on the path until I return.'

I looked at my communicator. 'We still have plenty of time to get back before curfew. I promise this time I'll wait for you on the way back and won't disappear again.' The grey crown was now coming into view. 'Look, we're almost back already.' I smiled at him. 'Tell you what, you were fairly cracking along that path. I didn't know you had it in you.'

The weak sun was beginning to set and despite the greyness of the sky, it cast a burnished light on the prison, making it glow as if it were a real crown of gold. How could nature make something as grotesque as that prison look so appealing?

Ridgeway's face had returned to a normal colour as we trudged along the path toward the crowning mound that was our prison. He looked almost content, but then I spoiled things by asking, 'Where are you from, Ridgeway?'

'I am not permitted to answer questions.'

'But we've been talking; you are permitted to talk to me, right?'

He nodded in agreement.

'Well if we are to be companions on these paths we may as well get to know each other. I won't tell.' I handed him one of my grain bars to seal the pact. 'Here, I'm not supposed to but who's to know if we hide the evidence.' It was like being back at the Montessori, bribing kids with my superior toys to make friends.

'Are you a Bas? I can tell by your height and breadth. We had a Bas on our Base once. He was the Commandant's man. He was from Central Esperaneo. Is that where you're from?' Somehow I needed to know.

'South is where I'm from,' he droned. 'From the area where the great rivers snake through the land from sea to sea.'

'How can a river stretch from sea to sea?'

'A canal joins them in the Flatlands, everyone know that.'

I ignored his cheek. 'The Flatlands? The Fertile Lands. I never met a Flatlander before.'

'It's not all flat. Mountains rise around the southern edges, but yes, the Fertile Lands is the correct name.' He looked to the sea like one retracing time. 'We worked hard to feed Esperaneo.'

'Yes, I suppose so. Is your family still there?'

His jaw clenched as if he had swallowed something unpleasant.

'I have no family any more. My parents, my sister, gone.'

'What about your mate?'

'Gone.'

'Gone? Gone where?' But as soon as the words left my mouth I knew it was a stupid question after all the bloodshed I'd learned of from our recent history. In the days of the great reform when

154

the Purists were in power they seized the land of the Flatlanders to grow biofuel, to feed the factories and the air Transports. The fortunes they made were enormous because these fuels were scarce, but the money went to a few and the Flatlanders were denied their heritable land. Food was scarce and many starved and died. Ironically the period was called the Time of Plenty.

'I'm sorry, I shouldn't have asked.' But the damage was done.

Chapter Nineteen

When we arrived back, the welcome-home routine was as before: warm clothes and available hot water, comfort food but no sign of Scud.

I bundled my outdoor clothes in a ball, remembering to extract the passport this time, secreting it into my work wear before chucking the ball in the corner of my room. So much had changed in the last few days. I looked at my reflection in the washroom mirror and searched for any resemblance to the native tribe. There was that hint of copper in my hair but that proved nothing. Kenneth said my grandfather lodged a fake passport with the authorities, but maybe the one I held was the actual forgery – could it have been tampered with again? If that were the case why would Ishbel be so careful about hiding it? My hands were in my hair, pulling and tugging, trying to make some sense to the riddles. Was Kenneth lying to get me to help him? Why would someone, presumably my mother, leave my obviously native grandmother in the book unless to preserve the truth? As I debated these thoughts with my reflection a cold finger of memory scraped its nail down my spine.

I must have been about five or six. It was one of my earliest strong memories because it was an event that showed a side to my mother I had never seen before and never seen since.

Ma was such a gentle person. Even though she worked hard during the day on the Base, and was often away on missions, she always made special time for me. When she was home she would dismiss Ishbel and prepare me for bed herself.

It must have been the main growing season and the camp had

experienced the best sunshine days since before the great flood. In my mother's absence Ishbel had allowed me to play in the vegetable garden with her while she weeded. Each military household was allocated a plot of land and required to use every inch for growing vegetables but were only permitted to keep one-tenth for their own use. The rest went to the communal food fund. Many households found the chore laborious even with a domestic native, but Ishbel loved growing food and managed to grow more than anyone else could in the space available. Our tenth was more than plenty for our household and, of course, all that was not used was pickled. This one day, my mother returned from a mission tired and tattered as usual. The Purists must have been in power at the time, before water restrictions, because I was in the bath. Ishbel had soaped and rinsed my hair. Ma lifted me in a towel and rubbed my hair then began to comb it dry. I loved when she did that because she sang to me and kissed my neck at the end of each line of the song. She began with strong brisk strokes but as it dried her strokes became slower and laboured. She groaned inwardly and bent as if something pained in her stomach. She dropped the comb.

'Native,' she shrieked. The violence in her voice spooked me.

Ishbel entered the room wiping her hands from her task.

'Look! Look at his hair.' She pushed me from her knee and roughed my hair with cruel hands.

'What's wrong with it? It's shiny and healthy,' the native said.

I could feel my lip tremble; I started to bawl and I shrank towards Ishbel. What had I done wrong? My mother had been absent for weeks and now she was back she was angry with me.

'Look, can't you see girl?' I remember Ma crying. Their voices in whispers.

Ishbel grabbed hold of my bare shoulders in her rough hands. She stared at my hair. She took me with her as she walked to the open window and closed it. It was as if she had to protect me from something evil that was about to enter our lives and steal me away.

She looked calm but her hands were damp with sweat on my skin. I thought I felt a small tremble in them but that might have been my own sobs.

'His hair is turning bronze,' my mother whispered through her tears. 'Oh lass, what have you done?'

Ishbel shook her head. 'It was the sunshine. It's bleached his hair.' She pulled the towel round me saying, 'Sorry Kathleen.' I'm sure she had called my mother Kathleen because I had been shocked she had a name other than Ma.

'Has anyone seen him? Anyone commented?' she hissed. She paced the floor like a guard at a gate.

'No, but I was going to take him with me to the cooperative tomorrow. Thank the Lord you noticed in time.'

'Thank the Lord? We must dye it.'

Ishbel looked shocked. 'It will fade in no time.'

'If anyone comes to the house they would notice,' she whispered.

I must have been crying. Great hard hurting sobs pounded in my throat and chest. My mother would have taken my hand wiped my tears and hugged me close, told me not to worry, I'm sure, before she delivered her warning.

'From now on,' she said, 'you must stay out of the sun – always. It is not good for you. Do you understand?'

I probably just nodded through my stuttering sobs. But I didn't understand.

'It's not good for your hair,' she told me and then she said something like, 'One day you'll understand.'

And now that day had come and I understood why for years every time the sun shone, which wasn't often, I was bundled into the house, or had a hat slammed on my head before its harmful rays could damage my hair – or bring out the native pigment. Ishbel didn't dye my hair, she shaved it. Hair dye was a banned substance after all. She convinced me it was the new pirate fashion and gave me a bandana to wear, and because I believed everything she told me, I played along. Now the mirror and my memories sealed the deal. How could I have been so blinkered?

There was a movement in my sleep quarters. I thought it might be Scud but it was Davie.

'Don't you ever knock?' I couldn't help it.

He never knocked, never announced his presence – just arrived. He glowered at me.

'Don't give me your teenage insolence boy or I'll knock your head off the door jamb.'

Even as he said this he was giving me his searching inspection look, that before today, I never understood. Even though the mirror had just shown me my face, I was sure 'native' was now tattooed on my brow. Had my appearance changed to show the new wisdom, the learned knowledge of my DNA? That was daft; he couldn't possibly see that in the piercing glance. I sat on my bed and signalled for him to take a seat.

'Have you found the bird?'

'No, not yet,' I said, then added, 'but I am sure I heard one.' The fact he was here again asking this question meant it mattered.

'Tell me.'

'By the south shore,' I continued. 'I went down to a little cove – to the toilet. And I heard one in a clump of green plants that only seem to grow there. I'll go back tomorrow and not make so much noise. I'm sure I can find one.' My zeal was overplayed but what the hey. 'I have a small camera here. I can take images if I find it.' I held up my communicator plug-in.

My grandfather snapped his fingers at me. 'Let me see that.'

I handed it over. 'It was a present from my father. It's just a plug-in.'

'What about your standard communicator?'

I considered lying but I knew that wouldn't work. 'It plugs into that.' Oldies could be so maddening. 'It's been adapted but it doesn't work here.' I didn't let on it had a radio.

He looked around the room and said almost to himself. 'We should have checked this before you entered the secure zone.'

The truth was the plug-in didn't work in the penitentiary, but I hadn't tried it outside on the island. What a fool. I could have tried to call Ishbel.

'Tomorrow,' he said as he threw the plug-in on the bed.

'What?'

'You can't go out tomorrow,' he said. 'Important visitors are coming and you must remain in your quarters until they've gone.'

'Who?'

'That's none of your concern.'

'Can I meet them?'

'Did you not hear what I said? Stay in your quarters.'

'When are they coming?'

'Thirteen hundred hours, so make sure you are in your quarters and nowhere near the library. I don't want them pestered by a small boy.'

I stood on my toes and grew tall at this but his smirk told me he was deliberately goading me so I shut up. He left me then, alone with a long night ahead filled with thoughts of planning. How could I hack Davie's computer? How I could find out who this visitor was. How would Scud react when told him I had found *Him*?

Chapter Twenty

I woke to the sound of an approaching Transport, jumped from bed, tumbled over the clothes Scud would later tidy and ran to the window. Davie had said thirteen hundred hours – they were early, really early. The day was already beginning to lighten. No rain as far as I could see. A crayola of purple streaked the eastern horizon and out of that purple pizzazz emerged a black speck almost like a mosquito flying low, sliced in half by the line of the horizon. It grew in size until fully formed, maintaining its course towards my window. There was no pull-up to the helipad, there was no reduction in speed. It was coming too fast to stop. The cliff face reflected in those two bug eyes of the front screen – it was going to crash.

'Suicide mission!' I screamed as I hurled myself across the room, ducked and cowered, arms over head. But nothing happened. When I lowered my arms I heard the whirring, the slow beat of the engine. When would I learn? I peeled myself from the floor and peeped out of the window, like a child hiding behind hands, wanting and yet not wanting to see. And there it was, just as before, hovering metres from my cell. It dropped its nose in a bow, then raised and levelled so that the two bug eyes looked at me blankly, and yet behind them I knew there was hope. If it wasn't Ishbel then it was someone else who knew my situation, not just on this island or in this prison but in this room. As the Transport drew back its full body came into view showing off full regalia of heavy armoury and decoration; the insignia was almost identical to Ishbel's but more elaborate, ringed with a red and gold border transforming it into a shield.

The Transport rose out of sight, its engine growling overhead until it touched down and cut. Would he be waiting for her as he had the night of my arrival? I tried to picture the scene: Ishbel leaving the craft, walking towards him as if she walked on glass, on tiptoes. I had to find out why she was here.

Breakfast was brought by a guard I'd never seen before. He was young with a similar appearance to Ridgeway; he might have been Bas too although it wasn't so obvious.

'Where's Scud?'

'The prisoners are confined in their cells today,' he snubbed.

As he closed the door I heard a buzzer sound. I tried to open it but it was locked with no way to force it. I hammered until my knuckles almost bled.

'Open the door!' I screamed. 'Open the door right now.' But there was no sound from the corridor. It was pretty hopeless. What an idiot – I should have been prepared and nipped out when the guard came in at first. I kicked the door. 'Open, open, OPEN.' All it returned was a sore foot.

The dot on the wall gloated. 'What the snaf are you laughing at?' I spat as I threw a pillow at it.

The tears were oh so close, but because this time the pain was physical, I could work them off by pacing the floor. The starburst glass still patterned the window, and I rubbed my hand over the rough surface wishing it would rip the skin to make it bleed. After a while my breathing eased and I reconciled myself to captivity. There was nothing else to do so I ate breakfast and settled to work.

The genetics articles available in FuB were as useful as an umbrella in an ash cloud. Beastie didn't even bother to restrict access, it just turned up blank. I read reports on corncrakes, but that lasted ten milliseconds because it was soooo boring. The room was a mess. Scud wasn't coming to tidy today so I sorted through some of the clothes strewn on the floor. Ishbel's pebble fell from one pocket. It was cool in my ravished hands. The indent she had worn down with her homesickness took my thumb as if it belonged. If I rubbed it hard enough and made a wish, would that make her come? Aeons must have passed in the stillness of my cell and then from nowhere a cold dread attacked me. What if the Transport was not Ishbel's but the Military come to claim me for their own purposes? What if my grandfather had denounced me or what if they knew of my heritage? What if they were experimenting on me?

What if, what if, what if? All these questions buzzed round my head like a fire cracker set loose in an empty oil drum. I threw the pebble across the room; it bounced off the window, and almost knocked me out on its return. The dot on the wall looked on disapprovingly.

'What?' I hissed at it.

The same guard returned at noon to collect the breakfast tray and leave me lunch. When I tried to juke round him he was ready, blocked me and backed out of the room, tray in one hand, baton in the other.

'Oh so that's the way it's to be? Batter me into confinement.'

'I'm only following orders,' he barked as he closed and locked me in.

'Oh yeah? Well remind him I'm not a prisoner!' I roared at the closed door.

After an hour the food lay uneaten. No way were they going to tamper with my genes. Despite my rumbling belly I must have drifted off to sleep because the click of the door jolted me back to the living, but I was too far from it to try another escape round the guard. Except it wasn't the guard. It was Davie. At last. I was so relieved to see him I forgot to be angry.

'Come with me,' he growled. I ran to the mirror, checked my appearance for stray freckles, eye tints, that sort of thing, then grabbed my holdall.

'Leave that and hurry boy.'

'But...?'

'You're not leaving with them. Just hurry or I'll lock you in again.'

The holdall went hurtling across the room but no way was I being locked up again so I hid my disappointment behind a teenage pout.

His face was red and his breath stank of something sour.

As I stepped into the library behind him I placed my hand on my thrumming throat to quell the beat. The table set in the middle of the room shone with gold goblets and half empty silver platters of food – it was a banquet of medieval proportions. Glass carafes of red and clear beverage were organised at one end; the carafe of red was almost done. Standing behind the table was a tall man with warm grey eyes and hair so blond his pink scalp shone through. He wore a uniform, similar to the one worn by Ma and Pa but with adaptations: the badges were in the wrong place and carried the same insignia as the Transport, shield and all. Despite these changes there was something familiar about the man. His features were perfect, like someone from a movie-caster – all the best bits assembled into the creation of a beautiful being. As we entered the room he moved to greet us. His brimming confidence infected me but Davie bristled, poking me in the arm, urging me forward. The man's eyes and smile welcomed me.

'Sorlie,' he said, chummy-like. Did I know him? Someone from the Base, perhaps. 'I'm Merj,' he said in a rolling purr. 'It's a pleasure to meet you at last.'

'Pleasure,' I echoed.

He shook my hand, his grip applying the correct pressure, not too limp, not too earnest. 'I have heard so much about you from Ishbel,' he continued before stepping aside to post sentry by my winged chair. And then I saw her, standing by the other side of the chair, Ishbel – alive. I wanted to rush forward but her eyes flashed no, her face masked, expressionless.

'Hello Sorlie.' Her voice was dull, mechanical.

When I remained by the door Merj moved again and beckoned me into the room. I saw Ishbel's eyes soften into a smile even though her mouth remained grim. She looked younger, fresher, as if the death of my parents had released her. Her uniform bore the same regal insignia as Merj who now leaned towards her and brushed some invisible particle from her shoulder. They smiled to each other. At first I experienced a stab of jealousy, but something was wrong, charged. Ishbel's arms were folded across her chest in defensive mode. The tension in the room crackled.

Slouched in the winged chair was a figure so tiny I hadn't noticed him at first. An almost religious type smothered in a large brown cloak, head bent forward as if in prayer; an ornate Hebridean hood was pulled over his head so all I could see were small withered hands spotted with liver marks and gnarled knuckles of age.

Davie coughed roughly at my side, grabbed my arm and tried to push me further into the room, but my feet rooted to the floor.

'Our esteemed visitor wishes to meet you Sorlie,' he said in a wily voice.

I glanced at Ishbel and she nodded for me to step forward. One withered hand lifted off the lap and like an idiot I just stared at it and then at the shoes of fine leather – a banned substance – on the feet of this esteemed visitor. Like my grandfather, this person flaunted the rules. Davie hacked again and nudged my back.

'May I present my grandson…'

'I know who he is.'

I was taken aback by the feminine strength and sharp tone of the voice from under the hood. Davie took a step back as if he'd been slapped but recovered quickly to stab me with his finger again.

I now took the hand offered to me and bowed. It was as light as a silk handkerchief but the dry palm was rough as if it had been used to manual labour. I felt that if I squeezed it too tightly it would crumble like the charcoal left behind in my father's beach fire, turned to dust to blow to the wind.

'Enchanté,' I said. I heard a small tinkle laugh.

The hand tightened its grip and the figure shuffled in the seat to move forward. A sweet perfume of lavender rose in the air and I gulped back the memory of Ma. A polite cough from under the

hood signalled that the visitor was about to speak, then my grandfather yanked me back and the cough from within the cloak rattled and gained momentum and racked its way through the frail
body. Ishbel crouched down and Merj offered a handkerchief;
they seemed quite a team. Davie propelled me towards the library
door. I struggled against the roughness of his grip.

'Wait!' Merj stepped forward and pushed Davie's hand away.
'This is not finished, old man.' I dared not look at Davie. He must
have been raging, but he was outnumbered. Merj led me back to
the sitting figure who had now recovered herself. She straightened and pulled back the hood that had obscured her face. The
red hair had faded and was woven through with grey; her green
eyes that had been so bright and clear in the hologram were now
yellowed and weak. Her skin was clear with few blemishes but
lines crinkled around the eyes mapping years of mirth, and yet
there was a pinch to her mouth as if that laughter was not always
true. When she smiled I saw she was enjoying my scrutiny. Her
smile showed me teeth grey with age but strong like Ishbel's. As I
looked to Ishbel now, the old woman tugged my hand to draw my
gaze back to her. Davie was right behind me and pulled me back
from her grasp. Her fingers fluttered in some 'no matter' dance.

'We saw you from the window Sorlie,' she said. 'How are your
quarters? Is the old man taking good care of you?'

'The boy wants for nothing.' There was a pressure in his grasp
that no one else seemed to notice.

'Are you here to take me back?'

'Sadly no.' She looked towards Davie and smiled sweetly but
her voice held no regret. 'Your grandfather was expecting someone else. My good friends in the Noiri had an unfortunate accident and asked me to deliver some specials to your grandfather.'

'A set-up more likely,' Davie said.

'Your grandfather always was paranoid,' she said. 'But I don't
suppose he would have been too happy to miss his wine delivery.'

'Don't talk of me in third person. You tricked me.'

166

Vanora sighed as if he were a child. 'It was a lovely opportunity to visit you and Sorlie.'

'Why can't you take me?' She looked shocked that I had the cheek to ask.

'My bag.' She held up her hand and I saw Ishbel move forward.

'Not you, I meant Merj.' Ishbel's face flushed. She stepped behind the chair and stared at the books.

'Bring me my bag Merj, dear. I have a present for Sorlie.'

'You are to give nothing to the boy. He has all he needs,' Davie said.

Vanora gasped and set off another fit of coughing. Ishbel moved forward but Vanora pushed her away. 'Get me a drink.'

I caught that familiar scent of lavender as Ishbel tiptoed to where I stood by the table.

'It's good to see you Sorlie,' she said in lowered tones as she poured a glass of wine.

'You don't smell of vinegar.' It was astonishing.

She laughed. This close I could see how tatty her uniform was. It was faded in parts and the emblem had been sewn over a bright patch that had at one time held the badges of the disbanded State of UKAY. The uniforms were a sham.

'Ishbel?' Merj called.

She stared at the glass as if counting the bubbles in the liquid.

'What's going on?' I whispered. 'Why is she so horrible to you?'

She smiled, almost to herself, and whispered, 'You've not long to wait Sorlie,' then rearranged her face into an expression of resignation so common of a native. Not much had changed in her world and yet the way she spoke to me told me that the woman who helped me escape was far from gone.

When she returned to Vanora the older woman's sweetness had curdled. She took the glass without acknowledgement and sipped before handing the goblet to Merj.

'You are growing up fast Sorlie,' she said to me. 'You will soon be able to join me. I need another good lieutenant.' She patted Merj's hand. 'I am not strong and my army in the north is growing.'

'Pah, army,' my grandfather said. She didn't even grace him with a look.

'Your mother,' Vanora paused. My heart thudded.

'What about my mother?'

'Your mother should have joined me.' Ishbel stood to attention, ignored. Maybe it was an act for Davie's benefit, but in that case why bring Ishbel?

'You're so like your mother. Don't you think so David?'

Was that a growl from Davie?

'Your grandfather needs to feed you up more.' I felt like an army drone being fattened for combat. I wanted to speak but could find no words.

'The boy is well cared for.'

'Don't get all defensive on me David. I'm just saying…'

'You have no idea what you're talking about.'

'No? Well no matter.' She fluttered her fingers again and turned to Ishbel. 'How does the boy look to you Ishbel? Is he well fed?'

'He is a little peaky, could probably do with some fresh air.' She smiled at me when she said this.

'There…'

'Don't you tell me how to manage this boy's life!' Davie roared. 'You didn't want him when he was orphaned and now you come swanning in here accusing me…'

'Let me go with them.' At last I had found my voice.

They both stopped and stared at me as if I had just committed a murder.

'Well?' I said to Davie. 'You don't want me. You hate me for being a native.' There, it was out. Davie grabbed my collar before I knew what hit me and began dragging me from the room.

I pointed to Vanora, 'And if you're so concerned for my health, take me.' I dug my heels in and fought hard against Davie.

'Take me, please!' I screamed. Ishbel took a step forward but Vanora's arm stretched out to halt her. This brought on another

168

coughing fit.

'Let go of me!' I shouted trying to shrug Davie off. There was no backup from the assembled company and I knew then that they would not help. I was on my own.

Just before Davie had a chance to push me through the door I glanced over my shoulder to take a last look at Ishbel, but her attention was on the coughing woman. As those warm grey eyes of Merj watched my removal, he smiled and gave me thumb and index OK and whispered something to the seated visitor. The head now lifted in a gasp for breath, an elegant neck stretched full and proud, a handkerchief held over mouth and nose. Those faded green eyes that looked at me wept old tears, but the act was blown. She couldn't hide her true self. The body may be weak but the will was strong and Davie had no intention of letting me stay any longer in her presence.

• • •

'Let me go!' My foot stamped like a child's but I didn't give a monkey's balls.

He stopped so suddenly that I jerked back on my heels, battering against the fist that gripped my collar. He started shaking me but in his rage his face twisted in fear. Unbelievable – this tyrant, this madman was quaking in the face of a withered old creature in a Hebridean hood.

I tried to break free, but like a rope in a cog his grip grew tighter.

'Stop this insolence,' he hissed.

'Why? What are you going to do? Get one of your guards to beat me up?'

He dragged open the door to my quarters and hurled me in so hard I fell against the desk and dunted my head. I was stunned – not just from the blow but from the violence and anger directed at me. He stalked after me. As he approached I grabbed the desk and tried to pull myself up, but before I could get to my knees he hooked my tunic in his fist, hauled me to my feet, and slammed me to the wall.

'Your days here are numbered, young man.' His eyes sizzled with hatred. 'Don't think that you are in an honoured position here. If it were not for that *mutant* back there you would have been dead long before this.

'Mutant! She's my grandmother.'

His eyes sparked around the room, but more in confusion than rage. Still I kept shtum about Ishbel; I had no idea if he knew of her identity.

'And what do you know of that meddlesome old hag?'

'Not much, just what my father told me.' My back was pressed against the wall my feet planted ready to spring – the door was still open.

'And did dear daddy tell you she has designs on being a great revolutionary, and hides on a ravaged island where she builds imaginary armies to take over the world?' Spittle flew round the room. 'That she has disciples who worship her, are brainwashed by her lies of native equality?' He slammed the door shut barring my escape route. 'No, I bet he didn't. She's a fraud. A mutant who thinks she can destroy the truth. Does she honestly believe natives can resume their professional status? When the natives find out she has been cheating them I hope they tear her into little pieces and send her to the recyk midden for reprocessing.'

As he worked his lather up I shrank further into the wall.

'Oh she's got a nerve coming here, heavy-handed, demanding to see you. Tricking me with Noiri contraband, goading me.' He pointed a shaking feeble finger at me. 'And what does she care about you?' He snapped his fingers, almost clipping my nose. 'Nothing. The whore brought you to me, remember, because Vanora doesn't want to be bothered with a child. But we'll show her. You're going to find me that bird.'

That did it for me. The bird, like his reason, was absent, but for the purposes of my health I merely nodded like a good little grandson with an evil grandmother. His anger seemed dampened by thoughts of the bird.

'Now, I've had enough of your snivelling, moping and mourning. Get over it.' Spit hit my face. 'Soon my job will be done and I'll have nothing to lose.' He reached down and hauled me to my feet. I couldn't speak for fear and from his stranglehold pinning me to the wall. The only sound I could make was a pitiful mewing, like a cub. But it was enough. A puzzle moved on his face, he opened his fist and I was dropped to the ground like a turd he had picked up my mistake. When his foot lifted and pulled back ready to kick me, I cowered to protect my head against the blow that didn't come. He spun on his shiny boot heels and locked the door behind him, leaving me to wonder what the hell had just happened.

I wiped the spit from me and found it mixed with my blood. It was then that I started chittering so violently my teeth rattled. Sitting by the wall under the starburst window, I curled into a ball and cried, letting the tears and snot run free. After a while I heard the Transport take off. There was the whirry at the window. I didn't look.

'Go to hell!' I screamed to the room. They could have taken me but instead they left me to rot with the rest of the prisoners. The only encouragement I had to hang onto was Merj's OK sign and Ishbel's strange words.

What planet did Vanora live on? Those uniforms were a joke. If what Davie said was correct, she was queen of the rebels yet still she abandons her grandson. She had looked so regal in her hologram, but her behaviour towards Ishbel was less so. Let them bow to my ass. I wiped my eyes and nose with the heel of my hand. My wrist was thin and white, tracked by protruding blue veins and a silver crust of snot. The utility tool was hidden with the passport; the puny knife could slice through those blue veins. Who would care? It would be one less native to worry about. All I needed to do was take out the knife. I ran my index finger across my wrist – X marks the spot. What stopped me was the memory of Davie's fear. All was not right in his world, but that didn't make it any prettier in mine.

• • •

My face looked like a bashed pumpkin; the skin was not broken on the graze on my forehead, but there was a bruise. Blood dripped from my nose. I could taste it in my mouth and throat. There was blood on the wall below the dot so I took a piece of towel and rubbed it off. What did Eye-Spy think of Davie's violence? Were they subjected to it too? Perhaps there was no 'they'. Maybe he kept this surveillance of me to himself. I gulped back this creepy thought and waited for power shutdown. If the only way out of here was to help Kenneth break into the system, then that's what I would have to do.

• • •

During the night the alarm sounded. The perimeter lights were strong. A single shot cracked then all went quiet. In my mind the tyrant goose-stepped to the helipad where the prisoner might be detained. They might be begging for mercy. Davie would smirk, draw his old revolver and shoot the prisoner in the head. Or maybe in his own confusion he would put a bullet in his own brain, but that was too much to hope for.

The whole incident lasted only minutes. The perimeter lights shut down to normal mode, which left me with the lighthouse beam clocking its path round the floor. Who could blame the prisoners for attempting a breakout after a full day's cell confinement? They had little to lose.

Scud woke me with a gentle shake on my shoulder, which was just as well because my body felt as though it had been wrapped in barbed wire before being thrown out a speeding Jeep.

'What happened to you?' he asked as he picked up the upended chair and the blood-smeared towel, which he only briefly examined before stuffing it in the laundry sac.

'I walked into a door.'

He twisted his mouth but said nothing.

There was so much to tell him, but the stakes had been raised by my discoveries. Then there was Davie's violence, but Scud's careful examination of the room told me he guessed the situation.

'There was a breakout in the night.'

'Yes – sometimes the defences here are not as great as the regime would like us to believe,' he said politely.

I didn't know what to say to this. It was one of his codes.

'What's with the funny accent?'

He raised his eyes to the ceiling and again said nothing.

'Em, tell Ridgeway he won't be required today.' I mocked his formal voice. 'I need to read in the library.' I rotated my arm and tried to ease my shoulder socket.

'If you say so, sir.' He never called me sir – was it another code? He seemed disinterested. He paced the room and picked at the broken glass on the window.

'The visitors yesterday, sir?' He said it casually but by the way he was holding his command band, he anticipated a zap.

'I got to meet them,' I said matching his casual tone. I knew then, at that moment, that my grandfather was not the one watching us from behind the dot. If he had been, Scud would have been writhing on the floor. 'One was Ishbel, my native. I got to see her again.' This was an innocent enough comment but the burst of joy in Scud's eyes told histories.

'That must have been nice for you,' he drawled.

'I thought they had come for me but it was a false hope.' The bitterness in my voice did not pass him. He gazed out the window and began to whistle a nonsense tune. I did not mention Vanora because he had already gone too far. And knowing Scud, he probably already knew.

His appearance had improved. His hair stubble was dark sand and suited him and his skin held a slight tinge of health, his eyes were still walnut. He was beginning to look almost Privileged.

He made the bed and cleaned the washroom while I ate breakfast. My resolve not to eat had rumbled off into the distance; I was starving. If they wanted to experiment on me they could do it anyway whether I starved to death or not.

'So you are working in the library.' His gaze flirted with the floor and the dot on the wall – shifty, that's what Ma would have called that look. 'What is it you'll be studying – anything I can help you with?' He was almost confident. The fingers of weirdom began to crawl over my neck. He was different in more ways than appearance.

'Why do you ask?' I said. Kenneth had told me Scud could help, but I didn't know how. He was not permitted to linger in the library and even though Kenneth assured me there was no surveillance there, Scud's command band would always reveal his whereabouts. I couldn't risk it. And anyway, this new Scud was creeping me out of my skin.

He studied the floor, the dot, the starburst with a sort of struggle going on in his face. It was the same struggle Ridgeway's expression fought with.

'No reason, just want to help that's all,' he said. We stood silent for a while. There was nothing to tell this new Scud and he yet seemed reluctant to leave. It was one of those sand-kicking moments that lasted too long.

'Tell me about the bird,' he said at last. Of course that's what he was waiting for.

'Yes, I think I might have found *Him*,' I said. 'I think I've found *Him*,' I repeated. 'Yes. Yes that's what I need to do.' I stumbled over words. 'Check some things. About the habitat and all.'

'Oh?'

'Yes, *Him* being so close to the sea.'

I hoped he understood my garbled message, but couldn't be sure.

I watched him as he turned Beastie on and began to clear my breakfast tray. What if the experiments were working and he'd morphed into a Privileged, not just physically but behaviourally? Surely that's not possible. But if that were the case how could I still trust him? I mentally thumped my head. Why hadn't I studied harder at genetics? I didn't even know what dilution actually meant.

'If that will be all, sir, I'll go back to my cell.'

That creeping sensation returned as one more of my allies deserted me.

Chapter Twenty-one

The library was unlocked, deserted and foosty. It was impossible to do anything because Davie's workstation was missing; all that remained of its presence was a small rectangle clear of the dust that covered the rest of the table. The old boy had second-guessed me and I had given up my outside recreation for a lousy dead duck deal. The room looked the same as always, minus the banquet table and the workstation of course, but the air felt thinner. The oxters of my work wear soaked and darkened with sweat – I had to get out. It was like being in one of those old science docyous where laboratory rats are set running round a maze and when one door opens another closes until suddenly they are in the middle with nowhere to go. And then I thought of the new Scud and the pseudo-regal Vanora and decided there was only one option left to me.

I raced back to my quarters and hit the messenger on Beastie.

'Call Ridgeway,' I shouted. 'Tell him to dress for outdoors.'

While I waited I stared at the familiar scene from the window. The seascape was grey, rods of rain stabbed landward. Flecks of sunsheen struggled to get to grips with the day as night-time chased it under the horizon and a faint moon hovered just above the tossed sea. The wind was almost visible as it bowed and buckled the monochrome waves. Only the birds were oblivious to the darkening world, wheeling, dipping and gliding on the therms; an afternoon play. Then something flashed out there. I rubbed at the window for a better view, but the position of the fractured glass was a problem. It flashed again. A buoy bucked recklessly against the wind. Where had that drifted in from? The flashes were inconsistent, like the lighthouse, so I counted them to try to take my mind off Kenneth. He would be waiting in his cave for me, getting his hopes up, imagining me hacking into a workstation that was now missing. In terms of international espionage, Kenneth would be lucky to get a job purifying water. I lay my forehead against the cold glass. Where was Ridgeway?

By the time he arrived ten minutes later I was prowling the floor, biting my already ragged nails and spitting the splinters of them into the sink. I could see by the cross of his brows that he was furious at being dragged out on such a dreich day even before he opened his mouth.

'Are you mad? Look at it out there.' If he noticed my bruises he didn't let on – not even a blink.

'I have to get out of here, even if it's just for an hour.'

'And do you have anything specific in mind? Apart from getting us soaked and possibly blown off the cliff, that is?'

I almost chuckled at his insolence.

'Be a sport Ridgeway, we'll be wet in the first five minutes. After that it doesn't matter.'

• • •

The outside door buffeted against a driving easterly gale. Ridgeway struggled to keep the old hinges from popping their screws. He made sure I had a good hold on the hand rail. It was the first time I noticed the old-fashioned lock. No electrics. The authorities obviously assumed this old door was enough of a deterrent to enter from such an imposing cliff stairwell. It certainly seemed like madness as we teetered down the precarious steps. The rock was slick and slimy with a combination of rain, sea wash and bird shit. Ridgeway's boots lost grip and he landed on his bum. At first I laughed, then thought from this position I need only put my boot to his back to push him off. If he slipped from the steps he would fall at least a hundred metres to the waves that hammered the jagged rocks below. He'd be bashed to smithereens. I thought of the keys in his pocket – they would be lost, he would be lost, so I let that plan go in the wind, but it gave me an idea for something else.

He soon recovered and scrambled to his feet, brushing his wet behind with a gloved hand. Despite the cold his face was red and sweating.

'Stuff this madness,' he shouted up to me. 'Why must you go out today?'

'I've something to show you,' I shouted back.

His grumbled reply whipped away in the wind and he left me to pick my own way down the slithery steps as first his body then head vanished into the mist below, but I knew he would wait at the bottom. When I reached him he was hood-bent against the wind like a bowing native. I took care on the last few treacherous steps. When I reached the last one I thought I was home and dry but the rock I stood on was soapy and my boot shot from its footing. I grabbed Ridgeway's jacket to stop my fall and almost pulled him over with me.

'This is madness,' he shouted again, but stood aside to let me lead.

'Come on, don't be such a native,' I hollered back.

He shot me a look that warned me not to push my luck.

'Don't you be rushing ahead again,' he said. 'Not in this mist, you'll get lost.'

We walked single file to the lower coastal path. I knew exactly where I was going and struck out. The distance between us stretched but I kept turning to check Ridgeway remained in sights. I didn't want him getting suspicious – not yet anyway.

At the cairn marking the junction with the path that led to Kenneth's cave I stopped. What I was about to do was risky, but my choices had diminished along with my Privileged status. If I stayed in the prison I would eventually tip the balance too far with my unpredictable grandfather and he would fulfil his promise to kill me.

I waited for Ridgeway to catch up. Now off the clifftop, the world was less windy and reduced our holler to a hoe.

'Down there,' I pointed.

He took a swatchie over the edge. 'You're mad if you think I'm going down there.'

'You have to. That's where the corncrake is and if we don't find it my grandfather might send you to Bieberville.'

He snorted. 'Don't you threaten me. You don't have that sort of influence with your grandfather.'

He was right but I needed to make him believe I had that influence. 'How do you know I don't? I'm his kin.'

'Because I've worked for him for years, and I know the make of that man. He cares nothing for kin. All he cares about is Black Rock and his position here.'

'That's a bit presumptuous for a guard is it not?'

Ridgeway straightened his back and looked right at me square in the eye. For the first time I could see that the bumbling, lumbering guard had been an act. He stood tall, his stomach pulled in and his eyes narrowed, turned hard.

'I'm more than a guard and you know it.'

Did I? What did I know? He pointed to the bruise on my temple. 'Where did you get that, stumbling about in the dark?' There was a bitterness in his voice. 'No, if he was so fond of you he would hardly beat you, would he?'

I touched the telltale sign. So he had noticed.

'And has he beaten you?' I asked. 'Can you tell me honestly that he never beat you or the other guards?' I watched his face and there was a slight flicker that hinted I was nearer to the truth than he wanted to admit.

'He's a violent man – we both know that. He would never have got into his position if he'd been biddable.'

The rain was dripping off our hoods causing a curtain of drops to draw past our eyes and fall on the jacket fronts. Anyone observing us from afar would see two helpless creatures, heads bowed, hands in pockets, waiting for some miracle to come along and sweep them to the promised land. We were a bit like the old sepia pictures of the last miserable inhabitants of this island.

The wind funnelled down the valley, nudging our backs and urging us towards the path, willing us to the beach.

'Come on, it'll be sheltered down there. You go first – it's not as hard as it looks, you know?'

He shrugged. I watched him kneel on the grass and take a tentative shuffle backwards, his big backside facing the sea. The big coward was going to down-climb facing inwards. He looked up once and the expression on his face as he searched with his feet for a hold was almost comical; his tongue stuck out so far I could have nailed it to the ground. He shoved the hood back and let the rain soak his hair. He chewed his lip and crossed his eyes under his dancing eyebrows. At last he must have found a ledge and lowered himself. I waited until he was two metres below before I rolled a boulder the size of a small lunch pack to the edge. My heart louped. I'd never done anything like this before. I thought of my parents who had both been in the Military and had had to kill for the State. And how many men had Davie killed? I guessed it was in my DNA. No, I shook my head. My grandfather had a choice. I had no choice in the same way my parents had no choice for their actions. This was not what I wanted to do.

I peered over the edge. If he fell now he would only fall about fifteen metres. He would be stunned, maybe break a bone. That would give Kenneth enough time. I hoped Kenneth would be in his cave waiting like a spider at the edge of a web, ready to scuttle out to his prey and have him bound before he had a chance to struggle. I aimed the boulder to the left of his head; I didn't want to kill him. I closed my eyes and gave it a shove.

'Below!' I shouted. I opened my eyes to see Ridgeway look up. The boulder bounced on a clump of grass, bounced again, changed trajectory and moved directly towards his head.

'Watch out!' I screamed. I saw him pull his arms off his perch to shield his head; the boulder skiffed his shoulder. He began to slide. His hands scrabbled for purchase, tore heather from the bank. His body tumbled and rolled and eventually stopped in a heap at the bottom of the cliff, motionless.

Oh Jupiter, I'd killed him. I levered myself off the edge and scrambled down to the prone guard. There was a cut on his forehead and lots of blood, but at least he was still breathing.

'Ridgeway?' I crouched down trying find the source of the blood flow.

'So you decided to come back young Somhairle?' I could hear the smile in Kenneth's voice, but when he saw Ridgeway he rushed to him and shoved me out the way.

'What happened?' he snapped.

'Have I killed him? The blood!' In my head I shouted this but the actual words were whispered.

My back was soaked in rain and sweat. Ridgeway lay like a starfish – I now saw a fountain pumped from his neck where a sharp shard of flint protruded. Kenneth grasped his neck with both hands and turned to me with thunder on his face.

'He's going to bleed to death. What have I done?' My voice rose to shouting.

'For the Lord's sake Somhairle, stop being such a native.'

This comment was as good as a slap across the face.

Still holding Ridgeway's neck in a strangle hold he placed the guard's head on his lap. The blood soaked his skin coat.

'Go into the back of the cave and bring me my hide bag.'

I ran to the cave which I found to be deeper than I'd first thought a few days ago when Kenneth abducted me.

The part of the cave he had taken me to had a sandy floor and walls damp with green algae. It was cold and stank of stale seaweed. I searched for the bag and found nothing but a midden of rusty cooking implements and jars, so I moved further into the dark until I came to an inner chamber. In there an electric light burned low, casting my shadow large and imposing on the walls painted bright corals and yellows, blues and greens. There were pictures of animals I didn't recognise, and transports and submarines. I wanted to stop and stare and make sense of things but I had to get back to Kenneth. There was a bed made up of animal skins and a bag on top. It was crudely fashioned like his coat, but with the absence of any other bag I guessed this was the one he meant. There was another hide vessel like a water bottle so I grabbed that too.

When I ran outside Kenneth was staring towards the cave entrance.

'Hurry lad,' he shouted. 'Go into the bag and find graft skin.'

There were five graft skins all in different sizes. I had seen them used once before when I had fallen from my gyrocycle and punctured my leg on a piece of glass. Because they were made from a rare substance derived of precious hydrocarbons, only medics were permitted to use them.

'Don't stand there gaping at it boy, give.' But his hands were full and bloody.

'Here, Somhairle, you hold.' Kenneth nodded to Ridgeway's neck. 'Place your hand over mine and press down really hard when I take my hand away.'

The blood was warm and sticky and smelled funny, like a rusted nail. The skin around the wound was cold and there was so much blood. My hands were shaking and I was scared my tremors would affect Ridgeway's blood flow. His pulse fluttered against my palm like a blinking eyelash.

Kenneth used his teeth to pull the cover off the graft, then in one nifty move he lifted my hand off the gash and clamped the graft over the wound. It seemed to suck onto the surrounding skin and immediately fused. Kenneth took a small vial and tube from the bag, inserted the tube into Ridgeway's vein and propped the vial on a rock above them to create a drip.

Kenneth untied the kerchief from his neck and handed it to me.

'Here, soak that in the rock pool over there and bring it back. Quick now.'

I did as he bid, washing my bloody hands at the same time. As I ran back I remembered the water bottle slung round my neck.

When I reached the physician and patient I handed the kerchief and the bottle to Kenneth. He looked at me with surprise and also, for the first time, with compassion.

'Thanks,' he said before he popped the stopper with his teeth, swigged a drink and poured a little around the wound. He dribbled some on the kerchief and dabbed some round the cut on Ridgeway's eye.

He handed the bottle to me.

'Here, have some.'

I could tell as soon as I put the bottle to my lips that it was not water but the banned substance Mash. But I was not as surprised as I should have been. I was now becoming used to this island of banned substances. To drink this was serious. Every Privileged and native had a taste for Mash. When the Product Locality Law first banned exports, production of Mash stayed high even though demand plummeted. The citizens of Lesser Esperaneo began a period of mass binge drinking on the low-cost glut. The Mash took over. At first it was viewed as a form of social control to replace the banned religions, but the control got out of hand. Dependency was high; the prisons couldn't cope even with the introduction of the island penitentiaries. The export ban was a political blunder. The Purists nationalised the distilleries and turned production into a military affair. All large-scale production went to barter for solar energy and weapons with the Dry States. A mass destruction of small stills followed but some survived – you just had to know where to look. It seemed I'd found one.

It was a prison offence to hold Mash. It was a prison offence to drink it. To make it was punishable by death.

Kenneth smiled as he watched me examine the bottle and fight with my conscience.

'You haven't quite caught on to where you are, lad, have you?' he said. 'There are no laws here.' He pointed up the cliff. 'Oh I

183

know that the penitentiary is just back there, but laws don't apply there either – you've seen your grandfather's library. What do you think he takes for a nightcap?'

I remembered the goblets and decanters on Davie's lunch table; Vanora's delivery, the Noiri consignment.

'Go on – take a drink; I'll not report you.' He patted Ridgeway's shoulder. 'And neither will he.'

I put the bottle to my lips and sipped. It tasted like iodine; my nose flared as the fumes ignited my tubes. The liquid warmed the back of my throat and grabbed it before sending a rod of fire through my breeches; my face numbed but at least my hands had stopped shaking. Suddenly I felt calm and yet my pulse still galloped. My toes curled in their boots with a satisfied glow.

Kenneth laughed loud and heartily and slapped the unconscious shoulder of Ridgeway. 'You want to see your face. Your eyes are almost popping their sockets.' He laughed the laugh of my mother, and although this made me sad, it was reassuring to recognise him as kin.

'Good, eh?'

As I put the bottle back to my lips he grabbed it.

'Not so quick, I don't want you getting tipsy. If we need to look after this fellow here, I won't be able to get up to the still for a wee while yet.'

The word *tipsy* was new to me but the swimming in my head gave me a clue to its meaning.

'Right now we need to deal with the problem in hand.' He took an old fashioned timepiece from inside his jacket.

'Tell me what you have found out and why you found it necessary to push Ridgeway down the cliff.'

'I didn't push him.'

He waved his hand in dismissal. 'Come on, be smart about it. We need to get you both back. What time do you need to get back?'

'I'm not going back. My grandfather is going to kill me.'

'Now don't start. Tell me what you found out.'

I pulled up the hair from my forehead and showed him the cut.

'This is what he did after Vanora wound him up.'

'Vanora? Of course, the Transport yesterday.'

'Right. That was her, with Ishbel. Vanora is crazy by the way.'

Kenneth stroked his matted chin. 'She didn't let me know she was coming.'

'She said she wanted me to be her lieutenant but she didn't take me with her. She provoked Davie and he took it out on me. He pushed me around and smashed me against a wall. He was murderous and unpredictable. He said he had nothing to lose now.'

Kenneth beckoned for me to move closer. He examined my head and, taking a clean rag from his bag, he dabbed some Mash onto the wound. It nipped for a bit then calmed.

'She was horrible to Ishbel.'

'Tell me, from the beginning.'

So I told him about being locked in my quarters and the Transport's bow – he chuckled at that – and then about my grandfather taking me to see the visitors. With each detail I watched Kenneth's eyes sink deeper into his forehead. Now and again he would nod. Was that a frown when I told him about the charismatic Merj? When I got to the bit about Vanora and Ishbel he sat forward.

'And Vanora? How did she look – well?'

'Old, decrepit, frail. She coughed a lot.'

'Did anyone try to give you anything?'

'Vanora tried to give me a present but Davie yanked me back before she had a chance.'

'What happened after that?'

I told him about Ishbel's strange words, about 'not long to wait'.

'What did she mean?' I asked.

'I don't know but Vanora was here for a reason. And you say she got the better of Davie. Good for her.'

'Not for me though.' I said, pointing to my head. 'I'm not going

185

back. She should have taken me with her but she didn't. And Ishbel, she did nothing.'

Kenneth patted the ground for me to sit. 'They would have good reason. But are you sure she didn't give you anything?'

'No. She came to goad him…and me.'

'Oh there would be more to it than that and you know it Somhairle.'

My head dropped. Did I?

'OK, you're safe now,' he said. We sat in silence for a few minutes, then Kenneth said, 'I wonder what he meant – he had nothing to lose.' He scratched at his beard. 'Did you manage to get to your grandfather's workstation?'

'No, I went to the library but his workstation had gone. And Scud was no help because now he's one of them.'

Kenneth's head snapped up. 'What do you mean?'

I could feel my chemical courage disappear.

'I mean Scud looks and acts like a Privileged.'

'This is bad.'

'What is?'

'They must have settled on a combination for a native dilution. I thought it would take decades of haggling to get agreement and I had hoped I had put enough confusion into the process to keep it in suspension until we had time to act.'

'What are you talking about? I don't understand.'

Kenneth's eyes held the worry of the world in them. 'Scud has, or had, a certain percentage of alleles that have been deemed by the government to be native. During the purge years every citizen of Lesser Esperaneo was DNA tested. The government had a definition of pure alleles and undesirable alleles. If a citizen had below a certain threshold of pure, they were classed as natives. Those above the threshold became Privileged, forming the two class system you know today – that you have always known. Not long after the Separation of Classes the fundamentalists in the Purists regime began work trying to find a solution to dilute the native alleles, or to eradicate it completely. Taking Scud as an example, if they had managed to change even a small percentage of his undesirable alleles it would mean the eradication of the native class. The world would be full of Privileged.'

'I don't understand why that's a bad thing,' I said. 'Isn't that what revolutions have been trying to do since the beginning of time, bring about equality? Everyone would be a Privileged, so what?'

Kenneth narrowed at me. 'Use your head laddie,' he snapped. 'Genes are only part of what makes us who we are. There are environmental factors that the blinkered government refuses to acknowledge.' And then he lowered his head and shook it. 'Changing the odd pigment here and there is easy but when you get into the behavioural genes, now that's where the problems lie.' He soothed the head of Ridgeway, almost unconsciously. 'Have you never heard of individual thought? This is what makes us who we are, not our class. Remember a percentage has been diluted in Scud. In many cases the psychological and physical impact may be so great the individual will die. It's worse than genocide. And what of the final solution? What is the perfect mix? Even Privileged genes can mutate.' He stared at me as if I was responsible for this mess. 'There is not, and never will be, a final solution. But how many natives will die before someone puts a stop to the madness? Now that is genocide.'

There was that word again – genocide.

'No, he may look "Privileged", he may act "Privileged" but the question is, has he ceased being Scud?' Kenneth sighed. 'I bet you liked Scud didn't you? Despite the fact he was a native and you have been brought up in a society that scorns natives.'

'My parents brought me up to respect everyone,' I bristled.

'What was it about Scud that you liked?' he asked me.

I thought about his humour, even after all his years of incarceration. His bravery, all the zaps he risked to get a message to me.

'Will we be able to change him back?' My voice sounded choked.

'Is that what you want? What about this equal world you saw a minute ago.' But he didn't bother to let me finish. 'And what about Ishbel? Your aunt – she was like a mother to you, would you like her to change? She loves you as her own child.'

I thought about what would happen if Ishbel changed but it was a stupid thought because she wasn't here; she was dressed up in a fake uniform taking care of someone else.

'Well? You realise if they have progressed with the experiments on this island the dilution, once refined, will soon be implemented nationwide. Would you like Ishbel to change?' he asked again, goading.

A blush swept over me at the memory of my old schoolboy fantasies about her, horrible now I knew the relationship. This was serious shit. I didn't want her to change. 'No, I suppose not.'

Kenneth moved and pulled his legs out from under him to give them a stretch. He settled Ridgeway's head on his lap then felt his pulse. The rain had eased to a smir but a cold seized my fingers and toes and spread inward to my core. As if reading my thoughts Kenneth unravelled the gut stitching, pulled the bottom of his coat apart and placed it over Ridgeway.

'I'm not sure you are yet convinced of the arguments Somhairle, so let me ask a question,' he said. 'What do you think happens to anyone with more than 15% native?' He thumped his chest hard and I knew what he meant.

I remembered Scud's suffering. The freckles that came and went – the freckles he said were not his.

'I don't know,' I said. 'I suppose it would be painful, but in the end you would be pleased that you were a Privileged and able to get a position in the Military rather than be a drone.'

Kenneth wiped a leak from Ridgeway's wound and checked the vial above his head. There was disappointment in his eyes.

'Unlike our friend Ridgeway here, who seems to be recovering well, our native kin will eventually die.'

I loathed being referred to as native, even though it was true.

'I bet Scud went through hell to get to the stage he's at now. He's probably on the threshold of anyone going through the experiment. Those with a high percentage of native genes, I am positive, will die. Just think of that Somhairle, billions of natives subjected to an excruciating painful death so that a handful can become Privileged. And suppose this part of the "final solution" takes place and the eradication of the full so-called native population is successful.' He looked at me, willing me to understand, but I didn't want to understand because the prediction was too horrible to comprehend.

'Yes, a world of Privileged. We will have solved our overcrowding problem, helped our fuel and food shortages. Ten billion reduced to five billion souls or less is not bad for a world solution is it? Yes, that math stacks up. But who would do all the work? Who would drone the Military? The Purists have already denied native children education to train for this task. Who would do it when there are no natives?'

Ridgeway began to groan.

'Who would the guards be? Or do you believe Privileged don't commit crimes?' He snorted at this. 'They are the biggest criminals of all. As ancient folklore states: "too many chiefs, not enough Indians". But the one thing the Esperaneo authorities, the Purists and the Land Reclaimists, conveniently overlooked in this great master plan of theirs was: who defines a native? They overlooked the fact that the definition is different in all three of the Global Zones.'

The realisation was so horrific I felt the Mash in my stomach cook to bubbling bile.

'How do you know so much? How do you know Scud? You even know Ridgeway.'

Kenneth looked at his watch, then at me. I knew that soon we would need to decide what to do next, but there were still too many missing pieces.

'How do you know all this?' I asked a second time.

His laugh was rusty, that of a tired old man whose pocket watch told him too many truths.

'To you I'm just a smelly old hermit who lives in a cave. Some scum or flotsam the sea has washed up and left on the shore. It hasn't always been so. Remember the Purist regime in this region only came into prominence just over twenty-five years ago, before you were born but not long in my lifetime. No, not long, but long enough for them to put their differences to bed and join forces with other groups in the regions to form the United States of Esperaneo.'

I knew the truth of Modern History had always been veiled with smoke and mirrors and anyone discussing it was punished either by work or family restriction. There was no gain in querying the State line. Everyone knew this. Propaganda through media manipulation was the norm, but no one at the Base seemed to care as long as life ticked along. That was my view of the world but, as Ishbel said, I'd been protected. My father told me some of this but not all. He should have told me the full story about Davie and Kenneth and my heritage – he must have known. Why didn't Ma tell me? What was the point in protecting me from the truth? Had they been foolish enough to believe the world would change before I became an adult? That Vanora would come charging in from her secret Empire to rescue me? What a monumental joke.

Kenneth stared at the sea. The rain had ceased but the wind still hurled its worst at us. He sipped his Mash and handed me the bottle.

'Here, you probably need this now. You're as pale as a native,' he grinned. 'Sorry, bad expression.'

Battling my nausea, I took a sip and enjoyed again that toe-scrunching sensation as the liquid seeped into my mixed genes. Kenneth settled his legs, crossed them at the ankles and leaned against the rock face.

'Vanora was not much of a mother, I have to admit.'

'She's horrible to Ishbel,' I said again.

'Yes, Ishbel has served her well but they may have been apart for too many years.'

He spat on the sand and Ridgeway stirred at the disturbance of his pillow. Kenneth took care to settle him then rolled over onto his side and onto his knees. I could hear his tendons and ligaments creak and crack as he groaned his way to his feet. He shook his legs out like a dancer and rubbed them hard. He chuckled then. 'Living in a cave for years plays havoc with your joints.' He checked Ridgeway's pulse then the drip.

'Come on Somhairle, he is stable enough to move now. We must get him into the cave – get you both dry. You grab his feet and I will take his top half. Be careful, his body is still in a great amount of shock.'

Ridgeway was a heavy guy when conscious but the dead weight of him was heavier than a builder's bag of wet sand. We half-carried, half-dragged him to the cave and through to the back chamber. It was a relief to lay him on a pile of skins. We eased off his sodden outer jacket before Kenneth gently placed him in the recovery position and covered him with more skins. He then dug around in the back of the chamber to produce a heater which he attached to a cable strung up the wall and fed through a hole drilled in the cave.

'Nuclear battery,' he announced with pride.

I blinked, and instinctively backed off.

'Calm down, it won't hurt. You were in more danger sitting out in that awful poisoned rain. Now slip your jacket off and get dry.'

'How long have you been here?' By the look of the cave set-up, it seemed that he had been installed here for a long time.

'Too long,' he said, ushering me to some skins piled against the cave wall. 'I started off with blankets but rabbit skins are much better for this type of living. Get comfortable, the place will soon warm up. I'll fix us something to eat in a bit.' He sat down beside Ridgeway.

'But why here? Why do you live in a cave, under the nose of the man you were hidden from as a child?'

'It was Vanora's idea, the first of her native network. At first I didn't question, but after all these years I suspect she had some perverse need to make a fool of him. I'm sure he loved her once. Her achievements in the city gave him a certain gravitas too.' He looked at me. 'You know what I mean?' I nodded.

'You said she was frail.'

I nodded again, not wanting to open my mouth for fear of swallowing the thick odour escaping from his foul breath. At close quarters he was rank.

'She was a beauty. Her hair was the colour of bracken in autumn and I'm afraid it blinded Davie to a few of her flaws. She was highly respected in broadcasting all over the earth. But some sections of society shunned her because of her accent, because of her looks, her red hair.' He grabbed a handful of gravel from the cave floor and let it run through his fingers. 'This land here was once called UKAY and dwelling within that land were many Celtic tribes. There was a lot of anti-Celtic feeling at that time, many reasons but mainly because of some political infighting and the power transfer in the industrial world. My mother seemed to rise above that while the Celts slowly descended into a subclass without even realising it was happening. They became a lower case society.

'Davie called her a mutant.'

'Yes he would say that. His kind really believe natives are stupid and mutated. And to be honest, some are. They can be led so easily by propaganda. The media were experts at that sort of native manipulation.' Kenneth settled his restless legs again. 'The media in the decades before the Purist victory had politicians in their pockets. They used their power to turn the heads of the sheep and aided and abetted in the rise of the cruel Purist Regime. I won't go into the whole bloody history but it was frightening at the time. Normal citizens of the land hounded by thugs, then thuggery became commonplace. Riots happened every day and the government was covertly backing it.' He snorted. 'Read your ancient history books boy, nothing changes, you can fill in the gaps.

'I studied genetics at university and by the time I was twenty was working in a laboratory, experimenting on DNA manipulation. We were on the cusp of a breakthrough into curing one of the most debilitating diseases ever. At least that's what we thought we were doing. The government backed the research and one day without warning the focus changed. We were to concentrate on the main DNA found in the majority of Celts. The Celts were to officially become an outcast race. Someone somewhere had decided the rules.'

Kenneth stopped and looked at me. His eyes were wild with memory.

'So you see Somhairle. I helped to create the processes they are now abusing up there.' He nodded towards the penitentiary. 'I should have seen it coming but some nightmares you just can't imagine. I suppose we should be glad it took this long.'

'Your mother was still in school when the Purists took power. It didn't take them long to expel all the immigrants of the last century, but what could they do about us? The native purge happened four years later. You either complied or you became an outcast. Every citizen's DNA was re-examined and in a matter of weeks the Privileged and native system came into effect.' He chuckled then in the midst of this shocking tale. 'You see, we were already halfway there. When the stats were examined, it transpired many Celts had been working as slaves for years in the guise of government-backed work schemes.'

The spell of Kenneth's storytelling had me frozen – or was that petrified?

'Davie must have seen it coming,' he continued. 'He protected Kathleen, your mother, had her passport changed and made a deal with the Military: she could serve them as an officer, help fill the growing military shortage and her heritage would never be known. As you can imagine, Vanora raged at this, cursed him, but Davie being Davie, he paid her no heed. He just beat her into submission. He was given Black Rock as a reward. His own little kingdom.'

Kenneth laughed that rusty laugh again and looked around him. 'Not much of a reward is it? The stupid fool didn't realise that they just wanted him out of the way. His mixed-heritage family was an embarrassment.'

'But what about Vanora?' I asked, finding my voice.

'He tried to murder her. Not just beat her up this time, but murder her.'

Although Kenneth looked at me for a reaction, this revelation didn't surprise me. I remembered the murder in his eyes – this was something he was more than capable of.

'Vanora, and her unborn child. He didn't want his spectacular career ruined because of a native. But Vanora too had seen the changes coming years before the Purists came to power and had been buying up gold and precious stones and storing them in secret locations. She had powerful friends in the United States of the West. Remember they have a different definition of a native, a different threshold. They didn't care that she was Northern Celt, her wealth was what mattered. So she fled.'

'Does he know about Ishbel?'

'No. And he never will, unless someone tells him.' He scowled at me but I shook my head, glad I'd followed my instincts.

'And now Vanora's back?'

'Back and vengeful. She's been back for years. Installed Ishbel into your home then set to work establishing her native network.' Kenneth began to laugh. 'Black Rock Davie believed he was a powerful man. And in his kingdom he is. He has done the government's bidding all his life.'

The bitterness never left Kenneth's voice now.

'He is nothing but a pawn.'

He stumbled from his seat, creaked to standing and paced the floor. 'Let's get something to eat, eh? Before I ruin your appetite altogether with this putrid tale.'

I watched him rig up a small cooker. He threw some vegetables in a pot and covered them with water from a stone jar that lurked in a dank corner. He clambered over a jumble of fishing nets and coloured buoys to reach into the back of the cave. He returned with a jar of preserved vegetables.

It was one of Ishbel's jars with the red wax tops and her mark stencilled on it. He saw me looking and smiled a sleekit smile.

'Ah, another missing piece of the puzzle for you, young Somhairle. You see my wee sister was also put to work for Vanora. Come, I'll show you.'

He pushed the nets aside and led me through to the other chamber where one corner was stacked high with jars – Ishbel's jars. A haunch of a small deer hung from the ceiling, dwarfing a couple of skinned rabbits suspended like gruesome afterbirth. There were also boxes filled with earth which he kicked, filling the cavern with a dull thud.

'The last of my fresh vegetables,' he said, pointing to the ceiling. 'Up there on the clifftop is a garden, a small patch of land, a ledge, hidden from the land by the cliff and hidden from the sea by a hedge of broom. No one would ever guess it was there, no one will ever find it. Sometimes I have trouble finding it myself. There I can grow enough fresh vegetables to see me through the growing months but I need the preserves for the winter. He grinned then and picked up another jar.

'Yes, you are right in your thinking. The rest of my food has come, *came*, from your garden on the Base, once Ishbel was established. But I am not the only recipient. A few others receive jars, in other hideouts.' He shook his head. 'We will have to revert back to our Noiri source now that Ishbel has been forced to abandon her post.'

I clasped my head in my hands against the bombardment of fantastical information.

'It's all part of Vanora's grand plan,' Kenneth said as he consulted his watch again. 'Well, our friend's recovery has been slow. You did too good a job on him Somhairle. It is too late to send him back now. Your grandfather will have rousted a patrol to search for you. But don't worry, he'll not find this cave. I've been here twenty-one years and they haven't found me yet.'

'Twenty-one years?' It was incredible. 'That's longer than Scud's been here.'

'Yes, we have both served our sentences, but they will soon be over.' He looked at me under his bushy brows. 'One way or another.'

'How have you managed to avoid detection all this time?' I found it impossible to believe, given the size of the island was not big.

'Oh Davie knows I'm here. He must have noticed the paths are not just trodden by deer. I think in a way he doesn't want me to be found. As far as he's concerned it's safer to have me here than out there causing trouble. He wants to stay locked up in his own kingdom, his own prison, his own delusions. That way he doesn't have to think about his embarrassing family and the one he gave away.'

Kenneth popped opened the jar, picked out a slithery red tongue of sweet pepper and sucked it down whole. The memory of the taste and the texture made my stomach lurch. I had forgotten how much I hated Ishbel's preserves.

'Mm.' He pushed the jar towards me. 'Here, try some.'

I shook my head. 'No, I'm not hungry.'

Part Four

Chapter Twenty-two

I turned towards the cave entrance and imagined the north Pa had pointed to that day on the way to the beach. To freedom.

Kenneth wiped the air in a majestic gesture. 'Welcome to Black Rock,' he said in ad-speak. 'Sunlight hours marginal, all the better to preserve your liver-spotted skin. Fresh sea breezes to scour clean your rotting lungs. Miles from the mainland – no need for pesky high security. Oh, and so you won't be lonely, here are a thousand prisoners to experiment on. Lovely isn't it? Run your empire from here – the ideal spot for an up-and-coming despot. Some reward, eh?'

Kenneth's hand shot out and grabbed my wrist. He consulted the communicator and dropped my arm as if it burned. 'It'll be dark soon, I wonder when they'll come.'

He smoothed the forehead and hair of Ridgeway. His bedside manner was touching, but his glower was murderous. He stared at the floor forever. The charged air stuck to me, a bad boak smell choked me. I swallowed a breath to break the hex but he beat me to it when he said, 'When I think of the Purists at that time, of their ideology, their stupidity, it's mind-blowing. Vanora wasted no time in such idle musings. From her island base she recruited natives, trained them covertly, then sent them to ground.' Kenneth picked up a walking stick that was propped against the cave wall and in the gravel drew a circle with tentacles spreading all airts. 'Her network, managed with the help of a few disciples.'

'It sounds like a religion.'

'Don't mock, Somhairle. This incredibly complex network began as a flea bite on the balls of the government, first turned to a rash and now a large infestation.' He tapped the circle with his stick. 'She and her network are highly effective. There's no mumbo jumbo about the results. She has developed a sophisticated comms encryption enabling her operation to function, making it impossible for the State to shut her down.'

Jupe sake, it was like loading your favourite sports season, settling down to watch and finding banned terror-zone material projected on the Games Wall. I looked at the pickle jars.

'I remember all the canning. Ishbel, always canning and pickling.'

'Yes that's part of it. How do you feed a massive secret army in a controlled continent without anyone noticing?' He didn't wait for my answer. 'You install an equally large army to feed and provide for them.' He held up the jar again. 'Ishbel did a good job.'

'What is it all for? The network, the army? If she has an army, why are we here?'

He chucked a look of joyous disappointment my way.

'Look, I'm not psychic,' I said. His mirth was tedious. 'Until a few months ago I lived a nice cushy life on the Base. Both my parents respected in the military, my schooling under control, my future mapped out, friends to wrestle with and my native always there for me.'

It was hard to ignore the chuckle Kenneth gurgled under his breath like a loon, but I continued just the same.

'The present reality is my native is my aunt, my parents are dead, my grandfather is a maniac and my grandmother is some loony international rebel, and you wonder why I don't understand?' I stood. 'I've heard enough. If I hear anymore my brain will implode. Come on, we've got to get moving. We've got to get off this island before the searchers come.' I paced the gravel, kicking it up and smoothing it out. Kenneth sighed, and that benevolent mask I suddenly wanted to punch returned to his hairy face.

'Vanora's army is to fight back, Somhairle. It is impossible to fight back through politics. It is not permitted for a native to vote.'

'Well say that, then. Stop playing games with me.' I thumped my head with my fist. 'In the last half hour you have told me enough family history to fill Academy Archive. "*It is not permitted for a native to vote.*" I snafin' know that! Tell me where we go from here.'

'Calm down.'

'And stop telling me to calm down. I'll calm down when I am out of this shit.'

'OK. But we need to wait a while longer.'

'Wait for what?'

He flapped his arm, wafting his own particular scent round the cave. 'Sit down, Somhairle.'

'No, I need to move.'

If I thought he was done, I was wrong. If I ever imagined cavemen in social isolation could lose the power to communicate, I was wrong.

'What a mess the Purists have made of things. They must be stopped. This DNA dilution is the last disaster Esperaneo can handle before the East wade in, and the Western States know that too. No, there can only ever be one winner in this game and that would be the Eastern Zone with their unique gene pool and wily systems.'

This guy wouldn't shut up. I looked around the cave, at the ochre and tempera primitive paintings Kenneth had doodled in his years here. How would future historians classify this period along with the Ice Age, Bronze Age, Apple Age? How about Mashed-up Age?

'Where is Vanora now?' I asked. 'This secret island…' Jupe, even as I said it I realised how ludicrous this story was.

He pointed north, of course. 'In the Arctic Archipelago. A group of islands inhabited for centuries by an indigenous people. You won't have heard of it because the Purists stripped it of its oil and left it fallow. It no longer has economic or strategic value and they believe there will be another tsunami there sometime soon – they can't be bothered with it, to be honest. The small population were immune from the native purge because their DNA is so different from ours and the establishment of a penitentiary there was uneconomical. These islanders took Vanora into their wilderness bosom twenty-odd years ago and she has run her operation from there ever since. She is revered and treated like royalty by the islanders and her disciples, as she is by all her covert cells around Esperaneo.'

'Can you please shut up your doors about Saint Vanora and her army?'

Kenneth blinked then stared at the floor for more beats than I could be bothered counting. A small moan teased from the unconscious lips of Ridgeway, like the murmur of a sleeping baby.

'What are we going to do?' I said. 'We can't go back.' The earlier hysteria had left my voice and my thoughts were as brisk as the keen breeze that rattled outside the cave.

'We have to stop the experiments,' Kenneth said.

More than twenty years he had lived in this cave. My eyes strayed to the heater rigged to a nuclear battery, the lights, the hide bedding, delicately stitched and fashioned. He had tried to make a home but it was miserable.

'*We* have to!' I said, struggling to contain my anger. 'Why haven't *you* done something? You've been here long enough. Why did you have to wait until I came on the scene?'

He speared me with a look that could slice carbon.

'I have done lots of things while I've been here. I've cleared the coastline of mines for when boats need to land. I sent messages to Scud using the beacon.'

The lighthouse, of course, that intermittent beam. Scud reciting the alphabet backwards.

'The flashing buoy?'

He nodded. 'I have caused power surges when an attack was due.'

Maybe he wanted me to hold my head in shame at my earlier accusation, but the truth remained that this creature had lived in these conditions yet achieved so little. Instead I slumped on the skins. 'Why don't you send a power surge now, then – send a message to Vanora? Tell her I've succeeded in escaping. Tell her to attack.'

'Tell her?' His eyes widened. 'We don't tell her anything.'

Ridgeway moved his head, his eyelids fluttered. Kenneth poured water into a cup and shifted Ridgeway's position so he could sup. His gentle touch reminded me of Ishbel as she'd tended to me when I was ill with fever. And now here was this man who claimed to be a scientist being as gentle with a guard as a physician would have been.

'I know what we could do,' I said. 'Why don't we take Ridgeway hostage and demand the experiments stop or we kill him. Pirates do it, why can't we?' Even as I said this I knew the cold and hunger of my escape was starting to nibble at my reason. I deserved to be laughed at.

Ridgeway opened his eyes and looked at me with the hazy pupils of a newborn cub, blind but not deaf.

'Grow up Somhairle,' Kenneth snapped. 'This is not some schoolboy prank. We can't stay here much longer. Davie will have someone out looking for you. He might even have alerted the mainland, but I doubt it. He probably wants to keep the problem of his troublesome and tainted grandson to himself. And unless I'm mistaken, Ridgeway's last known whereabouts were outside this cave. Your chips will also give away your location.'

'They won't find us,' Ridgeway rasped as he held out his hand to Kenneth, who clasped it in both his. 'I switched my communicator to random before we left the compound.' He nodded towards me. 'Our chips won't be picked up in this cave.'

He struggled to get up and Kenneth hooked Ridgeway's arm to ease him from the makeshift bed. 'It's good to see you again, Ken.'

They embraced in a way I'd never seen men do before: hugged then kissed each cheek, left then right.

Kenneth patted him on the shoulders as if he didn't want to let him go, before eventually resting Ridgeway's back against the cave wall. 'My good friend, I am sorry your young charge took such drastic steps to bring you to me.' Kenneth gurgled with delight and hugged Ridgeway again. I felt my face blush with the embarrassment of it all.

'He's not another long-lost family member is he?'

They looked at each other and grinned. Grinned! Not just a 'happy to see you' grin, but a big toothy, dimple buster.

'Almost,' Kenneth managed to say through his mashers.

Sakes! I'd seen traces of change in Ridgeway in our time together, but this transformation was more dramatic than the Scud metamorphosis. I almost began to wonder whether Kenneth had spiked the drip he had just fed him. Kenneth's change was just as startling; where had the rugged cave dweller gone? They were like two lovers in a soppy comfort-caster reunited after many years.

My brain was clanking like Beastie on a bad day.

'Oh yes, we know each other well,' Kenneth coughed, back to normal. 'We've known each other since university days.'

'What university days?' I pointed to Ridgeway. 'He's a Bas, he didn't go to university.'

'Yes he did, and so did Scud.'

'I knew you were on this island somewhere Ken, I just didn't know where. I couldn't believe my luck when I was transferred here.'

'Your luck? You don't think Vanora had a hand in that?'

Ridgeway shrugged. 'Maybe, I didn't think she could do that. And then when Sorlie arrived, well I guessed it was all going to kick off quite soon. I bided my time. Scud did well manoeuvring Sorlie into the corncrake project. It was easy enough to put the rest of the guards off the idea of escorting Davie's snivel-nosed brat out on a bogging windswept island. Those fat lazy slobs want as easy a life as they can get.' He patted his belly. 'I was just as bad but I think Davie secretly wanted me to have a heart attack.' He nodded towards me. 'I very nearly did that first day.' He shifted his weight and groaned, then rested his head back on the cool wall.

'Who do you think you are calling a snivel-nosed brat?'

They both ignored me. 'I didn't think I would find you so quickly. I had to be careful of the boy. When he disappeared that day I took my time looking for signs of you.' He opened his eyes and squinted at Kenneth. 'You could have left more clues.'

Kenneth chuckled. 'Some managed to find me.'

I was aware that my mouth was gaping at their sickly sugariness and I clamped it shut with an audible snap.

'Are you just going to ignore me? What's going on? Is he a spy or something, Kenneth?'

'No, he's not a spy. Maybe it is just a coincidence he landed here, or maybe Vanora planned it because she knew she could trust him.' Kenneth stroked his beard and did that staring at the floor thing again. I needed another drink to wipe the muddle from my head but Kenneth batted my hand away as I stretched it out to lift the bottle of Mash.

'Leave it, we've all had enough,' he said before turning back to the guard. 'It's crazy you being here. I mean, what happened to the safe civil servant with choices? Maybe now you need to choose again.'

'Choose what?' Ridgeway asked.

'Choose between going back to a job or helping us.'

A shadow passed over Ridgeway's face, fleeting yet deadly. 'Why do you think I'm here?' He pulled back his sleeve to show his immigration tattoo and slapped the skin on his forearm. 'Look at this – Bas yes, but still tainted. They get rid of the native and how long before they get rid of us?'

'That won't happen,' Kenneth said. 'They'll need you.'

'That's what you said about Davie harming me,' I quipped.

He visibly started at that and I caught a glimpse of his pleated brow.

'Oh yeah, that's right, we'll be needed.' Colour was flooding back to Ridgeway's waxy face, mottling its unhealthy pallor. 'We'll be needed to drone the army, do the native jobs. Maybe life won't be so cushy for a Bas after all, hey?'

Kenneth started to laugh.

'Are you mad? How can you laugh at this?' I snapped hard enough to wither his face into sobriety.

'This is our world Somhairle. A broken world we have been living in for twenty-odd years and whether you like it or not you are now part of it. Your soft Military Base life has gone.' He clicked his fingers. 'Just like that.' The complicity in his voice was acid, like this was some exclusive club I had to pass a test to join.

'My parents are dead,' I said grinding my teeth to stop the spit forming. Kenneth laid his hand on mine.

'I know and I am sorry, but you have to move on.'

Chapter Twenty-three

The two elders sat in silence allowing me a few beats to digest the information overload. I scratched at the gravel with Kenneth's stick and watched them. Sometimes they stared at the floor. Then, as if on instinct, they found that stupid grin and looked to each other. One or the other would catch me watching and then return his gaze to the floor. Every now and then Ridgeway would close his eyes and lean back against the wall and Kenneth would strain forward and peer at him with concern. The hypnotic slosh of the waves outside and the build-up of warmth from the heater made my mind droop, but I refused to sleep.

'Listen,' Kenneth hissed.

Both Ridgeway and I started at the break in silence.

'Flying seekers.'

At first only waves sounded, then a high-pitched buzz hurtled through the cave and bounced from wall to wall.

'They're heat-seeking and audio-seeking,' Ridgeway whispered.

'They would have been better with dogs – their heat seekers won't penetrate these walls.'

'Dogs? What are dogs?' I asked. Kenneth and Ridgeway glanced at each other and shrugged.

'Aw yeah, dogs, I remember.' Though my memory was pretty vague.

'It's unimportant. Quick, climb up here.' Kenneth clambered onto the skin beside Ridgeway and signalled for me to join them. He groaned as he pulled his knees in to his chest. I copied his pose until all three of us sat like relief sculptures, backs against the cold wall and our knees hugged tight. 'It might be uncomfortable but it will give you extra stability.'

He handed me a tongue of hide and passed one to Ridgeway, keeping one for himself. 'Whatever happens, don't move and don't make a sound.'

The whirrying of the seekers increased until a high intensity skirl ricocheted around the walls. The cold solid rock at my back began to vibrate, which set my teeth and bones rattling. Kenneth mimed with his mouth that I bite the hide. He and Ridgeway did the same. Nasal breathing made my eyes water so I leaned forward and swiped them on my cuff. I wasn't crying.

A clatter of stones crashed close to the cave mouth. S'truth, someone was scrambling down that steep face. What would they do to us if they found us? I felt my bladder start to nip and complain and tried to force the thought from my rattling head. People piss themselves in times of terror. I bit harder on the strap; it was not going to happen to me. I shifted in my pants, but the whites of Kenneth's eyes told me to be still. Ridgeway's eyes burned with enough fear to force my body into a state of paralysis.

• • •

They didn't find us. I don't know how long we sat in that petrified state. It could have been an hour, it could have been longer. At last Kenneth spat the hide from his teeth and the noise of the seekers was replaced by loud groans from my two cave companions. When I tried to move I found my feet and hands had solidified to brick and mortar and the simple act of splaying my fingers wrapped them with barbed wire. My toes stabbed with hot wiggling thorns.

'They've gone for the time being but they'll be back once they're recharged. With no evidence of us leaving the island he'll assume we're still here.' Kenneth's shaky voice didn't exactly fill me with confidence.

'What are we going to do?' I whispered.

His crinkling eyes held a trick when he asked, 'What do you think we should do?'

He probably expected me to mention pirates but all I said was, 'I'm not going back.'

'What about you Ridgeway, what do you think we should do? Somhairle here reckons we should become pirates and hold you to ransom.'

So he wasn't letting go.

'What do you think of that, eh?'

I felt my face crimson. He had no right to dump on me like that. He keeked at my face from under those busy brows and I could see the laughter lines stretched. 'Or maybe we could just use Ridgeway's key to get in. It is, after all, why you're here.'

I remembered Scud's words written with blood.

Did you contact   get them in here   only you can

My head throbbed, ready to burst. I hobbled to my feet and tip-toed to the cave mouth. At that moment I could have run into the sea and risked a drowning or a mine blast; I just wanted to escape from them, from this ridiculous ordeal.

'Why am I here? Come on, tell me.' They were determined to rip the piss out of me. 'What sort of game are you people playing?'

Kenneth put his hand on my shoulder to guide me back to sitting but I shook him off.

'I am sick of this. All you can do is talk in riddles. Why didn't Ishbel take me to Vanora? Why bring me to this hell to live in a prison cell? To find out I'm half native?'

'Not half,' he started, but I brushed Kenneth's comment away with the contempt it deserved.

'To find native kin. And everybody knows everyone else and everyone talks in riddles like some secret society. What's going on?'

'Somhairle.'

'Sorlie,' I shouted. 'My name's Sorlie. The only ones who call me Somhairle are – were – my parents.' I wiped my eyes and nose on my cuff and this time I allowed Kenneth to guide me to sit. I'd had enough. I would stay in this cave for the rest of my life and eat

Ishbel's bogging pickles if I had to.

'You are here as a catalyst, shake things up and to help pass a plan, but it seems Vanora failed to get it to you. That's why she was here.'

Ridgeway coughed and sat up. 'Was that visitor Vanora?'

'Yes, why? Did you see her?' Kenneth asked.

'I escorted her and her party to and from the Transport. I didn't recognise her. She seemed so frail. The woman who supported her – was that Ishbel? I've never met Ishbel.'

'Did Vanora speak to you? Did she recognise you?'

'I don't think so. No, there was nothing – they passed no words between them and seemed oblivious of me. Even when she stumbled and took my hand to steady herself she remained silent. Why? Do you think she was sending me a signal, that she recognised me?'

Kenneth narrowed his eyes then walked to the edge of the inner cave and ran a finger along a painting of a submarine. The ever-present sound of the sea sloshed in my throbbing ears as we waited for him to speak. Like the tide Vanora came, Vanora went. Game over. Reload.

Kenneth finished tracing the ship and rubbed his fingers to shake off a sliver of paint. He moved into dwam-time for a few minutes then spoke. 'What were you wearing Ridgeway?'

'My uniform.'

'Search the pockets.'

Ridgeway searched each pocket in turn. He stopped when he reached the side pocket and held out a button. 'I don't know what this is.'

Kenneth took it and beamed through his beard. 'Oh you wonderful woman,' he said as he took the button and slanted it up to the light.

'We don't need to break into the systems now. I am sure we have all the information we need here.' He laughed. 'She never did trust anyone else to do important jobs for her – control freak. But oh what an efficient freak she is.'

'She came to slip this to you, Sorlie. She knew you would get out and would give this to me. When she failed she made the decision to pass it to Ridgeway, whom she had seen on the way in. It was a risk. He might not have been assigned to escort her back to the Transport, but I am sure she would have thought of something.'

He put his arm around Ridgeway and squeezed his shoulder and suddenly I understood their relationship. 'She must have organised your transfer here.'

His face soured as he pointed to my bruised forehead. 'I think this is more fundamental. She shouldn't have goaded him. He only ever needed to be in the same room as her for the spit to start flying. He'd probably been drinking Mash.'

'He had.' I remembered the smell.

'The man is a fool and is only just beginning to grasp that. Of course Vanora never misses a chance to remind him of her Empire and how he sold his daughter into certain death,' he said whilst examining the button. 'The fact she asked to see you will have riled him. Sounds like she wanted him to know she has chosen you to be on her side soon, Sorlie. And the only way Davie has to hurt her is through you.' He looked at the wound again. 'Yes, I believe you're right, you are in danger. I was wrong; he could kill you at any moment. A man who has nothing to lose is a dangerous beast.'

'But why did she need to hand over the button in person?' Kenneth asked himself. 'She could have dropped it with the provisions but it sometimes takes a few days for me to retrieve them.' He tugged his beard again. 'Of course.'

'What?' This was baffling.

He held up the button. 'I think it's a thought map. A T-map. This must contain one of her plans. A T-map can only hold good for five days. She couldn't risk it being lost.'

'There are no such things as thought maps.' Both Ridgeway and Kenneth gasped at my statement. 'Come on, its mumbo jumbo.

Thought waves they can capture for sure, everyone knows that, but not images.'

'You have no idea what you're talking about, boy,' Kenneth said. 'Vanora has been using this technology for years.'

'Yeah right, and is she a mystic too?' I asked, sarcasm dripping from my words. 'And if it lasts for only five days, how did she know I would get it to you? How did she know I got out of prison?'

'I told her. When she missed the opportunity to give you the button she took a chance.' Kenneth stared at the floor for a bit, then shook his head. 'She *must* have organised your transfer here, Ridgeway. She never told me. I wonder why. It would have made all the difference to this operation.' He chuckled. 'Crafty old witch.'

I could see from the shadows casting over the walls that it was beginning to get dark outside and yet Kenneth dawdled as if we had all the time in the world.

'So, come on, what's in the button?'

'I told you, a T-map.'

He was crazy but I let him get on with it. Something had to be in the button.

Ridgeway looked pale. Maybe he was stunned by the mumbo jumbo, or perhaps still suffering the effects of his fall. Kenneth on the other hand was hopping about the cave like a loon, holding the button up to the light and passing it in front of the heater, mumbling to himself. I was beginning to wonder if I had stumbled into a freaking wonderland.

'What will you do with it?' Was I the only one who had thought of this major problem?

'Read it, of course.'

'How?'

Yep, that stumped him. He looked at Ridgeway who shrugged a 'search me'.

Then they turned on me in unison.

'Don't look at me, I can't help you.'

'It must be you,' Kenneth said, grabbing my arm. 'Let me see your communicator.' He scratched my wrist with his infested nails as he tried to yank if off.

'Hey!' I jerked my arm back. 'At least Davie waited until I had handed it to him.' Then another penny dropped. 'Wait a minute – the plug-in. Pa gave it to me just before all this kicked off.'

'Show me.'

I unstrapped it and handed it over. 'Pa loved gadgets and thought I would like this because it has a wicked imager.'

'When did he give it to you?'

'Last quarter, just after my birthday, which was strange but I wasn't complaining.'

Kenneth twisted it this way and that in his grubby paws. I didn't like the way he was levering his filthy fingernail into the grooves. He took the button and slid it over the surface. Nothing happened. He pressed it into a non-existent gap and I could hear metal grind against metal.

'Don't force it. Pa always said not to force it.'

'Well did he give you any instructions other than that piece of useless advice?'

I tried to snatch the plug-in back but he held it away from me like a bully who swipes your lunch bag just for laughs.

'No, he just gave it to me and showed me the upgraded imager and the special battery that needs to be inserted there.' I pressed the battery panel and a tiny card the size of a vitpill popped out. Kenneth's disgusting fingernail split as he fully ejected the battery and moved the button into the now empty slot.

He blew out some puffs of putrid breath and sat on the hide. 'Well, it's a bit of a cliché but we seem to have found a secret compartment.' He pushed the button flush and the imager sparked to life, sending out a smoky blue apparition that spread the length and breadth of the floor. 'Interesting,' Kenneth said. 'Fits to size.'

The blue carpet travelled up the stone walls turning them a milky moonstone, obliterating the paintings. The only sound from the apparition was a small hum like an electrical appliance running somewhere in the background.

'What…?'

'Shush.' Kenneth batted my question with his hiss.

The blue on gravel began shape-shifting, settling on an image of a plan, a blueprint of a castle-esque structure.

'Her mind, it's incredible,' Kenneth whispered, as a child would do in a magic show.

'It's a holo-caster.' I'd been watching them on my Games Wall since I was a tot. The woman was a sham. Had he forgotten she used to be in broadcasting?

The holo-caster showed a laboratory maze; the pieces fused together or fell apart like a jigsaw puzzle to show the interior of the castle. Within this image a man in a uniform stood at one end of a corridor. Above him more corridors unfurled, each separated into hundreds of single cells and in each cell, like a nucleus, a man sat on a bench or lay on a bed.

I looked at Ridgeway and he nodded. 'It's inside the prison.'

'Look,' Kenneth whispered, pointing to the periphery of the building. A door opened to the outside. It was my door, the one that opened onto the stone stairs. Descending those stairs was a man in a red raincoat leading a smaller person in yellow.

'It's me and Ridgeway.' I held my breath as I watched the pair teeter down the stairs which looked even steeper from this angle. As they reached the last step I expected them to veer from the prison on the cliff path, but they arched on the bottom step and continued descending by way of another stone stairway.

Ridgeway connected with my eyes but remained silent. We followed the progress of the imaging pair to where they stopped in a small cove directly below the prison.

'I know this cove; I've cleared the mines already,' Kenneth whispered.

The blue carpet shape-shifted as if in response to his words, and the images of Ridgeway and me standing in the cove jumped to us crawling along inside a tube, like a sewer or something. Then we were inside the grid of cells that stretched the breadth and height of the imager, stacked one on top of the other like a mountain of waffles without the sauce. There were hundreds of cells.

'We can't do this. How will we get them out?' Even as I said this, each waffle collapsed, one after the other like a house of cards, and the doors swung open. Orderly chaos ensued as prisoners spilled from the cells and converged like a colony of ants scurrying into every nook and cranny of the waffle stack. But where was the regal ant? I left the concentration of the colony and searched the installation. Something about this was wrong. Where were the guards? The image omitted this crucial piece of information.

My eyes journeyed the passages of the image until I found the long deep spiral staircase I'd descended that first day; ahead of it stretched the corridor which I now saw was one of many, but unlike that first day, there was now no guard on duty. The door at the end lay open, the large hallway deserted and dark. Finally my eyes reached the library. There he was, like a rat in his burrow behind the ornate door, barricaded with a table and the leather chair wedged against the other door. He was rooted in the middle of the room, his heavy revolver poised, pointing first to one door, then the other, ready for action. This was not a real plan, merely Vanora's wish.

Kenneth's gasp brought me back to the main action.

'Keep going, you fools.' The swarm had shifted as one towards their escape; then they swerved like a wave in the turning tide and surged towards the library. The boy in the yellow jacket had disappeared from the scene but the man in red veered the crowd en masse to the tube entry point and one by one they disappeared into it. One figure stood alone from the pack. He scuttled one way then another, undecided. One minute his head was bowed and twisting towards the swarm then he walked purposefully towards the library.

'What's he waiting for? Come on, hurry!' I screamed at the imager.

Kenneth placed a hand on my arm.

'Where will they go?' Ridgeway asked.

'Look,' Kenneth nudged me to look towards the moonstone wall. 'It's the sea.'

All the prisoners were walking into the sea towards five fishing trawlers anchored in the bay. Small landing craft scooped them up like collecting tadpoles into a jar.

'That's no good; there are hundreds of them and they can't swim,' I said.

'There are nine hundred and fifty four prisoners at the moment,' Ridgeway told us.

And just as quickly as it arrived, the blue carpet flashed, the moonstone evaporated and we were left blinking in the dim of the cave lights.

Kenneth sat back on his heels and slapped his thigh. 'You beauty!'

'What happened? Where did it go?' Ridgeway looked as though he was going to puke at any minute.

'I don't know. Maybe her thought powers were exhausted. It takes a ton of energy.'

'Yeah or maybe she ran out of spin.' But I could see these guys were hooked on the myth of Vanora. 'So, what happened to the prisoners? And what about the one who was left behind?' My voice sounded weak. Was the scuttling person me, left behind with my grandfather?

'This is lunacy,' I said. 'Ridgeway, tell him we can't do this. What about the guards? Where were the guards?'

'I don't know,' Ridgeway said.

'I suppose Vanora conveniently forgot about them in her plan.' I couldn't help my tone. It was OK for Kenneth to tell me that I needed to grow up, but he was delusional if he thought this was a sound plan to be acted upon in good faith. It was like re-enacting an action-caster in a live warzone.

Kenneth leaned forward and scratched his beard so fiercely

with both hands a flea circus trapezed in every direction.

'How many guards are there?' he asked Ridgeway.

'Not that many. In the main block the prisoners are mostly political or professional. There are no violent prisoners in there and they do all the work. There are a few guards on the perimeter.'

'So how many?' I snapped. Jupe, did every detail have to be dragged out of this pair?

'There's six on each shift, so twelve. When one shift is on the other shift confine themselves to their quarters. There's nothing else to do.'

'You said in the main block. What else is there?' I swear I saw the pinks of his eyes when I asked this.

He coughed. 'There's the Infirmary but we're not permitted to talk of this.'

I searched the cave with my eyes. 'Who's not permitting you? We permit you, don't we Kenneth?'

'Don't be flippant Sorlie.' At last my uncle looked serious. 'Don't they destroy the failures?' he asked Ridgeway. His voice held enough calm for me to believe for a nano I had imagined what he asked.

'Destroyed!' Even though I didn't understand the term, the shiver that wound round my neck like a rope to choke me gave me all the clues I needed.

Ridgeway looked as sick as I felt. 'They are only destroyed when the experiment has run its full course.' He squinted at me, pleading to be excused for what he was about to say. 'There are always a few…works in progress.'

My brain told me to jump and run. My body held me rooted. 'This is monstrous.' My voice could barely utter the words.

'Yes, it is,' said Kenneth, 'and it is not something I am proud of.' I baulked at his words. My nails bit the flesh on my palms, stopping the punch that was headed his way. He was the original architect of this horror after all.

'We will have to leave them.' He turned to Ridgeway. 'How

217

many guards in the Infirmary?'

'One during the day and one at night. Only hardcore projects remain in the Infirmary and they're sedated.'

'Then we leave them,' he said again.

My mind raced through the possibilities and each scenario ended in doom, so I concentrated on the front game.

Kenneth knelt on the cave floor, groaning like an old monk preparing for prostration. He lifted his stick and began to trace out the prison as depicted in the T-map and like a commander preparing for battle he talked us through his interpretation of the plan. When he had finished he sat back on his heels.

'Why can't we just use Ridgeway's keys to get them out?' I asked.

'I don't have access to the whole building.' Ridgeway sat up straight. 'Anyway, it would take forever to lead a thousand men down the cliff to the beach.'

'I know you have little faith in this Sorlie, but we have few choices.' Kenneth's voice was calm. Why was he so calm? 'Like everyone in her Empire you must believe in Vanora's power.'

Sakes, that's why. It was a religion.

As if he read my thoughts he took a deep breath and added, 'She would not have planned this and put you in danger if she believed we would fail. You must fully commit. We have no other choice.'

'Well actually we do,' I said. 'We could leave this island when the boats arrive and leave the prisoners. That sounds like a great plan.' But my words were as hollow as my resolve.

'Then what?' he asked. 'Those prisoners up there are clever, gifted professionals who just happen to have the wrong genes. Vanora needs them. To leave them here would mean certain death for them and no future for us.' He began pulling a small transmitter from under the bedding and moved to the mouth of the cave. 'It's almost moonrise. I can signal the boats and set the beacon to instruct Scud to deal with the guards. He'll know what to do.'

'Scud? Are you mad? You can't trust Scud. He's Privileged now,'

I reminded him. 'He'll betray us.'

'He only looks Privileged.'

'You didn't see him. I did. He's changed. You said yourself personality change will happen.'

'We have no choice; he is part of Vanora's plan.'

'Vanora doesn't know about his change.'

Kenneth wheeled on me and I saw a flash of his madness turn murderous. 'Choices, Sorlie.'

The silent Ridgeway rose to his feet and stood beside Kenneth ready to either restrain or pacify him, I couldn't be sure. 'We will be mindful of Scud's change. It is unlikely the guards will be convinced of his full change so early. They'll be reluctant to embrace him into the fold so soon. We have to take that risk.'

And then another part slipped into place. 'Ask your guard,' Scud had said.

'Scud knows you, doesn't he?'

'It's possible he recognised me from before.'

It was all too neat. My creeping doubts would not shift.

'What if the boats aren't there?'

'SORLIE!' Kenneth screamed; Ridgeway placed a hand on his arm.

'Twenty-one years she has been planning this,' my uncle spat at me, 'before you even entered the equation. The boats will be there.'

Talk about a leap of faith.

The back of his coat ruffled as he shook the anger off. He re-drew the sand plan at his feet. 'We head for the cove as soon as it's dark. Let's hope the weather remains typical and hides the damn moon. We'll wait at the entrance to the prison pipe. As soon as we receive a signal we go,' he glowered at me. 'We go.' He disappeared into the sound of the wash to make his fateful transmissions. When he returned he was much calmer, so I ventured with the question I dared not ask earlier.

'What about the mines? You said the beaches were mined.' I pointed to the tunnel entrance marked on the plan. 'That's sure to be mined.'

I watched his lip curl and his nostrils flare.

'Do you know I knew you would ask that, my doubting kin?' he smiled. 'As I said earlier, I have spent my years clearing mines from here. You should listen more, then your doubts might disappear.' I could feel a smile play round my lips; it had been a while since he had put anyone back in their box so I let the old fool bask for a bit. He blew his own smoking candle out, adding, 'OK, I might not have got them all but I'm sure I've picked off most of them around that cove. I've spent aeons wandering around there.'

Like a beaver preparing to build its dam he began dragging ropes and harnesses and bags into the middle of the cave, chanting, 'The boats will come, the boats will come. Infectious doubts be out.' He packed little devices into his hide bag and took a swig of Mash. The bottle was handed round 'for courage'.

He checked Ridgeway's pulse and under his eyelids.

'You'll live, at least through the ordeal of helping us get into the prison.' He thumped Ridgeway's back. 'Of course you might get killed on the way out.' His chuckle was sickening. 'Just don't stand on a mine or drown if the boats don't turn up.' He winked at me, but there was a dullness to his eye that conflicted with his mirth.

He tidied the heater and coiled the wires as if he were going on vacation rather than a rescue mission.

He stuck a tympan in his ear and cocked his head to one side.

'Right, time to go, the tide has turned.' He held two pairs of infrared glasses, put one on himself and snapped the other in two, then handed one lens to me, the other to Ridgeway. Cyclops style.

'I'm not putting that on.'

'Then you'll be blind.'

Ridgeway motioned me to put the lens to my eye then pulled a thin transparent band over it to hold it in place.

'I agree it's not ideal but it will do the job,' Kenneth said as he flapped his arms wide and corralled us from the heart to the mouth of the cave.

The tidal air blasted my cheeks hollow and I stepped back expecting Kenneth to be behind me. From the dim light of his torch I saw him smooth the skins of his bed; he ran a caressing hand along the wall paintings. With a fingertip he traced the outlines of the boat shapes. He had lived in this cave for twenty-one years; he was saying goodbye because he knew that one way or the other, he wasn't coming back. My face heated at my intrusion into this unusual scene. I turned and followed the bowed head of Ridgeway into the wind and the moonlit night.

· · ·

Ridgeway stopped short of the cave entrance. When I caught up with him he held his hand out to halt me.

'What is it?'

'Something's not right, can't you hear it?'

A rhythmic clanking like links in a chain could just be heard above the roar of the tide.

'The boat – it's come back.' But of course Ridgeway didn't know about the boat. 'It must have come round to pick us up. Come on!' I struggled to get past but Ridgeway held me back with his bulk.

'What's going on?' Kenneth, finished with his fond farewells, had joined us.

'There's a boat in the cove, like the last time. Come on!' I said.

'What last time?' Kenneth asked.

'The first time I came here, there was a boat. Wasn't it for you?'

'No,' Kenneth said. 'Something's not right. We meet the boats at the pick-up point, not here.' He clung to the cave wall as he edged himself through the entrance and onto the beach to peer towards the sea. 'I can see it with my night vision; it is one of Vanora's fleet right enough.' Still Ridgeway held me back, only just allowing us to edge forward with stealth.

The second we emerged from the cave entrance a hunter's light blinded us.

'What the…' I held my hand up to my good eye. The light was intense but dulled behind the infrared.

'Stay where you are, old man,' a voice I recognised hollered from below the light.

'Who are you? What do you want?' Kenneth demanded.

'The boy.'

'The boy stays with us; it is part of Vanora's plan.'

'Vanora has changed her plan. She wants the boy taken from the danger zone and brought directly to her.'

They talked about me as if I wasn't there.

'Maybe the boy doesn't want to go.' I could almost hear the doubt in Kenneth's voice. 'How do we know you're from Vanora?'

At this a figure emerged into the beam-light, like an old game show host hamming it up for his stage entrance. It would have been funny if it wasn't so creepy, and the gun in his hand was no joke. The hunter light bounced off the blond hair, which almost sparked in a halo of light.

Kenneth stepped forward with such purpose that I guessed he hadn't seen the gun.

'And who exactly are you to be ordering me about?'

'It's Merj.' As I spoke I juked round Ridgeway to stand in front of Kenneth. 'He was with Vanora and Ishbel up at the prison.'

'Well, young Merj,' Kenneth kept up his superior tone. He placed his hands on my shoulders and tried to edge me to his side. 'Tell me why do you feel you need a gun? If you have orders from Vanora, show them to me or send them to my tympan.'

Merj waved the gun at Kenneth and Ridgeway. 'If you two don't step back I'll kill you both.'

'And what about the prisoners back there?' Kenneth continued on his own agenda. 'We need Sorlie to help us release the prisoners.'

The smooth laugh Merj gave was all the answer we needed. What happened to Mr Charisma? And where was Ishbel?

'It's OK Kenneth, I'll go.' Kenneth opened his mouth to speak but I held his words. 'No, you don't need me. I didn't believe in the stupid plan anyway. It seems Vanora has come to her senses.'

Kenneth pinched the sleeve of my jacket but I shook him off and walked into the beam.

'Don't do it, Sorlie.' He moved to stop me, but Ridgeway stayed him.

'Let him go, it's what he wanted all along. He doesn't give a damn about the prisoners.'

'That's rich coming from a guard,' I said.

Merj threw me a rope. 'Tie them up, Sorlie. We don't want that pair of lovelies wandering around while we execute our new plan, do we?'

The look on Kenneth's face as I tied them together would make a rat weep.

Merj was taller than I remembered from that brief meeting in Davie's study. As I got up close to him I choked back my own fear and hoped Kenneth and Ridgeway wouldn't do anything stupid. At least he hadn't asked me to kill them. As I walked back into the beam, I took my cyclops eye off and stowed it in my pocket; the split light was disorienting.

'Where's Ishbel?' I had to ask. I was treated to that smooth laugh again.

'You'll be handed over to your whore once the ransom is paid.'

I aimed for his eye. He yelled like a loon when my small blade dug deep into his left cheek. He dropped the gun as he pulled the knife out with one hand and grabbed my throat with the other. Then both hands were throttling me. My mind booted the Cadenson and suddenly I was back in the Games Space. With both his hands on my thrapple I hooked my arms through his, undercut him and kneed him in the guts. It winded him for a millisecond then, like a raging bear, he fell on me again, pinning me to the sand – Jake's old move. I executed the 'heave off and roll over'. Before he had a chance to get to his knees I crouched and levered my arms under him and hurled him towards the rocks where Ridgeway had fallen. If this had been a bout in the Games Space the machine would have called a halt and started counting.

I took a knee and knuckled down to catch a breath, watching Merj roll over and place a hand on the sand to pull up. That's when I saw the pretty pink trinket twinkling on the beach beside him.

A hot white flash threw me off balance; I was showered with sand and something wet. Merj was huddled in a heap on the shoreline; in front of me on the sand lay his hand and half his arm. The memory of my mother whammed through my brain before reality struck. By the time I scrambled towards the old lovelies they were already free of their loose bindings.

'I thought you said this beach was cleared of mines?' My words came in hoops and gasps. My body was shaking, so I took great breaths to try to get a grip on my nerves.

Kenneth was scratching sand from his hair. 'It is. That wasn't one of the beach mines. That would have blown you both to bits.'

'Then what was it?'

'A butterfly mine would be my guess. Designed to maim. They're pretty little things to attract children to pick them up. I wonder where it came from.'

'Is he dead?' I looked back to the body on the shoreline, which was now being rummled back and forward in the tide.

'No, I don't think so,' Kenneth said.

'What do we do about him? Finish him off?' Listen to me, psycho-killer.

'Leave him, it was an accident. He's as good as dead and he's just a rogue piece. There might even be a bounty on your head, Sorlie.'

This was incredible. 'Then he's working alone.'

'Let's hope so. But if he is still in Vanora's pay we don't want to set her off.' He looked back at the body. 'No, just a rogue piece with ideas of piracy.'

• • •

I expected Kenneth to take us up our original descent chute, but he moved us in the opposite direction.

'The explosion wasn't loud but it might have given away our location. We'd better stay low.' The light from the hunter's beam lit our way initially. We could have disabled it, but decided it was more useful left as a decoy. We had just started on the negotiation of a series of narrow terraces, zig-zagging up another cliff face, when Kenneth stopped. He turned and placed a finger to his lips.

'Listen,' he mouthed.

'Oh no, not the seekers again.' We were committed to the cliff, so they were sure to find us out here. Kenneth batted my words with a silent shush.

'No, listen,' he hissed.

At first all I could hear was the sea, then a sharp scraping noise rattled the air like a gate hinge needing oil. The corncrake. There was no mistaking it. My cheeks split into a smile and Kenneth nodded. If only Scud could hear it. I quickly switched my communicator to record, a futile act maybe, but it felt right. It was surprising the wee bird ventured out after the commotion on the beach; maybe it wasn't so shy after all. The moment was too brief. Kenneth led the scrabble up the cliff, grabbing vegetation for purchase. After one slime-rimed step up, he stopped again on a ledge about three feet wide to catch his breath. I turned to face the cliff and clung on to some precarious heather; a funnel of wind was hurtling up the couloir, chafing the backs of my legs.

'Hurry up,' I said to myself behind gritted teeth, but he was pointing at something.

'Look!'

With the hunter's beam out of range and the cloud sweep from the south, darkness had crept up on us. I pulled my lens over my eye and followed Kenneth's direction. There was a flat piece of turf and cultivation ahead. I shuffled along the ledge until it widened to safety.

'It's my garden.' He cupped the branch of a small shrub. 'The raspberries were good last year but will be better this year,' he said with a dramatic sigh. 'Oh well, the birds will have a feast.'

'Can we please get off this cliff?'

'Sorlie's not great with heights,' Ridgeway kindly added. Cheers!

We had no sooner dropped to the shingle beach of the ruins when we were climbing again, traversing the wall of the cliff face. Above, on the clifftop, searchlights ranged the landscape like lighthouse beams. Out in the blackness of the sea the buoy's light was keeping a constant flash sequence of Kenneth's setting. He maintained a line below the level of the clifftop and teetered us along a small two-feet-wide ledge. The rock was slick with sea wash and guano, and at one point the ledge disappeared into a mere notion of a path. Kenneth reached over the void, hooked his hand on a jutting rock and spanned the gap, one foot across then the other. The precipice yawned between us but Kenneth danced across as if he were on a soccer field. He took a rope from his bag and chucked it back to Ridgeway. Ridgeway tied it round my waist without instruction from Kenneth, then he pushed me against the wall so he could pass me. With his hand on my elbow, he eased me along the ledge.

'Don't look down,' was his helpful advice. 'Feel the rock, feel how solid it is. The holds are bigger than a Jeep. Use your hands. There is a big jug-hold there just above the gap. Take your lens off, if it will help.' Was he mad? I'd be blind.

My hand searched above me and two fingers found a notch to hook into.

'Good,' Ridgeway said. 'Now shuffle your feet to the edge and step one foot over.'

My bowels grumbled and my mouth filled with fear dust. The legs that had served me for sixteen years decided to pack in. I was stuck. Then my right leg took to shaking of its own accord like jelly on speed. I couldn't go forward, I couldn't go back.

'It's OK, we have you. If you slip we'll catch you.' Kenneth shouted as he held his hand out. Catch me with what? A rope tied around me with a bowline knot; there was no guarantee it would hold. I felt the rope tighten as if he was pulling.

'Don't!' I screamed. Kenneth had made the step over look so easy. 'I can't.'

'So what are you going to do, spend the rest of your life here?'
Ridgeway whispered in my ear as he nudged me further towards
the gap.

'Fucking move!' he bawled in my ear, and I was suddenly
grasped by Kenneth and pushed into the rock face on the other
side of the gap. My undergarments felt a little damp, but that
might have been sweat.

Ridgeway stood beside me. 'Lord, we are going to have to do
something about that phobia.'

A peek behind Ridgeway showed me the gap wasn't as bad as
I'd imagined.

'Let's hope he's not afraid of water.' Ridgeway grumbled.

'Maybe it's an act,' Kenneth said. 'Our little warrior seems to be
good at acting.'

'I am here, you know.' But they both ignored me.

Chapter Twenty-four

Contrary to the thought map, we did not arrive at the rock steps from the prison, but on a ledge just below them where we picked up the lower path. When I pointed out the error of the plan to Kenneth he threw me one of his disappointed looks, but remained silent. The way down to the hidden cove was not obvious but Kenneth knew the way. The lovelies had left the rope tied to my waist.

'How much more?' I asked.

'Nearly there. You're doing fine,' was the breezy response. 'You're almost used to it now. That last part was pretty exposed and you hardly blinked at it.'

I had to admit, Kenneth's cheeriness reassured me.

We arrived at the bottom of the cliff onto a boulder the size of a truck. Kenneth creaked to his hands and knees and crawled to the edge. He peered over, then sat back and scratched his head. 'Uh huh.'

'What?'

'The inlet pipe is below the water line.'

'Oh great! The plan didn't tell us that either.'

'Stop doubting Vanora, Sorlie,' he snapped.

What was I supposed to do? We were walking, or rather stumbling, into a situation that was laid out for us in a T-map.

'I thought you had cleared the mines, didn't you notice the pipe was under water then?'

I was treated to that dramatic sigh again. 'I came to clear mines, not look for pipes.'

'What's the pipe for anyway?'

'It's a cooling system,' Ridgeway said, looking round with his monocle glass, 'and if there is an inlet pipe there will be an outlet pipe.'

Both Kenneth and Ridgeway walked the perimeter of the boulder while I tried to remember what the plan had shown. Were there one or two pipes? And if there were two pipes, why hadn't Kenneth seen the other?

'There it is,' Ridgeway said, pointing to a trickle of slime that ran from a patch of green algae about three metres above the beach.

'Come on Sorlie.' There was infectious excitement in his voice like some rogue set on mischief. He was a guard; all he needed to do was walk up to the prison and let himself back in – why was he doing this?

I scrambled to keep up to where the two men were beginning to lower themselves off the rock and down to the small stretch of soft sand. Kenneth had forgotten I was tied to the other end of his rope and nearly pulled me over, but stopped in time to grip my wrists and jump me off the boulder to land in a heap.

'There, can you see it?' Ridgeway said. Jupe, no wonder Kenneth didn't notice; it was a tiny grill, only about a metre across, well camouflaged into the rock with its covering of algae. Drops of water seeped from its bottom lip and slavered down the rock face.

Kenneth untied my rope end and handed it to Ridgeway, who began climbing to the grill, hooking the rope around a jutting boulder as he went. He threaded the rope through the grill and descended again, still holding the rope end. Both Kenneth and Ridgeway wrapped the rope around their bodies and heaved. Splinters of debris showered from the grill and a wrenching sound cracked the air. Both men fell backwards, a flying grill narrowly missing them before it thudded in the sand. An **O** in the cliff mouthed its astonishment at being exposed.

The lovelies lay on the sand chuckling like schoolboys who had just pulled off a monumental prank, Kenneth more so than his partner-in-crime. I had the impression Ridgeway was humouring him.

'OK, so we have a way in,' Kenneth said as he extricated the grill and threw it behind a rock.

'What about the boats?' Ridgeway asked him.

Kenneth scratched his beard then rummaged in his bottomless bag. He sat on the sand clicking a small device like an antique video game shooter. The lightbuoy's constant beacon broke sequence for several revolutions then regulated. Kenneth stopped his clicking, held his breath and narrowed his eyes away from the beacon towards the horizon. He held his hand over one ear and fiddled with the tympan in the other. The buoy broke sequence again and the breath hissed from Kenneth's mouth. 'They're here.'

'Are you sure?' This time Ridgeway dared to doubt, but Kenneth's dagger look quelled any further dissent.

'Let's go, then.' Ridgeway straightened his back, showing no sign of his earlier fall. Whatever was in the drip's miracle juice had a future.

My hands were already on the rock and I had started to climb before I realised what I was doing. The T-map was in my head. It wasn't just Ridgeway's enthusiasm – something in my blood line was pushing me forward. This job needed doing; these two old men, who knew each other so well, were risking their lives for this. Vanora needed me to be here. Or did she? I still wasn't sure. She needed me to get out of the prison and to bring Ridgeway, the T-map and plug-in to Kenneth. I tried hard to ignore the image on the plan: the old man in the library with the gun, the undecided figure whose fate we never discovered. What else did Vanora need from me? Merj's kidnap attempt still bothered me.

My communicator told me it was past midnight. It had taken us over three hours to get here from the turn of the tide.

• • •

Although the cove beneath the pipe entrance was sheltered, a desolate wind howled round the coast, creating an eerie chorus in our amphitheatre. The short, steep climb required my face to the rock and my nerve in my boots. Unseen from below was a small ledge where Ridgeway waited for me. He held out a hand, then pulled me up and over the last crease of rock. Without waiting for Kenneth, he said, 'Do you want to go first or shall I?' Close up, the opening looked no bigger than a truck tyre.

'It's not big enough. Why is it so small? What's it for? Not sewage?' It didn't smell like sewage.

'No, I told you, it is the outlet pipe for the cooling system.'

'Cooling system of what?' The rusting of the grate and the dribble of water which teamed with slime growth on the pipe entrance and floor all evidenced a moribund system.

'The small nuclear reactor that used to power the building when it was military.'

The word 'nuclear' pushed me back and Ridgeway's sharp grab reaction just prevented my fall.

Kenneth, with perfect timing, chose that minute to join us and placed steadying hands on my shoulders.

'Calm down,' he chuckled, 'you'll come to no harm.' This was what he said before, but radiation scared the shit out of me. 'On you go, Ridgeway. Come on Sorlie, help him in.'

As Ridgeway grasped the lip of the pipe we each took one foot and hoisted him further into the aperture.

'Watch out, it's on a slight incline,' he shouted. 'I'm using the tight walls to lever me in,' he continued as he began to grunt his way up the pipe. Kenneth helped me. The pipe stank of sour breath and rust and another unidentifiable metallic substance that tasted rancid on my tongue. There was no glow or heat or evidence of anything deadly. Sweat burst on my brow.

The pipe was at an incline of only a few degrees, but the slime that covered its bottom meant each hand and knee scramble up was followed by a slide back. Behind me I could hear Kenneth grunting and swearing to enter the pipe and then a voice far off. 'I can't get in. You go. I'll man the boats.'

So we were on our own, just as the plan had shown. I don't know how long I shucked up the pipe, pushing with my knees, elbows, head and hips, anything I could find to make contact with the wall and stop me backsliding. My infrared lens persisted in clouding over. Each time I tried to wipe it the damn thing slipped from my eye; one minute I would see the big backside of Ridgeway in front and the slime covered walls of the pipe, the next I would be plunged into a total frightening blackness until I scrabbled to place the lens back on my eye. The smear on the lens thickened with every wipe, leaving a kaleidoscope of blurred images.

Suddenly Ridgeway stopped.

'Sorlie? Kenneth?' His whisper came through the miniscule gap between his body and the pipe.

'I'm right here. Kenneth couldn't get in the pipe; he stayed behind.'

He swore under his breath. Even though I couldn't hear his exact words, the slump of his body told me how he was taking the news.

'Right then Sorlie,' the voice came stronger now, as if he tried to twist to face me. 'When we enter the reactor room an alarm is going to go off. When that happens the power will automatically shut down. That means we have ten minutes to get to the main prison door and the security control room before the electric locks kick back in.'

'What about the guards?'

'You saw the plan; there were no guards in the prison. We have to assume Scud did his job.'

'What if he didn't?'

'I don't know. But we have to trust in Vanora's plan and hope Scud is still with us.' He was nippy but there was something dejected in his voice as if he didn't quite believe it either. 'We have to have faith in Vanora's power. You heard Kenneth, you saw the beacon change; the boats are here, that part came true.' On this point I think we both had a fear that Kenneth might have been manipulating the truth.

'OK, Sorlie, are you ready?'

The fluttering in my gut was urging me to let go of the pipe and slide back to the beach, but that just wasn't an option any more.

'Are you ready?' he asked again.

'Yes.'

'Stick to me like a fly on shite and keep your lens on, you'll need it.'

He rotated his body to lie on his back and began work on a small manhole cover on top of the pipe. He chipped at the bracket with a driver, then wedged his baton into a wheel. With brute force and strangled curses he tried to lever it open. Once or twice he stopped and lay back for a few seconds then bent to the task again. There was no room to manoeuvre, so any help my puny strength could have added was redundant. He took in a huge breath, gritted his teeth and with an almighty grunt heaved. Rust and muck showered his face and hands, but he never flinched, keeping the pressure on. The hatch squeaked open.

'Ready?' He didn't wait for an answer. The minute he shoved the hatch and torpedoed through the gap, a shrill siren screamed into life. A hand came down and hauled me through the hatch onto a crossbeam gantry which we clattered over to reach a door. Ridgeway touched it and it slid open. Within seconds of leaving the tube we were in a corridor. He knew exactly where he was going and it struck me that ever since he had seen the T-map he had been working the layout of the prison over in his mind. We ran, or rather stumbled, half blind along the corridor to stairs. We clanked up two flights. The climb busted my gut and lungs and yet this bulking guard, who had so recently suffered an injury, was sprinting ahead like an Olympian, fuelled by Kenneth's magic juice.

Another door barred us at the top of the stairs. Ridgeway shoved it and then tugged. The door held firm.

'Damn.' He slammed a frustrated palm to his brow.

'What? What is it?'

'It's bolted from the other side. Idiot, I should have remembered.'

'What are we going to do?'

'We're going to have to find another way in.'

'How? We don't have time, you said only ten minutes.'

'I know.' He punched the door. 'Damn.' And then it began to open a crack.

Ridgeway hurled me against the wall and unholstered his gun. The crack widened to reveal a beam of emergency light from the corridor beyond.

As quick as a lizard swipes a fly in its tongue, Ridgeway's hand jabbed and snatched a creeping figure from the doorway.

'Scud!' I said too loudly.

'Shush,' they both hissed.

Ridgeway shook Scud from his grasp.

'How did you get here?' I asked.

'I'll explain later, come on.'

'The guards?' Ridgeway asked.

Scud ruffled his fingers together like a successful pickpocket. 'A little something special in their bedtime brews tonight. Vanora's visitation delivered mucho goodies. I got some too. Left in the library.' His voice was as rich and cloying as corn syrup.

It was Scud but not as I knew him. The guard's uniform hung on his wiry body, but it suited him. His now blond hair had more than one day's growth. Even in the poor light I could see how pale his eyes had become – the sign of a true Privileged. But, unlike a true Privileged, here he was helping us. The closer I examined his change, the deeper the doubt crept into my bones.

'You can take those lenses off now,' Scud said, but Ridgeway signalled for me to keep it on.

Ridgeway reclaimed his lead and took us to a circular room fitted out with monitors and imagers. Empty chairs faced half-filled beakers and picked-at food packs. It was like the legend of the Flannan Isles lighthouse, when the three keepers disappeared without a trace. This was the surveillance control room, the room behind the dot on the wall, but there was no time to dwell on that.

One grid monitor viewed the waffle stack of the prison cells; it looked exactly as it had laid out on the cave floor. How had she known?

'We need to open the cells,' Scud said.

'How will we stop them all panicking and rushing out?' The T-map images had shown chaos, but orderly chaos.

'This,' Scud said, holding up his wrist and showing off his command band. 'And this.' He held up his other arm – a communicator.

So it was true. Scud really was the inside agent.

'Each level will release, one at a time; I have appointed a leader in each section – they know what to do.' As he was saying this he grabbed my hand, tugging at my communicator. As I resisted his grasp, he drew in some breath between his teeth and snapped his fingers. 'Quick.'

He dragged me towards a control panel with multiple switches and ports. I shook him off.

'I know what I have to do.' It was incredible. Even though no one had told me, I did know what to do. One of the ports was similar to the plug-in button. My hand gravitated to this and I positioned the plug-in over it. As soon as they connected magnetically, the monitor on one level showed cell doors swinging wide. Heads appeared in doorways. Soon the cell landing was awash with men.

'We'd better help,' Ridgeway said. Scud followed him to the door.

'What about me?' I tried to move but the plug-in resisted. I wrestled with the communicator but it was welded to my wrist.

'You have to stay here until all the doors are open. Vanora's key should release you then.'

'Why can't I take it off?'

'Because you can't,' Scud said, and then they were gone. I watched the door swing closed behind them. Trapped. The more I wrestled to tug the communicator from my arm, the tighter it bit into my wrist.

The progress of the orderly line threading the corridors shown on the monitor reminded me of the convoy of prisoners destined for Dead Man's Ferry; but unlike those chained wretches, these men on the screen were controlled by chemicals and electrical pulses and they would soon be free. The men were of differing hair and skin colour; some of the pigments were blotchy, but they all had the weary tinge Scud carried before he became Privileged.

Emotion bubbled in my chest and almost choked me. I saw Gobo, his white hair shorn, his skin shedding and mottled like a patchwork quilt. The rims of his pink eyes were swollen and red with weeping sores. He shuffled like an oldie and stumbled to his knees. The leader of his pack, a man with an ear to ear smiley scar, lifted Gobo by the scruff of his neck and half carried, half dragged him after the line of men. Scud conducted the procession at one end and Ridgeway was leading them towards the reactor room and the pipe at another. One body broke from the rank and ran in circles, his arms flapping. When he ran into the wall under the surveillance, I almost choked. His eyes had no pupils: he was blind. Scud held up his communicator arm and the body became a juddering heap on the floor. Scud turned his back on the surveillance then and bowed his head, forehead pressed to the wall. Poacher turned gamekeeper? The mass of men stopped and witnessed the scene, then allowed themselves to be herded once more. There was Toad, his thick lips now shredded, loose skin hanging in ribbons and his front teeth protruding in a gruesome grin of agony. The only sounds from the control monitors were the dragging of a hundred pairs of boots, some supporting those who could not support themselves. Ridgeway was right, we could never have manoeuvred this sorry bunch down the cliff face.

When one corridor was clear, Scud moved to another level to repeat the process as another set of doors automatically opened. It was obvious now that the plug-in was controlling the whole operation; it was a marvel of micro-engineering. Ridgeway, still with the first group, conducted them into the reactor room. I watched him on the monitor as, like a gambler at a slot machine in a Pleasure Zone, he fed the men one by one into the pipe. The slope would be to their advantage, creating a flume for them to slide down. I imagined them catapulting through the opening onto the beach. Jackpot!

The incarceration had rid the prisoners of excess fat, so even brutes could fit the space that Ridgeway squeezed through. I just prayed that Kenneth could help them into the boats.

Minutes dissolved in the fascination of the escape. Hundreds of cameras revealed angles of the prison I had never seen before. I viewed my cell from the dot on the wall. Beast station sat idle on the desk. The room dazzled white and small; how had I survived in that bubble for so long without going bonkers? Unlike Kenneth, I felt no need to say goodbye to my island home. Another screen showed the two doors leading into the library: the one from my quarters and the heavy ornate door from the prison. Both remained resolutely shut. The plan predicted the old man behind those doors, but Vanora couldn't have known what the reality was, could she? She only guessed it, or wished it. Wherever Davie was, he must be scared. With his kingdom crumbling around him, would he run, or would he hide in a sewer like a deposed dictator? A pang of guilt swept through me like fire. He was my grandfather – an old, confused, sick man. And then I noticed the other room. In a dim light I made out a row of about a dozen beds carrying bundled-up bodies suffering unspeakable horrors – the Infirmary. To be left behind. To be destroyed. Destroyed in more ways than one. My guilt was doused by hatred for this tyrant, a replica of what my grandfather felt for them and for me. There was something strange about the light in the Infirmary. It was muted and something stirred within it. A movement passed across the wall, like a shadow puppet, stretched and grotesque. It travelled over the greyed sheets of the beds, scraping across each body with its outstretched claw. As the shadow shortened I could see it wasn't a claw but a hand clutching a gun. A dark figure appeared into the line of the camera.

'No,' I groaned.

As if he heard me, he faced the camera and grinned. Then he lifted that ancient gun, turned, aimed it at the head of the mound in the first bed and fired. The figure jerked once then was still. I jabbed a call button.

'Stop this murder,' I screamed. My grandfather took no notice of this call as he moved to the next bed and fired again, but from the corner of my eye I was aware of Scud and his hoard pausing.

I tried another button and shouted, 'Murderer!'

This time Davie halted his slaughter and looked up. He was three beds down the line and from the blood washing the floor, I could see he was being systematic.

'You will be next, mongrel.'

'Why are you bothering with me and them, what about the escaping prisoners?' He ignored me and continued on his bloody journey.

'Don't you care? All your hard work escaping.'

'Out of the frying pan into the fire. Out of the frying pan into the fire.' He repeated it over and over as he moved down the line.

I tugged at my wrist strap but it held tight. I counted the beds left on his murder spree. Six.

'Why do you want to kill me? I am your grandson.' I had no clue where the Infirmary was in connection to the control room.

Four.

Three.

'Stop the prisoners! They're escaping!' My desperate words were ignored.

Two.

One.

'Your turn, Sorlie.'

I thumped my hand on the other call button. 'Scud, he's coming for me.' But Scud had moved on to another section. With my free hand I hammered each button, some twice. 'Scud! Ridgeway! Anyone!' But an escape was being executed as per Vanora's instructions and I had no idea whether they heard me or not.

Davie's coat paddled the blood on the Infirmary floor as he spun and left the room. I tugged; the strap bit, breaking skin and drawing beads of blood. Then suddenly my hand and arm were flung from the port – the plug-in's job was done. The monitor showed Ridgeway still feeding his human slot machine. Scud was on the top level conducting the hordes but showing a worried eye to the camera. I reckoned I could reach Ridgeway first. There was no sign of Davie.

I yanked the control room door open and fled down the corridor. I knew the steps were just beyond the door. My fingers touched the latch when a boot struck out and I sprawled on the floor. Before I could catch a bearing he throttled the scruff of my neckband and hauled me back to the control room. The gun pressed into my back. His strength was immense. He threw me into the control chair, the gun still trained on me.

'Why haven't you killed me yet?' I was dead anyway.

'Because I want to enjoy your terror.' A crazed smirk was on show.

'Like my mother's terror.' Wow, where'd that come from?

He took a step back as if I'd punched him. 'What terror is this?'

'The terror she felt when she was dragged off by the Military.' There was a flicker of doubt behind that smirk. 'Oh no wait, you missed that, didn't you? You were off doing important work for the State.' What was I doing? But the smirk had slipped and with it, all the tension in his face; his features sagged and so did the hand holding the gun.

'I was protecting her. She looked Privileged, she deserved a good life.'

'She was given a Hero in Death status.' My hatred dripped from each word.

'That wasn't supposed to happen.' Was that snot on the end of his nose? Was that a tear that stood out on his eye? And then like a starburst revelation, I knew this was the debt Ishbel claimed he owed. A guilt Vanora used to torment him.

'She was a lovely child.' His face masked in memory. The gun dropped its aim. 'I thought I was protecting her,' he repeated. 'She was such a good girl. Privileged.'

'Memories are the one thing the State cannot take from you,' I whispered, afraid to break the spell. 'My mother Kathleen told me that every time she went on a mission.' The sound of her name felt good and gave me courage.

'Did she really tell you that? That was my mantra; I gave it to her. To remind her of our good times. To remind her I loved her.'

He was crazy. 'And she gave it to me because she loved me and wanted me to have a little piece of you. I have your Privileged genes. She wanted to protect me as you did with her. She destroyed my passport.'

He searched my face for some form of recognition and I prayed he did not see Vanora. 'I'm Kathleen's son. We could fight back,' I wheedled. 'Together.' But he seemed not to hear.

'Memories,' he smiled. Then something on a monitor caught his attention. He tightened the grip on the gun.

One monitor showed Scud running down stairs, having finished his human round-up.

I shifted the communicator round my wrist; it had dug in deep. 'I found the bird, Grandfather,' I whispered. He lifted his head and stared with confused eyes. I thumbed the playback. The room filled with the sound of the sea, and then rising from it the creaking, scratchy call of the corncrake. The confusion left him as he listened, the gun almost forgotten.

'We could take this to the government. You will get the place you deserve.'

His smile had an eerie edge as he lifted the gun once more to aim at me.

'Ma had forgiven you. She never held it against you. She knew you were trying to protect her. She loved you.'

'You think so?'

'Yes.'

'I don't.' Confusion cleared completely from his face.

'Why do you want to kill me? I'm your grandson.'

'You are a mongrel and this mongrel line has to end. It ends with you.'

'You're wrong. What about Ishbel?'

'Vanora's lieutenant?' his sneered. 'Your whore can not help you now.'

'Ishbel is your daughter. Vanora's daughter,' I whispered.

He sank into the chair, his winter eyes iced over. I watched his expressions move with a thousand possibilities.

'No. Not possible.' But doubt flickered on his brow. He believed me. I could see he believed me as his mind slipped further into the past.

'Vanora gave birth to her after she left you.'

'You lie to save yourself.'

'She has your height, your stature. I've seen her passport, her name under your name.'

'No.' He spoke as if in a dream.

'If you kill me she'll be all that is left of your blood line.' I watched the gun waver. 'Just think, a native, alive, ripe and ready to carry on your line.'

His eyes clouded, but the gun stayed trained on me.

'Memories are the one thing the State cannot take from you,' I whispered in prayer.

The sound of running shook him from his dwam. His eyes flicked to the door. I lunged at him, grabbed for the gun. His boot caught me between the legs. An explosion of pain and sound rocked me. My body skittered across a wet floor. There was no further pain, but my ears were ringing. I was splattered in blood. And then Scud was beside me.

'Don't look,' he said, but of course I did.

His face was blown off, his mane of silver hair matted, seeping with thick black blood that reached out on the floor towards me.

'I killed him.'

'It was an accident, I saw.'

'I killed him.'

'You did us a favour, now come on. Let's get moving Sorlie.' Scud didn't even look at him. He lifted me to my feet and manoeuvred me into the corridor towards the reactor room.

'I killed him. I'm sixteen and I'm a murderer.'

'Forget him, come on.'

The taste and smell of his killing crawled over me. I gagged and spewed the contents of my stomach onto the corridor. Scud rubbed my back, still trying to usher me along. I spewed again, bile this time, my stomach empty. I moved to wipe my mouth with the back of my hand but it was covered in blood and brain. I gagged.

• • •

Scud pulled up before we entered the reactor room. 'On you go, hurry or you'll miss the boat.'

'What do you mean?'

'Ah'm not coming.'

'You have to come, to tell them it was an accident.'

He looked disappointed. 'There's nae need fur that. You'll be a hero. No, ah'm stayin' here.'

'Are you mad? Why?'

The Privileged eyes narrowed and something alien crept there. 'Ah've some reading tae catch up on.'

'But why? There's nothing here for you.' I motioned to the reactor room. 'Scud, we're nearly there. Free.'

'Look at me,' he said, dusting down his uniform. 'Ah'm Privileged now. Ah don't belong out there.'

'Yes you do. You helped with the escape. Vanora…'

'Vanora will have no further use for me. I've done my bit. She's not wanting a mongrel like me muddying things.'

'No, you're wrong. We're the same, I'm part native too. A mongrel.' That word almost choked me but it was the truth.

'We're not the same. You were brought up Privileged and you will always look on me as a native. Ah don't belong with you.' There was a glimmer of the old Scud in the beseeching look he wore. 'Ah don't belong anywhere but here.'

'Are you mad? You're just institutionalised, you'll be looked after, I promise.'

'Ah'm staying.'

'You can't stay here on your own.'

'Why not? Ah can live like a king fur a while. All those books. There will be enough provisions tae last me until they come.'

'What about the guards?'

'Oh yeah, the guards.' He shrugged.

'The guards will kill you.'

'No they won't. They've been a victim of Davie's brutality too. We'll get along just fine. Ah'll cook them up something special for when they wake.'

When I opened my mouth to protest again Scud took my arm and squeezed it.

'Make your grandmother proud. Make Ishbel proud,' he said, then tapped his nose as he used to, although this time I had no clue to its meaning.

'Now go, before ah huv tae punch yer lights out and carry ye there.'

I watched his straight proud back as he walked away and closed the door behind him.

The last of the men were out.

'Where's Scud?' Ridgeway asked, peering at my bloodied state.

'He's not coming.'

'Is he dead?'

'No, but Davie is.' My voice choked at the memory and I knew it would haunt me forever. 'I killed him.' Ridgeway showed no surprise.

'You did the world a favour then.'

'Didn't you hear me? I said I killed him.'

But he ignored me. 'If Davie's dead, why did Scud stay?' He moved towards the door as if to go back for him. I held up my hand.

'Leave him, he's too far gone.' My voice sounded unconvinced but Ridgeway heeded my words and wasted no more time before he lifted me into the pipe and with his great shove I began to slide. In those few seconds in the flume the final picture of the T-map came to my mind. The person left behind – undecided. I had thought it was me. I had screamed 'come on' because I thought I'd been left behind, but it had been Scud. Vanora knew this – that had been part of her plan all along. But had she planned for her grandson to become a murderer? Nothing would ever be the same again. I felt tears chafe my bile-burned throat. I stank of death. It was me or him. He was going to kill me. Maybe it would have been better if he had.

• • •

The sea was so full of bobbing bodies, I could have walked across them to the busy convoy of small inflatables, a few metres offshore. Splashing bodies were being ladled on board head over heels.

Heavy rain pattered the sea and pelted a triumphant Kenneth as he stood on the big boulder, arms windmilling, roaring instructions like Moses directing the parting of the Red Sea. His instructions were unnecessary because whatever Scud and Ridgeway had programmed into the command bands still worked. The men were automatons, blindly walking into the sea like some sort of mass suicide. Once the boats had scooped their fill, they disappeared into the dark before returning empty to replenish their load. Ridgeway adjusted the lens on his eye and I followed. Out in the bay a huge black turret bulked from the sea and another rose beside it, followed by one more. Their fat rounded bodies stretched horizontally; a city of sea-monsters emerged as we paddled in the waves. The inflatables buzzed around the beasts' skirts.

'What are they?' I shouted to Ridgeway.

'Submarines?' Kenneth shrieked into the wind like a banshee.

'Yes,' he said. 'Old nuclear subs.' He spelled it out with great pleasure but this time I didn't care. Nuclear or not, I just wanted off this damned island.

A commotion erupted on the beach. It was Toad, frozen at the water's edge, his eyes bulged like onions. When he backed up the beach, a man with white hair grabbed him and nudged him forward, but he dug his heels into the sand, petrified. The white-haired man gestured to another and together they hoisted him onto their shoulders, waded into the water and flung him in the nearest boat.

'Come on, let's go,' Ridgeway said.

'Well, this is all going very well.' Kenneth scrambled off his boulder. 'Where's Scud?'

'We leave him here,' Ridgeway said. Kenneth looked sharply at him then lowered his head.

'I don't think that's wise.'

'What do you want to do, destroy him?' I said. Kenneth winced as a piece of my spittle flew at him, but he just wiped it off his sleeve and walked towards the boats. He didn't even notice the blood on me.

'There's been enough bloodshed tonight,' I screamed. Kenneth spun his heels on the sand. Ridgeway whispered something to him. Kenneth narrowed at me, summing me up.

'Well, Vanora's going to love you,' he sarcied to me, then turned to Ridgeway. 'Take the boy to the boats, then go back and deal with Scud.'

'No,' Ridgeway said.

'No?'

'No Kenneth, we leave him.'

Kenneth turned to me. 'Sorlie, you were the one who didn't trust him and you were right. If he stays he will be a danger to our plans. He knows too much.'

'He won't betray us.'

'How can we be sure?'

245

'Oh – so now we have to be sure.' His sarcasm had infected me. I pointed to the prison. 'We have just followed a plan from a snafin' thought map dragged out of an old woman's brain and one of those images was Scud staying behind, remember?'

'But she broke the connection before we knew what happened,' Kenneth stuttered.

'Yeah, I wonder why. Maybe it was deliberate, I don't know any more. All I know is Scud stayed behind; that's what she wanted. It's what Scud wants. Game Over. Reload.'

Ridgeway settled the matter. 'No, Sorlie's right. Scud got us in, he dealt with the guards, he helped the escape. We don't have time to go back for him.' He began wading into the sea. 'It's what Vanora wanted. The Military will kill him anyway when they eventually decide it's worth spending some of their precious fuel to come out here and check things out.'

A wave of sickness assaulted me again. If this is what Vanora planned all along, what fate did she really have in store for her released army? Suddenly the boats didn't look so inviting after all.

I left the shoreline and put my head against the cool boulder. I spat in the sand to push the nausea down. It was sheltered from the wind, calm away from the commotion. That's when I heard it again – the rasp and the scrap of the corncrake. I searched the black cliff face, took off my lens, wiped it and tried again. There it was again. I looked up to just below the prison stairs. There she was. Perched on a ledge. Ishbel, smiling down at me. She held a finger to her mouth to stop me alerting the others. When the corncrake call came again I was transported back to our kitchen, to the game we played, matching the extinct animals to Ishbel's sounds. A game she excelled in. She had never left me. It was Ishbel who threw the butterfly bomb at Merj and it was Ishbel who called the corncrake to me as we climbed the cliff, her call I played to Davie. She had followed us along the cliff-pass to watch us leave. I started to climb the cliff.

'No!' she mouthed, flapping her arms towards the boats, pointing north. Kenneth roared for me to get in the boat and she signalled again for me to leave. When I held my hand up as if to wave she OK'd her thumb and finger as Merj had done in the library. Then she was gone, disappeared over the cliff rim. I had no idea what she was up to but I didn't care, Ishbel was still on my side and that mattered more than anything else.

• • •

Ridgeway and I were destined for one of the subs.

'Your chips need to be deactivated before you can be allowed up top,' one of the seamen explained.

Kenneth the caveman had escaped being chipped and would be permitted to ride on one of the heavy trawlers set to tow the subs once they were sunk to two hundred metres under the ocean.

Hundreds of men clambered up ladders slung over the sides of the black hulking beasts and crawled all over the decks like maggots on a carcass. Men in uniform directed them towards three different entry points. How would they all fit in?

Kenneth read my mind. 'Don't worry, they've fitted out the torpedo space for them. We can get more than three hundred in each. You must hurry though; the sooner these beauties are below water, the better. Only the ballast and air pumps will be used, no other power. The wake of the trawlers will hide all evidence of them. And remember, these trawlers have legitimate business in the northern seas.' His mirth had returned. 'Come on Sorlie, one more day of discomfort and then we'll be free. I'm sure Vanora will have a feast prepared to welcome her army and victorious kin. Things will change now. We have our chance. It is up to us to make our future work.'

I wished to share his excitement, but too much had happened. Maybe when we reached the north my feelings would change. My doubts must have shown because Kenneth suddenly became grave.

'Whatever happens, Sorlie, you will still have Ishbel and me looking out for you.'

The two who cared. The 'we' Ishbel had told me of on the Transport so long ago. I knew I should have told him of Ishbel's presence on the island but something held me back. Now I just wanted to leave the bloody mess behind.

● ● ●

Ridgeway and I waited on the sub-deck until it cleared of prisoners.

The lights of two fishing trawlers were blinding as they moved into position, as heavy fumes polluted the salty air. A cable stretched from them and tightened on a Sub to the left. As the trawlers moved forward they screamed with the pain of the strain until the vessel began to sink under water. Another cable tightened ahead and the other sub began its forward, downward motion.

'We better get below,' Ridgeway hollered above the squeal of the trawler engines.

The seaman led me up the ladder to an open hatch. At the top I paused and placed a hand in my pocket and found Ishbel's pebble. I wondered if she would go to the prison. She would find the body. How would she feel about her father's death and my part in it? I turned towards Black Rock for the last time. Its ghostly outline stood in silhouette against the rain-slated seascape, its total blackness broken by one single light shining from the cliff face. I knew that window so well and I pictured the new-look Scud standing there as he had done on many other occasions, still trapped, looking through the starburst glass at the blackness beyond. Maybe Ishbel would persuade him to leave. I bowed my head in thanks to them both and allowed myself to be lowered into the cramped doorway that led to Freedom.

Acknowledgements

Writing is a solitary business but it also involves teamwork. I would now like to thank;

Colin Baird, Frances Wright and Liz Small, the early readers who weeded out the rubbish and cleared the path for future drafts. Alan Green, the tough guy, who cut me no slack and embarrassed me into killing my darlings. The experts; Sebastian Russo, the scientist and Dez Burt, the sub-mariner – they both gave excellent advice, and any errors in the novel are due to my misunderstanding of the facts and are mine alone.

Thanks to all at Saraband Books, in particular Sara Hunt who always believed in this book and whose advice helped to shape this novel into what it is. Also Jennifer Hamrick and Heather McDaid for their slick edit.

Lastly I would like to thank my family for keeping me in the here and now, especially my sons, John and Gary and my sister Liz, who is my runner's conscience and librarian extraordinaire.

About the author

Moira McPartlin's debut novel, *The Incomers*, was shortlisted for the Saltire Society First Book of the Year Award and was a critical success. Moira is also a prolific writer of short stories and poetry, which have been published in a wide variety of literary magazines.

GEORGE LAMMIE

Read on...

Sorlie arrives in the Atlantic Archipelago to find Vanora's empire in decline...

Ishbel fights to keep Scud alive...

the Noiri's hold on Esperaneo's supply chain is increasing ...

and there is a new player in town.

Who holds the real power in Esperaneo? The State? Vanora? The Noiri? Or The Prince?

And who will heed the *Wants of the Silent?*